# CON...

**Badge No. 1314**

**Rank:** Rookie Officer

**Skill/Expertise:** Thorough and meticulous. First in recruit class (outstanding achievement in academics, firing range, self-defense).

**Reason Chosen for Assignment:** Her tall, leggy blond looks are likely to appeal to the target of this undercover operation— and her fellow officer. Will she be able to stay focused under his heated, intense gaze?

**Badge No. 0539**—Alexander Blade

**Rank:** Sergeant

**Skill/Expertise:** Chameleonlike ability to change appearance and personality in order to convincingly assume any covert identity.

**Reason Chosen for Assignment:** Razor-sharp instincts make him a natural for this risky operation. But it might be more difficult for him to resist the beauty of his passionate partner.

Dear Reader,

The year may be coming to a close, but the excitement never flags here at Silhouette Intimate Moments. We've got four—yes, four—fabulous miniseries for you this month, starting with Carla Cassidy's CHEROKEE CORNERS and *Trace Evidence,* featuring a hero who's a crime scene investigator and now has to investigate the secrets of his own heart. Kathleen Creighton continues STARRS OF THE WEST with *The Top Gun's Return.* Tristan Bauer had been declared dead, but now he was back—and very much alive, as he walked back into true love Jessie Bauer's life. Maggie Price begins LINE OF DUTY with *Sure Bet* and a sham marriage between two undercover officers that suddenly starts feeling extremely real. And don't miss *Nowhere To Hide,* the first in RaeAnne Thayne's trilogy THE SEARCHERS. An on-the-run single mom finds love with the FBI agent next door, but there are still secrets to uncover at book's end..

We've also got two terrific stand-alone titles, starting with Laurey Bright's *Dangerous Waters*. Treasure hunting and a shared legacy provide the catalyst for the attraction of two opposites in an irresistible South Pacific setting. Finally, Jill Limber reveals *Secrets of an Old Flame* in a sexy, suspenseful reunion romance.

Enjoy—and look for more excitement next year, right here in Silhouette Intimate Moments.

Yours.

Leslie J. Wainger
Executive Editor

Please address questions and book requests to:
Silhouette Reader Service
U.S.: 3010 Walden Ave., P.O. Box 1325, Buffalo, NY 14269
Canadian: P.O. Box 609, Fort Erie, Ont. L2A 5X3

# Sure Bet
## MAGGIE PRICE

INTIMATE MOMENTS™
Published by Silhouette Books
America's Publisher of Contemporary Romance

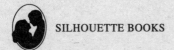 SILHOUETTE BOOKS

ISBN 0-373-27333-9

SURE BET

Copyright © 2003 by Margaret Price

This edition published by arrangement with Harlequin Books S.A.

® and TM are trademarks of Harlequin Books S.A., used under license.
Trademarks indicated with ® are registered in the United States Patent
and Trademark Office, the Canadian Trade Marks Office and in other
countries.

Visit Silhouette at www.eHarlequin.com

**Printed in U.S.A.**

# MAGGIE PRICE

turned to crime at the age of twenty-two. That's when she went to work at the Oklahoma City Police Department. As a civilian crime analyst, she evaluated suspects' methods of operation during the commission of robberies and sex crimes, and developed profiles on those suspects. During her tenure at OCPD, Maggie stood in lineups, snagged special assignments to homicide task forces, established procedures for evidence submittal, and even posed as the wife of an undercover officer in the investigation of a fortune teller.

While at OCPD, Maggie stored up enough tales of intrigue, murder and mayhem to keep her at the keyboard for years. The first of those tales won the Romance Writers of America's Golden Heart Award for Romantic Suspense.

Maggie invites her readers to contact her at 5208 W. Reno, Suite 350, Oklahoma City, OK 73127-6317. Or on the Web at http://members.aol.com/magprice.

For opposites who attract

# Chapter 1

"Anytime you want to move your tennis shoe off my windpipe is good for me."

Keeping her foot in place, Morgan McCall gazed down at her fellow police recruit, whom she'd tossed onto his back on the padded gym mat. "I wouldn't have my tennis shoe on your windpipe if you'd quit acting like I'll break if you fight back."

"I fight back, you'll start using those karate moves of yours," Lonny O'Brien pointed out. "Then where will I be?"

Morgan's mouth curved as she stabbed a loose pin back into her disheveled blond topknot. "On your butt, with my foot on your windpipe."

"Case closed."

Around them the echo of voices—and occasional grunts and groans—filled the Oklahoma City Police Department's gym as the members of their recruit class practiced self-defense moves. Rubber-soled shoes squeaked against the shiny wood floor. From somewhere in the distance, the staccato dribble of a basketball echoed off the high ceiling.

With sweat gleaming on his flushed, freckled face, O'Brien speared a look toward the gym's bleachers. "You too busy mashing my windpipe to notice your stalker's made another appearance?"

Morgan's smile melted. "I noticed."

She hadn't needed to catch a glimpse of him to know he'd shown up. *Again.* The tall man with dark, shaggy hair tied back from his unshaven face had first appeared at the academy a week ago. She'd spotted him shaking hands with the major in charge of training, so there was no doubt he had authorization to be there. Later, the man strode into class alongside her criminal investigations instructor and slid into the seat behind hers. She hadn't had to see his face to know his gaze stayed on her the entire hour. She'd *felt* it, as physical as a touch. The instant the instructor dismissed class, she swiveled and looked directly into brown eyes as hard and sharp as stone.

She'd found herself fighting not to jolt at the sudden and unexpected punch of power. Sheer willpower had kept her from blinking or shifting her gaze from the sharp-planed face that gave nothing away. For humming seconds they'd stared at each other while something undefinable sizzled in the air.

"Who are…" Her words had faded away when he stood, turned his back and walked away. She'd remained in her chair, her heart hammering while she watched him stride out the door.

He had shown up at the pistol range the next day, his interest intensifying when she stepped to the target and aimed her Glock. Two nights ago he'd lingered in the humid June shadows and observed her participate in arrest reenactment exercises. She had lost count of how many times he'd settled on the gym's bleachers and studied her self-defense moves.

With his measuring gaze consistently directed at her, the other recruits had dubbed him "McCall's stalker." Morgan had kept to herself the fact that each time he appeared, an electric current zipped through her veins.

It was a familiar sensation. That same frisson of awareness that brought all of her nerve endings to full alert had stirred her senses only once before in her life. Then, it had left her with a broken heart and physical scars.

The man who now seemed to size her up with a hunter's focused interest possessed a similar power that drew her even as it set off alarms. She had no idea who he was or why he was there. In the academy's military-like climate, she wasn't at liberty to question his presence, merely accept. She figured he was a cop, but had no clue if he was local, state or federal. All she knew for sure was she wanted nothing to do with a man who could jolt her so thoroughly with one look.

Keeping her gaze off the bleachers, she shifted her foot from O'Brien's throat. "I'll spare you, rookie, only because you've got such a cool wife and baby. Otherwise, your windpipe would be history."

"Gee, thanks, *rookie*," O'Brien rasped as he shoved his six-foot frame up off the mat. Using the hem of his gray academy T-shirt to swipe his sweat-soaked forehead, he slid another look toward the bleachers. "Found out yet who the guy is?"

"No." Morgan snagged the pair of hand towels she'd left folded on the edge of the mat. She tossed one to O'Brien, then looped the other around her neck. "We graduate in two days," she said, blotting one end of the towel against her throat. "I plan to hit the street and do my job. That's all I care about."

"That, and becoming OCPD's first female chief," O'Brien amended.

"I keep telling you there's nothing wrong with setting lofty goals. You want to get anywhere in this department, you'd better do the same thing, starting now."

"Yeah, well, *my* most pressing goal is to be an awesome host at our graduation party. Anna's made so many hamburger patties I'll have to sweat over the grill for hours to cook them all." He scrubbed the towel over his head, leaving his sandy hair standing in spikes. "You'll be there, right?"

"Wouldn't miss it. I promised Anna I'd make tiramisu for dessert. And my mom's sending over pots of flowering plants to decorate your patio."

"Must be nice to have a garden center in the family."

"It has its advantages."

"You bringing a date along with that fancy dessert?"

Morgan raised a shoulder. "Maybe." She far preferred a vague answer than having to explain she'd long ago sworn off dating. And everything else that had to do with nonplatonic relationships.

Amusement slid into O'Brien's blue eyes. "If you're having trouble finding a date, you could ask stalker-man."

"And you could wind up on your butt again before this class is over."

"No way. My pride is bruised enough for one day. Anyway, it looks like your guy's leaving. Maybe he won't be back."

"There's a happy thought."

Morgan shifted to get a view of the far side of the gym where the subject under discussion made his way down the bleachers. Dressed in worn jeans and a denim shirt, he moved with the unhurried stride of a man who did not know what it was like to be off balance either mentally or physically. When she found herself wondering what it would take to make him move fast, she bit back a curse.

She didn't *care*. Didn't want to be drawn to any man. Had no desire to ever be drawn again.

Just then the shriek of the training instructor's whistle split the air. Morgan glanced at the clock bolted high on the wall. "Time to hit the showers."

"I get a shot at you tomorrow, McCall," O'Brien said, snapping his towel at her sneaker-clad feet. "Wear your padded undies because I plan on tossing you on your butt."

"In your dreams, pal," she bandied over her shoulder, then jogged off toward the women's locker room.

She was almost there when an academy instructor barked her name. After weeks of training, she automatically halted and stiffened to attention. "Yes, sir?"

The instructor's black buzz cut was as severe as his expression. "Report to the major's office."

"The *major's* office?"

"Nothing wrong with your hearing, McCall."

Knee-jerk reaction had her wondering if she had failed to do something required of her, skimmed over some rule, left a task uncompleted. Just as quickly she pushed away the thought. Would the time ever come when her past mistakes lost the power to reach out and grab her by the throat? She *knew* she hadn't screwed up.

Not lately, anyway.

Just a few years before, she had pulled herself out of the black hole she'd dug for herself and vowed to never again lose direction, lose *herself*. Since then she had made a point to live by the rules. Go by the book. Follow instructions with precision. When she joined the academy she had focused on doing her best, being the best, making her family proud. Having let them down once, she had a lot to make up for.

Letting logic take over, she directed her thoughts to the memo she received the previous day that advised she would graduate at the top of her recruit class. Surely that was the reason the major had summoned her.

Beneath her gray academy T-shirt, Morgan felt the sweat from her strenuous workout pooling between her breasts. She glanced toward the locker room, then looked back at the instructor. "Sir, do I have time to shower first?"

"Negative, recruit. Report to the major's office now."

"Yes, sir."

Morgan hesitated when a tingle of eerie awareness drifted through her. As if drawn by an invisible force, her gaze returned to the bleachers, where her stalker had spent hours observing her. She might not yet have a badge, but that didn't prevent a deep, intuitive disquiet from sweeping through her.

Standing there, she knew instinctively that the dark-haired man with the stiletto-sharp eyes was the reason for her summons to the major's office.

# Chapter 2

Minutes later Morgan stood at attention before the major's imposing desk, using all of her inner control not to gape at the man. "Sir, how can I work an undercover assignment when I'm still in the academy?"

"The chief's ordered you to, that's how," Edward Henderson stated. The training center's commander was a big bear of a man clad in an immaculate uniform with razor creases. His office with its cool black furniture and stark white walls was as pristine as his appearance.

"You'll still graduate with your class." As he spoke, the office's fluorescent lights reflected off Henderson's bald head. "You won't attend the ceremony, is all."

"Not attend, sir?" Thoughts of her family flashed through Morgan's brain. Her grandfather and father had served on the department. Her three brothers and two older sisters were active-duty Oklahoma City PD officers. Morgan had looked forward to her entire family serving as a cheering section when she accepted the silver badge she'd coveted most of her life.

Henderson gave a curt nod. "Missing graduation after sixteen weeks of hard work is a disappointment, but it can't be helped. The media air coverage of these ceremonies on the news and print a picture of the recruit class in the paper. They'd clamor to run a piece on you, being the eighth person in your family to wear an OCPD badge. One of the bad guys targeted in this operation might get a glimpse of you and remember later where he'd seen you. That's a risk we can't take."

The major's use of "we" had Morgan shifting her gaze to the man standing on the opposite side of the room. When she'd entered the office, the major introduced her to Alexander Blade, a sergeant in one of OCPD's undercover units.

*Her stalker.*

Blade now stood with a shoulder propped against a built-in bookcase, one thumb hooked in the front pocket of his jeans. Unease rippled up Morgan's spine while he watched her through those unreadable dark eyes.

"I have a memo to you from Chief Berry." The comment pulled her attention back to the academy's commander. He opened a desk drawer and retrieved an envelope. "Per the chief's orders, you're assigned to Sergeant Blade's undercover operation for its duration. I'll swear you in and give you your badge before you leave today. You will no longer report here for duty."

"Yes, sir." Morgan broke her "at attention" stance long enough to accept the envelope. Her brows slid together. "Sir?"

"What is it, McCall?"

"There's...a postgraduation barbecue at recruit

O'Brien's house. It's private. No media. Am I allowed to attend?''

"Negative. We'll inform the members of your recruit class you're on special assignment. They'll receive orders not to contact you." Henderson rose. "You're to cut off communication with them until after this assignment ends. Understood?"

"Yes, sir." Coming from a family of cops, Morgan knew being chosen for undercover work could boost her career. Which would put her on the fast track toward a rise in rank after she'd served her time on the street. Still, the instant flare of disappointment at having been jerked so suddenly from her fellow recruits was a jolt. Over the past months she had purposely paid more attention to her studies than to those with whom she'd shared a classroom. She hadn't realized until this moment she had formed an unintentional emotional bond with her peers.

"Sergeant Blade has the use of my office to brief you," Henderson continued. "Until further notice, you report to him."

"Yes, sir." The sense of unease already in her stomach tightened. Before she could switch off her mind, Morgan felt again the memories that still oozed blood, and wounds that had never healed. All because of a man whose very presence sent electricity up her spine. She wasn't into self-deception—around Blade she felt that same hard, hot ball of awareness.

She had promised herself if her hormones ever again stirred like that for a man, she would run in the opposite direction. Right now the only way she could do that was to stop being a cop before she ever got started.

Since she had no intention of walking away, she was stuck.

The door's quiet snap had her looking across her shoulder. Henderson was gone, and Alexander Blade was advancing across the office like a hunter who'd gotten a bead on his prey. She forced herself to stand motionless while anxiety shredded her insides.

"This assignment come as a surprise to you, McCall?"

He talked like he moved—slow with a warm-honey tone to his voice.

"Not totally, sir." She matched his gaze, look for look. "The training staff wouldn't have let you hang around here for a week staring at me if you were just some crazed stalker-pervert off the street."

His mouth hitched on one side. "My 'hanging around' had a purpose. I wanted to check you out. And I needed to know how you handle yourself when you're aware you're being observed."

"Since I'm here, I take it I passed?"

"Barely. Every time I walked into a room your spine stiffened and your shoulders went as tight as wire. Your body language sent the message you knew I had my eyes on you. That won't work for this assignment. You'll be watched, yet still need to act like you're unaware."

Although it stung he'd read her so well, she gave thanks he didn't know the underlying reason for her reaction to his presence. "What's the assignment?"

"We'll get to that." He raised a dark brow. "Speaking of passing tests, you get a perfect score for knowing how to stand at attention. Your academy days are over, McCall. Relax."

"Yes, sir." Morgan assumed a "parade rest" stance, her long legs slightly apart and her arms behind her back. For sixteen weeks the training staff had insisted each recruit adopt a military bearing. Now, the stance and talk were habit.

Blade narrowed his eyes. "I said *relax.* We won't get

far if you go around acting like you're in boot camp and I'm your DI.'' He waved her toward one of the visitor chairs in front of the desk. ''Have a seat. We need to get comfortable around each other.''

Morgan slid, stiff-spined onto a chair. No way would she ever feel at ease around a man who could make alarms blare just by walking into the same room.

Blade moved behind the desk. Instead of settling into the major's high-backed chair he leaned and used an index finger to flip open the cover of the file folder. ''You have an impressive record. Top of your recruit class in all areas—academics, in-the-field training, self-defense, pistol range.''

''If you're going to do something, you should do it right.''

He cast her a quick, weighing glance. ''That philosophy has been pointed out to me several times in the past.'' He looked back down at the file. ''I expect you're like every rookie—anxious to hit the streets and start taking down bad guys.''

''Yes, sir.''

Blade's gaze sliced upward. ''McCall, do you need me to define the word *relax?*''

Morgan clenched her fingers on the envelope containing the chief's memo. ''No, sir. Like you said, I've got a handle on academics.''

''Then stop calling me 'sir' before it becomes habit. I don't know of one wife who addresses her husband that way these days.''

''Wife?'' She kept her face expressionless. ''Am I going undercover as your *wife?*''

''To be exact, we're going undercover together as husband and wife.''

"Yes, s—" She pressed her lips together. "What am I supposed to call you?"

"We'll both use our real first names. We answer to them by reflex, so that's one less area in which we might slip up."

As he spoke, Blade walked around the desk, leaned against its front. The move put him in a position of dominance by forcing her to have to look up at him. She would much rather have faced him on her feet.

"For the duration of this assignment, my name is Alexander Donovan. You're Morgan Jones Donovan. I call you Morgan. You call me Alex."

"All right." When he continued to stare at her, she added, "Alex."

"Before you leave today I'll give you a packet containing, among other things, a sketchy history of your fictional background. We'll get together a couple of times over the next few days to flesh it out."

"Fine." She would simply have to ignore her hormones, she resolved. Approach this assignment as she did everything—with cool common sense. No emotion.

Blade crossed his arms over his chest. "You ever hear of Carlton Spurlock?"

Morgan had a quick vision of a tall, distinguished man with a smooth smile and dark hair going silver at the temples. "Local land developer. He shows up a lot on the business and society pages."

"Right. Spurlock inherited millions from the grandmother who raised him. She died about three years ago and left him her estate in Hampton Hills."

"The snooty part of town," Morgan commented.

"After she died, a rumor surfaced that Spurlock had refurbished his swimming pool's cabana into a first-class casino. The Feds got an undercover officer inside who nailed Spurlock for interstate racketeering and running an illegal gambling operation. During his trial, the Feds screwed up and the judge dismissed the charges. The details are in the packet I'll give you. Because of the screwup, the Feds had to back off. But they still want Spurlock. Now, so does OCPD.''

''For gambling?''

''Murder.''

''Murder?'' Intrigued, Morgan leaned forward. ''Whose?''

''The first person was a jockey named Frankie Isom. Hours before his murder, he rode a horse to victory in a million-dollar futurity.''

''Why did Spurlock kill him?''

''We're not sure.''

''You said Isom was the first person murdered. How many more?''

''Five we know of. A woman named Krystelle Vander and a man named George Jackson, head of security at Remington Park. Jackson was retired OCPD.'' Morgan thought she caught a flash of emotion in Blade's eyes. Then it was gone and they were simply cool, brown and unfathomable.

''Krystelle Vander was Spurlock's lover,'' Blade continued. ''She owned a town house, but spent most of her time at his mansion. She had a thing for gambling. Football, baseball, horses, casinos—you name it, she laid bets. A few weeks before the jockey died, Vander told a friend she was worried Spurlock planned to dump her for a younger woman. She said she'd given him the best years of her life and wasn't going to let him get away with it.''

''*Did* he dump her?''

''Apparently. She'd met George Jackson at the track and knew he was a retired cop. On the day of their murders, she called his office. We know that because Jackson typed notes on his computer while he had Vander on the phone. She was hysterical, claiming Spurlock had broken off with her. She said she had evidence proving Spurlock ordered the jockey's murder. Jackson told her to meet him, then left his office. A patrol cop found their bodies in a parking lot of an abandoned warehouse.''

Beneath the harsh office lights, Blade's stubbled face looked hard, even dangerous. But then, he was talking about murder. Morgan eased out a breath. ''I take it Spurlock was questioned?''

''Yes. He confirmed he broke up with Vander. He claimed he was at home the night she and Jackson were killed, playing poker with three buddies. The men—all pillars of the community—verified his alibi.''

''Do you believe them?''

''I believe they played poker. Because the victims were killed someplace other than where they were found, I suspect Spurlock either committed the murders or was behind them.''

''Why?''

''Vander's phone records show she regularly called gambling contacts in Reno, Las Vegas and Atlantic City. She also made calls to a local number. When the cops dialed it, they got a recording that just said leave a message. The number checked to Emmett Tool, a former CPA and ex-con who did time for gambling charges. Tool claimed he used the phone in his bookkeeping business. The homicide detectives got interested in Tool after they found proof he kept books for Spurlock.''

Morgan nodded, her mind working to process the information. ''Did they suspect Tool was also involved in the murders?'' she asked after a moment.

''They didn't know. At the very least, they thought

Tool might have incriminating evidence about Spurlock's gambling operation. Under his prison release agreement, Tool had to report his gambling receipts to his parole officer. That's where my unit stepped in and I began surveilling Tool. After witnessing several transactions where he met known gamblers and exchanged money, I hauled him in.''

''Did he implicate Spurlock in the murders?''

''He intended to. Tool had a wife and kid to support, so he sweated going back to prison. His lawyer worked a deal: Tool's testimony about Spurlock's involvement in the three murders and illegal gambling in exchange for immunity. Since Spurlock was violating federal gambling laws, we called the FBI. As a part of the deal, we moved Tool to a hotel for questioning.

''The first morning he was there room service delivered breakfast. When I showed up for my shift I found two FBI agents dead of poisoning, but no sign of Tool. The theory is Spurlock got tipped that Tool was about to turn informant. He arranged the poisoning and had Tool snatched.''

''Do you think Tool's dead?''

''I know he is. A week after he disappeared, a burned body turned up. Dental records confirm it was Tool.'' Blade pushed away from the desk and settled into the chair beside Morgan's. ''Right now we have nothing solid on Spurlock.''

''Where does our parading as husband and wife come in?''

''The notes in George Jackson's computer said Krystelle Vander claimed she was too afraid to try to get out of Spurlock's mansion with the evidence she had that proved he murdered Isom.''

''The jockey,'' Morgan confirmed.

"Right. Vander told Jackson she hid the evidence in the gold bedroom." Blade's mouth tightened. "The way things stand, Isom's murder is the only one we have a chance of nabbing Spurlock for. To do that we need Vander's evidence."

"Can't you get a warrant to search the gold bedroom?"

"Not when we don't have a clue what type of evidence it is. Spurlock's place is guarded like a fortress. That means the department has to use human intel to get the evidence. That intel is you and me. Our goal is to get Spurlock to invite us inside."

"How are we supposed to do that?"

"The mansion next to his belonged to an oil man who drilled one too many dry wells and went bankrupt. His girlfriend immediately ran off with some CEO worth billions. The bank seized the oily's mansion, all furnishings and personal possessions. The bank has agreed to let us use the place gratis. You and I are moving in."

*"Together?"*

"Yeah." One corner of Blade's mouth tipped up in a smirk. "Most husbands and wives live under the same roof. At least until the shine wears off the marriage." The light undertone of disdain etching his voice sent the message he had little regard for that particular institution.

When Morgan remained silent, he angled his chin. "Relax, McCall. The place may not be as large as Spurlock's, but it's big enough to be classified in the huge category. It's three stories, has a handful of bedrooms, bathrooms, even a small gym. The only room we have to share is the kitchen. I'll make sure there's plenty of food stocked in the freezer that can be zapped in a microwave. If your taste runs to meals that don't start out frozen, bring your own food."

"I will." She swiped a palm against the back of her

neck where her muscles had tightened. "Why me? I have yet to work the streets. OCPD has tons of experienced female officers. Why pick me to work this assignment?"

"Because no one has your particular expertise."

"Which is?"

"For one thing, your knowledge of gardening. Specifically growing roses in Oklahoma."

Morgan blinked. "Gardening? *Roses?*"

"Your mother owns the largest landscaping-and-gardening business in the city. Growing up, you worked there on weekends and during summer vacations. You helped out there full-time before you left for college."

"Sounds like you've done a good job of checking me out."

"Yes, I did. Welcome to working undercover."

"So what does my knowing about roses have to do with this assignment?"

"Spurlock inherited a love of roses from his grandmother. There are hundreds of rose bushes on his property. He cultivates new breeds, which have won numerous awards. Serves as the president of the local rose society. Land development may be his lifeblood, but roses are his passion. Your displaying a similar regard for roses will draw him to you. To us." Blade paused. "Here's a lesson about undercover work, Morgan. Any hard facts you give the bad guys you'd best be able to back up. *You* can discuss growing roses—and probably anything else—in Oklahoma with Spurlock. No way he can trip you up because you know what you're talking about. No other female cop can do that."

"There are two others. My sisters." For some reason she couldn't define, Morgan felt a wicked little streak of satisfaction at having caught Blade in a mistake. "Carrie and Grace are both OCPD cops. *Seasoned* cops. They also grew up working at our mom's business. Your background check should have red-flagged them.''

"It did.''

She frowned. "So, why aren't you talking to one of them about this assignment?''

"I considered them both.'' Watching her, Blade leaned back in his chair, stretching his long denim-clad legs out in front of him. "In fact, Grace and I worked an undercover assignment a few years ago. She's a good, solid cop and I would prefer to use her on this. Unfortunately, neither she nor Carrie are right for this operation.''

"Why?''

"One of them is a brunette. The other a redhead. Frankly, I need a blonde.''

"Hair can be dyed.''

"True. But neither of your sisters can grow the additional inches in height you've got on them.''

Morgan conceded Blade was right—Carrie and Grace had inherited their mother's slim, shorter build. *She* copied their paternal grandmother's tall, willowy height. "Just because they're a few inches shorter than me doesn't mean Carrie and Grace can't handle whatever comes their way.''

"I'm not saying it does. There's just other things to consider.''

"Such as?''

"You're new on the force, haven't worked the streets. There's no chance you've ever pulled over Spurlock or any of his hired help and written them a ticket. No chance you maybe walked into a restaurant or a store in uniform the same time Spurlock was there. I can't be sure of the same thing where Carrie or Grace are concerned. And I don't want to take a chance.

"Add to that, Spurlock has a thing for good-looking

young blondes. Tall, *leggy* blondes. One might say he cultivates them, like he does roses. Your meeting the physical requirements of his ideal woman and sharing his passion for roses will lure him. Perhaps even fascinate.''

As he spoke, Blade's gaze traveled from the toes of Morgan's gym shoes up her legs, past her rumpled workout shorts and T-shirt to the top of her head where she'd piled her long, blond hair. ''You're exactly what I need to get Spurlock's attention, and keep it. That's the bottom line.''

Blade's intense inspection sent a current zipping beneath her flesh. ''Are…'' She paused when her voice wavered. ''Are we supposed to knock on Spurlock's front door and introduce ourselves as his new neighbors? Then once he sees I'm a tall, *leggy* blonde, he'll invite us in?''

''Not that easy,'' Blade said. ''There's no knocking on his front door. After the judge dismissed the gambling charges against him, Spurlock didn't close his casino. He just made it invincible. He built a twelve-foot brick wall around his premises, complete with motion sensors and security cameras. Cameras that at various times do sweeps across his neighbors' property. The only way to get in is through the wrought-iron gate blocking access to the driveway. Goons who look like they could bench press a patrol car, and fanged-dripping Dobermans guard the gate around the clock. No one gets in unless they're friends of Spurlock's, or are vouched for by someone close to him.''

''So you hope Spurlock will let down his guard because we're his neighbors? That he'll invite us over to dinner? To maybe gamble? Then once we get in, we look for the evidence Vander hid in the gold bedroom?''

''Right.'' Blade's eyes narrowed. ''You make our objective sound easy. It won't be. It's going to take time. We can't act too eager, too pushy. We move in, mind our own business. We get Spurlock's attention in ways that will make him feel comfortable, maybe even curious. Sooner or later he'll approach us.''

''And you're betting my physical attributes will speed the process.''

Blade looked at her for a long, silent moment. ''The man's not blind,'' he finally murmured before shifting in his chair and snagging a manila envelope off the corner of the desk. ''This packet also contains pictures of the mansion we'll move into. There's a swimming pool, cabana and flower beds. A lot of them. They're in bad shape because no one's taken care of them since the bankruptcy. I want you to spend most of your time working in the flower beds.''

''If we can afford a mansion, wouldn't we have a gardener?''

''We do. But you, Morgan Donovan, have a green thumb. You prefer to spend hours everyday working in your gardens. Dressed, of course, to get Spurlock's attention.''

Morgan lifted a brow. ''Not many women wear spandex and stilettos while pulling weeds.''

''I'll leave the specifics to you. In general, I'm talking tight. Revealing. Eye-catching.'' He handed her the envelope. ''There's a credit card, driver's license and social security card in your undercover name inside. Shop for those types of clothes. Pick up a couple of evening gowns. Nightgowns, too.''

''Nightgowns?''

''Once we stir Spurlock's curiosity he—or one of his thugs—might knock on our door anytime, day or night just to test us. To make sure we're who we say we are. It'd be hard to explain why your choice of sleepwear was a police academy T-shirt.''

Morgan scowled over the fact Blade had pegged her actual sleeping attire.

His gaze swept over her disheveled topknot. "Spurlock likes his women to wear their hair down and poofy. Big hair."

She stifled a groan. "Poofy. Big. Great. Just my style."

"I've put pictures in the packet of him with some of his past squeezes, including Krystelle Vander. You'll want to go for the same look." Blade rose, stared down at her. "That's the overall view of the assignment. Think you can handle it?"

Her chin lifted. "You don't have to worry about me doing my job." Gripping both envelopes, she rose. "When do we move in?"

"In about a week. Until then, you and I work on getting used to each other while we flesh out your cover background. Since part of that is learning a little about each other's quirks, habits and how each other lives, we'll work at both of our places. My address is in the envelope. Be there in the morning at eight sharp. The following day we'll work at your house. Knowing as much as we can about each other will cut down on surprises after this operation starts."

Surprises, Morgan thought. She'd had enough of those to last a while. "My family," she said. "I need to tell them not to show up for my graduation. And give them a reason why. Plus, Grace, Carrie and I live together. If I suddenly disappear they'll call out the troops."

"Good point." Blade paused, then said, "Since your family is comprised mostly of cops you can tell them you've been pulled to work an undercover assignment with me. Just be vague and keep the specifics to yourself."

"Fine," she said, then began to turn.

"Morgan." Blade's hand gripped her elbow, shifting her back to face him. "There's something else you need to get used to."

"What? Hey—" She jerked her chin as his hand cupped it, but his fingers held firm.

"My touch." His dark gaze roamed her face, betraying nothing. "Remember, we're going undercover as husband and wife. You need to get used to my touch. I'll need to get used to yours."

His fingers were warm; something jolted and tensed in her belly. She couldn't imagine herself ever doing anything so emotionally dangerous as reaching out and touching him. "Fine. No big deal."

"When you go undercover it's essential you look the part, but it's far more important you play it well. We're a husband and wife who have the hots for each other." He released her, his eyes probing her face. "Our touching each other may feel like no big deal, but whenever Spurlock's watching, we both have to act like it matters. A lot."

"Message received." She took a step backward. Then another. Not in retreat, she assured herself, but for needed distance. Her breath had clogged in her lungs, and her pulse throbbed hard and quick. Her hands weren't quite steady as her fingers clenched on both envelopes. "I'll…see you tomorrow."

He studied her as if trying to read her thoughts. It frazzled her to think he might succeed. Might find out how much just his presence unnerved her.

Finally he gave a curt nod. "Tomorrow, Morgan. And a lot of tomorrows after that."

''No.'' He'd thought about stopping at the quick mart for coffee, but that would have made him run late.

''I've got muffins in the oven. And I was about to put on a pot of coffee.'' As she spoke, she thrust her hands into the pockets of her shorts, pulled them out again. ''Want some?''

*There it is,* he thought. Neither her eyes nor her expression betrayed her emotions, but body language said it all. He could almost feel the shimmer his presence injected into her nerves. Convincing people they were husband and wife wasn't going to happen unless he figured out how to get her to relax around him.

''If it's the muffins that smell like heaven, I'll be happy to join you.'' He raised a brow. ''Are you feeding me because all I had to offer you yesterday at my place was tuna fish, stale bread and flat soda?''

''You got me pegged,'' she said, then headed down the hallway, its wooden floor dark-stained tongue-and-groove. ''Consider this a pity breakfast.''

''I'll consider it whatever you want, as long as you feed me,'' he said, following her. ''Did you notice yesterday how I take my coffee?''

''Black,'' she said across her shoulder.

''Right.''

''Was that a test of my powers of observation?''

''One of many.'' He found himself doing his own form of observation as his gaze slid down to her hips, lingered, then lowered. She moved with an elegant stride he attributed to her tall, slim build and those mile-long legs.

Endless, tanned legs that he felt certain would send a tinge of envy through most professional dancers. And just might tempt a man to beg for a chance to feel all that alluring flesh wrapped around him.

Disconcerted by his thoughts, Alex jerked his gaze upward and switched his mind off his future partner's legs. Rule number one in undercover work was to maintain emotional detachment. He and Morgan McCall had a serious job facing them and he was too professional to let some out-of-the-blue sexual itch cloud his thinking.

"My remembering how you take your coffee doesn't involve rocket science," she commented. "You didn't have any cream, milk or sugar in your kitchen."

"Good point. I always put off going to the grocery store until my back's to the wall, so it's easier to drink coffee black."

"Not going to the store is another bad habit. That means you probably eat too much fast food and not enough fresh fruits and vegetables."

"Keep honing those observation skills, and you'll make detective in no time, Officer McCall."

"That's the plan."

No surprise there, Alex thought. Any woman who aced every class in the academy definitely had her sights set on moving up the ranks. Good for her—let her ride a desk, push papers and get ulcers. He would rather deal with a hundred bad guys than spend one minute slaving over departmental budgets and policies.

He trailed her down the hallway, noting the rooms they passed were typical of an older house—small with high ceilings and plenty of windows to let light in. The layout was conventional, too. A living room to the right, small dining room to the left, with a steep wooden staircase at the end of the hall. The furniture he glimpsed was done in calming neutral tones with accent pieces in deep roses and smoky grays. Everywhere he looked, lush green potted plants and flowers speared out of pots and vases.

"Nice place," he commented.

"Thanks. I take care of the yard. The decor is mostly

Grace's doing.'' At the end of the hall, Morgan made a sharp left turn. ''It's hard to believe now, but this place was a dump when Carrie and I bought it.''

''You fix it up yourselves or hire a contractor?'' he asked as he followed her into the kitchen where copper pots and pans hung on a rack over a small butcher-block island. Gray slate topped the counters. Small, colorful pots of what Alex guessed were herbs lined the wide windowsill.

''It was a family project. My grandparents, parents, three brothers and Grace pitched in with the renovation.'' While she spoke, Morgan gestured Alex toward the long-legged stools on one side of the butcher-block island. ''Carrie and I signed the papers on the house the day before Grace's husband died in the line of duty. Lieutenant Ryan Fox,'' Morgan added, retrieving a copper canister off the counter. ''Did you know him?''

''Vaguely. I've crossed paths with all three of your brothers. And I worked that short undercover gig with Grace. Ryan and I just never connected on the job.'' Settling onto one of the stools, Alex laid the manila envelope beside a stack of file folders. ''I hear he was a good cop.''

''The best. And an awesome brother-in-law. Losing him…'' Her voice trailed off, and Alex saw grief flicker in her blue eyes. ''It was a terrible time for all of us. Having this house to come to, to work on together, was a sort of cathartic experience for the family.'' She swept her gaze around the room. ''Hard to believe three years have passed.''

''How's Grace doing these days?'' he asked quietly.

''Better. She eventually sold her house and moved in here with Carrie and me. It's good she's not alone.''

''Lucky you guys get along so well.''

''We're typical sisters.'' Sending him a sardonic look,

Morgan scooped beans out of the canister and dumped them into a grinder. "We live in harmony as long as Carrie remembers to shovel her heaps of makeup, jars, tubes and potions out of the bathroom every so often." Morgan turned on the grinder, its motor filling the air with a soft whir. "What about you?" she asked while setting the coffeemaker to brew.

"What about me?"

"Do you have any sisters? Brothers?"

"I'm an only child." And on the night a faceless killer fired a bullet into George Jackson's head, Alex had lost the only person who had ever cared enough about him to hang on and not let go.

The now-familiar mix of grief and anger had Alex setting his jaw. He would never forget the sight of George's body dumped in a weed-infested parking lot. Never forget having to watch the casket of the man who'd been like a father to him going down into the earth. An ache built around Alex's heart, a kind of distant grief he knew he would never be rid of. Whether Carlton Spurlock had pulled the trigger or ordered others to do the killing, George's blood was on his hands. Spurlock was accountable, and Alex would see he answered for his crimes. No matter how long it took, no matter *what* it took, he would nail the bastard.

Narrowing his gaze, he studied Morgan while she slid a tin brimming with muffins from the oven. This woman, who looked a hell of a lot more like a varsity cheerleader than a cop, was the weapon he would use to take down a killer.

"Hope you like these," she said as she drizzled a swirl of pale-orange glaze over each muffin. "It's a new recipe I wanted to try out."

"Judging by the way my stomach is growling, you

don't need to worry about me liking them." Leaning back on his stool, he crossed his arms over his chest. "Your scores in every segment of the academy were off the charts. You grind coffee beans and whip up a batch of homemade muffins with no effort. Then there's your obvious gardening ability. Is there anything you don't do well?"

"Not anymore."

"Anymore?"

"Long story." She settled plates of muffins and mugs of steaming coffee on the butcher block, then slid onto the stool beside his. "The bottom line is, if I want to learn how to do something I get a book, read the directions and then I do it." Lifting her shoulder, she sipped her coffee. "Everything is a step-by-step process. What's so hard about that?"

"Put that way, sounds like everything ought to be easy."

"My thoughts exactly."

Her apparent inner drive to do everything one hundred percent made it a snap for him to compare Morgan to another woman. A woman motivated by a burning need to lead in her career field, to be the best in anything, *everything*, at the exclusion—and expense—of all else.

Even after so long the bitterness over his failed marriage was still there, simmering with a foul taste he'd almost grown used to. Almost. He would never forget the betrayal and hurt that had slashed through him when he finally realized his own lack of desire to move up the police ranks had earned him the disdain of the woman he had loved.

He sipped his coffee—which was the best he'd ever tasted—thinking perversely that he ought to be glad Morgan shared the same no-holds-barred ambitions as Paula.

That would make it a hell of a lot easier for him to keep his mind on the dangerous job facing him and the rookie.

"There's nothing hard about learning something when you've got instructions," he commented. "Unless maybe you're talking about something like quantum physics." He took a bite of muffin, savored it…and decided he had truly stumbled into heaven. Yeah, the woman had learned how to cook. "Problem is, not everything comes with directions. And even if something does, following them isn't always the smartest thing to do."

She sampled her muffin, washed it down with a sip of coffee. "What about the detailed biography of my undercover character you had me write yesterday?"

"What about it?"

She retrieved a file folder near her plate, flipped it open. Alex recognized the pad inside as the one she'd used to jot notes on yesterday at his apartment. Her handwriting was precise, the letters angular. Exact.

"The biography starts with Morgan Jones's fictional birth," she continued. "Takes her through an unremarkable childhood on to her move to Las Vegas where she worked as a cocktail waitress. There, she met Alexander Donovan. It was instant attraction, which quickly turned into lust, followed by love. They married one month ago, and just wound up their honeymoon at a resort on the north shore of Lake Tahoe."

"Is there a question in there somewhere?"

"I'm getting to that. You told me to include every detail of her life I can think of to make her a well-rounded, real human being. And to memorize those details. Practice going over them in my head until I think and react like she would. So, isn't Morgan Jones Donovan's biography my instruction manual for this assignment? Don't I use it the way an actor uses a script?"

"Not hardly." Alex swiveled on his stool to face her. The span between them was small enough that their knees bumped. Purposely he adjusted by sliding his jeaned thighs against her bare ones.

And instantly felt her stiffen.

He told himself the acute annoyance that shot through him was due to the fact this same reaction to his touch after they went undercover could plunge them both into deep trouble. They would deal with the body language, he promised himself. First things first.

"An actor on stage or in front of a camera doesn't have any room for deviation. He's required to give a certain response that's programmed to get an expected reaction. No surprises. No glitches in timing, no missed cues. Everybody knows the ending before they even get started. That's not the case here—the biography you wrote on Morgan Donovan isn't by any means a script."

He glanced down, saw she now had her hands fisted in her lap. Her shoulders were back, as rigid as cold steel. Not good.

Locking his gaze with hers, he shifted closer, wanting to read her eyes. They looked cool and impersonal. At least she had a talent for keeping her feelings from being reflected in her face. It was the body language that needed work. Badly. Among other things.

He glanced at the pad she'd written the biography on. White paper, black ink. She wouldn't see the shades of gray he saw there, not until she'd gotten some experience under her belt.

"When it comes to working undercover," he continued, "there is no such thing as a script. All you have is a general scenario of what you're dealing with. You'll get surprises no one can foresee. What you can't anticipate is what will happen from minute to minute and how it will happen. Or what individuals are going to show up, or who might all of a sudden decide to make themselves scarce. And sometimes those are the people who are far more dangerous to you than the ones right there in your face, because you don't know what the hell they're up to. It's all a big question mark. The main thing you need to remember is, if you screw up, you don't have an audience to toss tomatoes your way. Instead, you've got bad guys who fire bullets. Real bullets.''

She nodded, her gaze serious. ''I went online, found some articles written by cops who'd worked undercover,'' she said, her voice even. Businesslike. ''I've been studying them.''

''Articles,'' he repeated. Could this woman be any more by-the-book?

''Yes. In one the author compared undercover work to walking a very thin wire over a very long drop. With no net below. It's dangerous. I understand that.''

''Let's be sure.'' He retrieved the manila envelope, dumped out a handful of photos into his palm. ''Like I told you the day you snagged this assignment, we know from the notes George Jackson—the retired OCPD cop who was the head of security at the race track—left on his computer that Krystelle Vander called him. She was hysterical, claiming Carlton Spurlock ended their relationship. She told Jackson she had some sort of evidence proving Spurlock ordered a jockey's murder. Jackson told her to meet him, then left his office.'' Alex handed Morgan the photos. ''We don't know where they met or what happened later. We just know they wound up dead.''

Alex studied Morgan while she scanned the photos of the bodies found dumped in the parking lot of an abandoned warehouse. He knew her recruit class had been subjected to crime-scene photos during their weeks of training. So he wasn't surprised her hands remained steady, her eyes impassive while she gazed at the leggy, model-thin Vander sprawled on her back, naked save for a pair of red-sequined stiletto heels. Bruises mottled the woman's tanned face; her head was twisted at an awkward angle. Her arms and legs were flung out, her long, blonde hair matted with dried blood.

When Morgan got to the photos of George Jackson, Alex looked away. He didn't need pictures to remind him of how a single bullet to the head had ended George's life. Of how the blood clotted against George's thick, gray hair had looked almost black in the glaring lights the lab techs had set up at the crime scene.

"You knew him, didn't you?" Morgan asked quietly.

Alex sliced his gaze back to her. She had finished looking at the photos and was sitting there, watching him. "Yeah, I knew him. He was the best beat cop this department ever had."

"What I mean is, he mattered. To you."

"What makes you think that?"

"Because when you say his name, there's something in your voice. Some change. Emotion."

Alex couldn't say George's name without it hurting his throat. He figured if Morgan was perceptive enough to catch that, she deserved the truth. "Yeah, he mattered. A lot. George Jackson is the reason I became a cop."

"Is he the reason you're on this assignment?"

"He and the other five people Spurlock murdered." Alex gathered up the photos. "I wanted you to see these because I don't want you to forget for one second what he's capable of having done on his behalf."

Nodding, Morgan met his gaze. "Seeing these, seeing what he did, especially to the woman, it would be hard to forget." She watched Alex slide photos back into the manila envelope. "Do you think Spurlock is the one who pulled the trigger? Poisoned the FBI agents? Set his accountant, Tool, on fire?"

"Those questions are some of the unknowns we're dealing with in this case. What I do know is when it comes to bad guys, the more money one makes in his criminal endeavors, the less likely he is to be violent, directly at least. In other words, the man at the top may have people working for him who break arms and legs, but he, in creating his own illusion of respectability, usually doesn't get his own hands dirty."

Alex clipped the envelope shut. "That's another factor I added to the equation when I pegged you for this assignment, instead of a more seasoned cop. We're not dealing with some fried-brain doper who might pull a gun if you look at him wrong. Spurlock is at the top of the heap when it comes to the dregs of society. He rubs elbows with some of this city's elite, even a few politicians. He'll think long and hard before he gets his own hands dirty."

"But he will if he needs to," she said quietly.

"Count on it. A cop works undercover long enough, he'll eventually find someone he thought of as a pussycat suddenly turn into a lion."

"And he has to deal with that lion without a script."

"Exactly."

She met his steady gaze, uneasiness drifting through her. "I think I understand why you chose me. But nothing changes the fact I'm an inexperienced rookie. That means there's more chance I might make a mistake."

"If this assignment required you to do technical things like fill out paperwork for search warrants or even read someone their rights and interrogate them, I would have made other arrangements." He raised a palm. "This job doesn't call for you to have a seasoned cop's technical expertise. It requires you to have certain physical characteristics and know about plants. You can do this, Morgan.''

She gave him a slight smile. "I hope you're right.''

"I am. You just have to trust me. Trust that I won't let you go into this unprepared. That's why I had you create Morgan Donovan's biography. Doing so is the only way I have ever found to train a cop to convincingly portray a character. You've got her in your mind now. That's the first hurdle.''

"What's the second?''

"You become her. Mrs. Alexander Donovan can't be someone you just think about when you're with me. You have to give birth to her, *be* her.''

Morgan shook her head. "I don't know the best way to do that. If you'll explain how…''

"You're wanting me to give you a set of instructions from a textbook. Forget it. It all has to do with emotions, feelings.''

"Emotions and feelings,'' she murmured.

"Right. You start by getting used to having me around.'' He settled his hands on her board-stiff shoulders. "Relax,'' he said quietly, kneading at the tension he felt there. "You're Morgan Donovan now. The guy touching you is your husband. You jump every time he gets within a few inches of you, Spurlock is going to wonder why.''

"You're right. I know you're right.''

"Close your eyes.''

She gave him a wary look. "Why?''

"Because I'm your husband and I give the orders. You follow them.''

Her expression instantly went from apprehensive to derisive. "That unsavory character flaw isn't in Mrs. Donovan's profile."

"No kidding." Kneading her shoulders, Alex grinned. "Just go with me here, Morgan. Close your eyes."

"Fine."

"Yesterday I showed you photos of the mansion we're moving into," he said when she complied. "You studied them. All the furnishings, appliances, even the pots and pans got included in the bankruptcy. You've seen how each room will look when we move in."

"Yes."

"Picture the master bedroom."

In his own mind he saw the image of the sumptuously attired room with vanilla-colored wallpaper sprawling with pale flowers and soft coral tinted carpet. The massive four-poster bed sitting opposite the green-marbled fireplace was the size of a small lake. Its thick mahogany headboard matched the chest of drawers, dresser and nightstands.

"See it?" he asked quietly.

"Yes."

"Now, picture yourself there as Morgan Donovan. It's early in the morning. You're still in that big bed, just waking up." Wanting to enhance the image, he matched his voice to the lazy kneading of his fingers against her shoulders. "You stretch like a cat, maybe even consider going back to sleep. What, if anything, is Morgan Donovan wearing? How does she feel? Did she do something last night to make her feel that way?"

The instant the words were out, a vision stabbed through Alex's brain of Morgan lying in the expansive bed beneath him, her warm, lush body moving in sync with his, those long legs wrapped around his. For the first time in years, he felt his blood move for a woman. *This* woman who sat inches away, her golden lashes feathering her cheeks, her unpainted mouth looking soft and moist. Ripe.

He became aware of how quiet the house was, how the two of them were alone, how the heat of her flesh rose through her T-shirt into his palms. He could smell only her now, the tang of lemony soap that clung to her skin. Clean, fresh and simple. The raw hot churning inside him wiped his brain of all thought of what was supposed to come next during this lesson.

When Morgan felt his fingers go still, then tighten on her shoulders, she opened her eyes. Alex's unshaven face and black, shaggy hair lent him the air of a buccaneer. Still, it wasn't his appearance that shot a ripple up her spine. It was the realization his dark, unreadable gaze had focused on her mouth.

Her throat went dry.

How could the mere feel of a man's hands on her shoulders—not even her *bare* shoulders—spark an inferno inside her? Good Lord, they were working. He was trying to teach her how to stay alive during an undercover operation, and her system was revving like an overloaded blender. Sitting this close, it was impossible not to feel the heat of his body, not to breathe in his spicy male scent. It had been a very long time since a man had put his hands on her.

She didn't need this kind of distraction, she thought, gritting her teeth. Had made certain she would never again let herself get distracted. She'd gotten her life back on track by taking step A, making sure it lead to step B, and so on until she had every aspect under control. *She* was in control, she assured herself. Not her emotions.

"Is…" She cleared her throat to rid her voice of a sudden huskiness. "Is that all?"

His gaze skimmed up from her mouth to meet hers. Something flicked in his dark eyes, then was gone. "Not by a long shot. Close your eyes again."

Angling her spine a little straighter, she complied, thinking this training exercise would be far easier if he took his hands off her shoulders. Moved to the far side of the kitchen. Maybe down the hallway. Yelled at her from a nice, safe distance what she needed to know about assuming her undercover persona.

"Picture how Morgan Donovan gets out of bed each morning," he said.

*Concentrate,* Morgan told herself. Think about the operation. "Okay."

"How does she walk? Brush her teeth? Does she come downstairs and grind beans and bake muffins? Or maybe she prefers instant coffee and a bowl of granola?"

*Maybe she skips breakfast and jumps your bones first thing.*

The unbidden thought had Morgan's eyes shooting open. In a lightning move she sprang off the stool.

"What the hell?" Alex rose, took a step toward her just as the door connecting the kitchen to the garage swung open.

"Well, good morning."

"Carrie." As she struggled to settle her pulse, Morgan didn't have to wonder if the heat pooling in her cheeks had turned into a flush. She saw verification in the arch of one of her sister's perfectly plucked eyebrows. Mouth pursed, Carrie flicked her gaze between the two people she had just walked in on.

*Doing nothing wrong,* Morgan added. The only thing wrong was the crazed direction her thoughts had taken about Alex Blade. She set her jaw. Her hormones were mistaken if they thought she was game to take another wild ride with a man who could make her pulse pound just by walking into a room. Not after the misery she'd put herself—and her family—through last time. She had dug herself out of one pit. She had no intention of winding up in another.

Shoving her hands into the pockets of her shorts, she fisted them. She noted Alex looked totally at ease in his worn jeans and white T-shirt with one hip leaned against the butcher-block island while sipping his coffee. Of course he looked totally unaffected, she told herself. He was used to preparing partners to work undercover. *He* was only doing his job. Working.

"Carrie, this is Sergeant Alex Blade. I told you I'll be working with him. I don't know if you two have met." Morgan could hear the edge in her voice, but she couldn't help it. Any more than she could stop from adding, "We're working. He's giving me pointers on how to get into my undercover persona."

"They must be doozies," Carrie murmured before moving across the kitchen. Even though she was just coming off working the graveyard shift, she looked wide-eyed and rested. As usual, her stunning auburn hair was a mass of long, silky waves, her makeup flawless, her snug shorts and cotton top pristine. Even the uniform pants and shirt she'd changed out of at the briefing station looked wrinkle free, draped over one of her forearms.

Her mouth curving, Carrie held out a hand to Alex. "We haven't met, but I've heard a lot about you."

He dipped his head as he shook her hand. "Try not to hold it against me."

"It was all good. In fact, Grace and I breathed a sigh of relief when Morgan said it was you she's assigned to work with. We won't worry near as much about her."

"Glad to hear it," he replied.

Carrie lifted her chin, sniffed. "Morgan, tell me you've baked something decadent I can indulge in before I catch some shut-eye."

Morgan let out the breath she hadn't been aware she was holding. "Orange-glazed muffins." Relieved to have something to do with her hands, she retrieved a saucer from a cabinet. "Take two upstairs with you," she said, sliding muffins onto the plate. "Do you want coffee?"

"More than anything. But if I drink it, I'll never get my beauty sleep." Carrie glanced at the clock on the stove's panel. "Is our shopping trip with Grace still on for this evening?"

"Yes, we're meeting her at the mall at six."

After Carrie disappeared down the hallway, Morgan met Alex's gaze. "You told me I could give my sisters a vague idea of my assignment. I did. They're both more into fashion than I am, especially Carrie. She's the clothes horse. We're shopping tonight for my undercover wardrobe."

"Fine." Watching her, he settled back onto the stool. "Morgan, is it this assignment or me that has you wound up like a junkie late for a fix? Or both?"

She studied the sharply defined planes and angles of the face that gave no indication of what he was thinking. For as long as she could remember, she'd wanted to become a cop. And she'd done it. Maybe she hadn't been there to graduate with her recruit class, or wear the badge she now carried tucked in her purse, but that didn't make her any less of a police officer. She'd proven the one tumble she'd taken in college over a man didn't mean she couldn't pull herself back up.

In an unconscious move she fingered the nearly invisible scar near her right temple. Her bad judgment in men had led to a car wreck that almost killed her. She had finally paid back every cent her parents had spent on her medical bills their insurance hadn't covered. She'd carefully budgeted her city paycheck so she could make quick repayment of the student loan she'd taken out when she'd adopted her party-hearty boyfriend's lifestyle and lost her full-ride academic scholarship.

Now, just as she was getting her life back on to the course she'd always intended it to be on, here was Alex Blade, stirring her senses as only one other man in her life had. The emotional scars from that encounter had penetrated far deeper than the physical ones.

Which was good, she thought perversely. Remembering the pain, the suffering she'd endured was all the reminder she—and her hormones—needed to keep her mind off the man and on the job.

"I'm tense because this assignment was so unexpected," she said truthfully. "I thought I would graduate from the academy, and ride the streets for the next six months with a field training officer. Instead, I'm working undercover." *With you.*

"Being a cop, you can't take for granted what you'll be doing next. Where you'll be assigned. Or who you'll be working for or with. None of that is up to you."

"Every cop in my family clued me into that a long time ago." Slowly she relaxed her shoulders, her arms, her hands. She had to get used to this man. Loosen up. "I understand the point you made about Morgan Donovan."

Keeping his eyes on her, he sipped his coffee. "What point?"

"I can't just think about her. I have to become her. Get out of bed like her." She moistened her lips as he continued watching her, saying nothing. "I have to brush my teeth the way she does. Eat like her. Think like her. Think of you as she would her husband."

"That's right," he said after a moment. "Morgan, I need you to level with me. Do you think you can pull it off? Our lives may depend on it."

"You don't need to worry. I know my assignment. Spurlock is a killer. We have to take him down. I'll do what it takes to do that."

"Good." Alex shifted his gaze from her face to the pad of paper on which she'd compiled notes. "Ready to get back to work?"

"Ready."

# Chapter 4

Days later, Alex steered a shiny black Lincoln into the drive behind a nondescript two-story brick house. The Lincoln had been the pampered baby of an Atlanta drug dealer until his conviction. Atlanta PD had acquired the Lincoln and a white BMW convertible through an asset forfeiture program. To cut down on chances of the distinctive vehicles getting recognized by other local bad guys, APD had swapped the cars for two primo pimp-owned Cadillacs the OCPD vice squad had seized.

Alex braked the Lincoln behind the BMW convertible that gleamed like a milky pearl in the morning sun. The Beemer drove like a bullet and was the perfect vehicle for the new bride of Alexander Donovan, a man with money to burn, a newly purchased mansion in Hampton Hills and one felony gambling conviction on record.

He turned off the Lincoln's engine, then paused as he stared out the windshield. He couldn't quite picture Morgan McCall sitting behind the sassy convertible's wheel, not dressed in the loose-fitting clothes she habitually wore and her blond hair slicked back or piled carelessly on top of her head. The image just wouldn't gel. He hoped to hell he'd been right to trust her to buy the right outfits for the job during the two shopping trips she and her sisters had embarked on.

His mouth formed a caustic curve at the thought of the list Morgan had made of the clothes and other items she planned to buy. Making a list wasn't so bad—showed she was organized. Problem was, he remembered another woman who made a list or chart or graph for everything. Anything. Even one to document the time line she expected his move up the PD's ranks to take. Too bad Paula never bothered asking if moving up was something *he* wanted.

"Hell," he muttered as he climbed out of the Lincoln. It was just his bad luck the perfect woman for his present assignment might have been cloned from his ex.

The narrow wood steps leading up to the house's back porch creaked as he took them two at a time. He crossed toward the door while nudging back the French cuff of his starched white shirt to check the time on the solid-gold designer watch he'd strapped on that morning. One of the FBI's whiz-boys had inserted a few handy microchips inside the watch, one being a bug detector. After two consecutive clicks on the stem, Alex would instantly know if any surreptitious audio surveillance devices were in his and Morgan's vicinity. A different sequence of clicks would transmit an SOS to a pager worn by their control officer.

He knocked twice on the door, paused, then rapped four times in quick succession. The code told the cop inside that Alex belonged there and, if he had someone with him, he hadn't been coerced into bringing them there.

When the door swung open, he tipped his head at the trim, attractive federal agent clad in tan shorts and a black T-shirt. "Morning, Rackowitz."

"Back at ya, Blade."

He had worked with Sara Rackowitz several times on joint federal and local law enforcement operations, and was pleased she'd been pegged to act as his and Morgan's control officer. A smart, capable cop, Rackowitz was blissfully married with two rambunctious sons.

"Things go okay this morning?" Alex asked as he stepped into the small kitchen with its faded wallpaper, chipped counters and yellowed linoleum. The safe house had gone unused by the department for the past couple of months, lending it an empty feel.

"Like clockwork." Rackowitz tucked her dark, straight hair behind her ears. "I picked up McCall, her luggage and about ten sacks of groceries from her house a couple of hours ago."

"*Ten* sacks?"

"Yeah, she said you had the freezer at the mansion stocked with frozen food, which isn't exactly her idea of fine dining. So she got up early this morning and went to the store. The groceries and all but one suitcase are now stashed in the BMW. McCall took the remaining one upstairs. She's still there, transforming herself into your wife."

Alex hid a wince, thinking of the mental comparison he'd just made between Morgan and his ex. "Were any of her neighbors out when you picked her up?"

"Didn't see a soul."

"Good." The Donovans' cover was that they were new in town, so he hadn't wanted Morgan's neighbors spotting her leaving her house in the guise of her undercover persona. Nor did he want her seen driving the BMW convertible before she transformed into Mrs. Donovan. All little details, but they were ones that could turn an operation dicey if the wrong person saw her. This assignment was his one chance to take down Carlton Spurlock for six murders. *George Jackson's murder.* Alex didn't intend to leave anything to chance.

"The moving van got to the mansion around eight-thirty," Rackowitz reported.

That wasn't news to Alex. He had checked before he left his apartment to make sure the van—manned with a mix of federal and local undercover cops—had arrived on schedule. He had purposely planned for Morgan and himself to make a later appearance commensurate with a rich, privileged couple who had the money to hire things done.

Rackowitz walked into the small alcove off the kitchen and retrieved her purse and keys off the scarred wood table. "Since I'm your yard and pool girl, I'll head over there now and start mowing. Glancing down at her T-shirt and shorts, she smiled. "At least this is one assignment where I'll get to do some serious work on my tan."

"Who said a career in law enforcement has no perks?" Alex asked dryly. "Just remember, with all the activity at the mansion it probably won't take long for Spurlock's security cameras to start sweeping the property."

She wiggled her dark eyebrows. "I wore my tightest shorts to make sure he gets an eyeful."

Alex chuckled. "For a Fed, Rackowitz, you're not so bad."

"Yeah, well, for a local cop, you'll do."

"Keep a watch out for Wade Crawford from our Vice detail. He'll show up at the mansion sometime this morning to get the security alarm up to snuff and install the cameras and straight-line."

"Will do."

"Before you go, let's check to make sure my watch talks to your pager." His gaze swept the waistband of her shorts. "Where is it?"

"In my pocket. It vibrates instead of making noise that might draw the wrong kind of attention."

"Good." Alex hit a sequence of clicks on the watch's stem.

"Feels like there's a crazed moth trapped in there," Rackowitz said, dipping her hand into her pocket. She withdrew the pager, checking its display. "Got your personal code to send in the cavalry." She reset the pager, slid it back into her pocket. "Anything else?"

"I'll tell you in a minute."

Alex walked out of the kitchen into the living room furnished with a sagging dirt-colored sofa and matching chairs that looked as if they'd been acquired from a cut-rate motel. A phone sat on the table beside the sofa. He picked up its receiver, heard the dial tone, then hung up. Crawford would install phones in the study and master bedroom at the Hampton Hills mansion. Those would be linked to this one to provide instant communication. Pick up one, the others would automatically ring. The specialized phones also acted as omnidirectional microphones, doubling as both a security feature and bug. The phones were almost impossible to tap and could be swept as often as necessary to ensure their integrity.

Alex turned and looked at Rackowitz, now leaning against the kitchen door. As their control officer, she would live in the safe house for the duration of the assignment. Any contact he or Morgan needed to make with law enforcement would be through her. Rackowitz working each day on the mansion's grounds and pool made communication among all parties easy. If Alex did find it necessary to visit the safe house and picked up a tail in the process, the attractive Agent Rackowitz could be explained away as his mistress.

"I'm glad you're assigned to this operation," he said. "Too bad it uproots you from your family."

"Spurlock had two FBI agents poisoned when he snatched his accountant, Tool, out of our custody." As she spoke, something cold and hard settled in her dark eyes. "One of those guys was a pal of mine. This is personal, Blade. I want Spurlock in the worst way. And Tool's lucky the big guy already charbroiled him. Otherwise, he'd be on my takedown list, too."

Alex thought about George Jackson and felt the still-sharp drag of grief. "I know what you mean."

"Anyway, Frank and the boys will get along fine without me for a while. They're looking forward to going to Waterworld every day and pigging out on frozen foods and takeout." Her expression turned pained. "I'll just have to rent a dozer to shovel out the house when I get back."

"No doubt."

"McCall," Rackowitz said, her gaze flicking to the narrow staircase at the far end of the living room.

"What about her?"

"Great skin, gorgeous hair, awesome bod. They sure come out of the academy looking young these days." Rackowitz shook her head. "You positive someone as green as she is can pull this off?"

"If I didn't think so, she wouldn't be here."

"Yeah, well, I trust your judgment." She slung her purse strap over one shoulder. "I'm off to mow your lawn and clean your pool, Mr. Donovan. I sure hope you believe in giving big tips to the hired help."

Alex lifted a brow. "You want a tip, Rackowitz? Don't talk to strangers. You'll stay safe that way."

"You're a load of laughs, Blade. See you and the little woman in a while," Rackowitz added before heading into the kitchen and out the back door.

Alex shifted his gaze toward the staircase. It was time he had a look at his wife.

He was about to head upstairs when he heard the creak of a door overhead, then footsteps clicking along the hallway's wood floor. Remaining in the center of the living room, he kept his eyes on the staircase, waiting for Morgan to step into view.

The instant she did, the blood drained out of his brain.

She'd sure as hell bought the right clothes, he thought, struggling to ignore the buzz in his head.

A black leather miniskirt clung to her thighs like wet paint and showcased those long, bare, tanned legs. She'd put on makeup—enough of it to make her eyes a cool, luminous blue and her mouth brooding. And extraordinarily tempting. Her blond hair was teased and cascaded across her shoulders, looking mussed and tousled, the way it might if she had just spent a session in bed with a lover. A very long, heated session.

Alex could see enough of her electric-blue tank top not concealed by miles of golden hair to tell there was nothing but woman underneath.

When Morgan glimpsed him standing in the center of the living room, she hesitated, then walked toward him. "I hope this outfit is okay." She might look like a man's darkest fantasy, but her voice and demeanor were all business. "Since my job is to get Spurlock's attention, I thought I should try to do that the instant we arrive at the mansion."

When Alex managed to drag in a breath, a kick-to-the-glands perfume wafted off her flesh into his lungs.

She eyed him guardedly. "Something wrong?"

"No." He worked on getting his breath back. It was now a snap for him to picture her sitting behind the sporty little Beemer's wheel. This woman had been born to drive that car. Born to make a man weep from wanting to get his hands on her. "You look…good. Fine."

She arched a brow. "I look like the poster girl for a porn palace." She cast him a long, weighing glance. "You look different, too. Totally."

He'd shaved, had his hair trimmed in a businessman's cut, and donned a tailored, gray silk suit and red tie. "Alex Donovan, at your service, Mrs. Donovan."

She glanced toward the kitchen. "Where's Agent Rackowitz?"

"Already left for Hampton Hills. She'll either be mowing or cleaning the pool by the time we get there."

"I like her." Morgan raised a bare shoulder. "She doesn't project the uptight image of a Fed you always hear about."

"Uh-huh." Alex was just now getting around to noticing the black ice-pick heels that made her long legs look endless. Before this moment he had never realized a woman's legs could be considered a work of art.

She ran her palms down the leather skirt that could double as a wide belt. "Alex, you're staring at me like I'm not what you expected." As she spoke, she tossed all that long, golden hair back in a gesture so utterly sensual it delivered a punch straight to his gut. "If the porn queen look isn't what you had in mind for me, say so. Carrie gave me lessons on fixing my hair and slathering on makeup, but she may have gone overboard. And if the clothes aren't right, I can take them back. I saved the receipts—"

"No, you're exactly what I want." And was totally unprepared for. If she had this effect on him, she'd have

Spurlock drooling the instant he laid eyes on her. "You nailed the look, Morgan. Trust me."

"Okay." She glanced at the solid-gold Rolex he'd strapped on her wrist the previous day. Hers had been modified with the same microchips as his. "Are we done here?"

"Almost. We just need to take care of one more thing before we head to Hampton Hills." As he spoke, he closed the distance between them while pulling a small brown envelope from his pocket. "The Donovans are husband and wife. They wear rings."

"Rings." In the black stilettos, she stood eye to eye with him. "I hadn't thought about a ring."

"Work undercover long enough, you learn to think of every detail." They were standing so close he could almost feel the heated, come-get-me scent pulsing off her flesh. The varsity cheerleader had transformed into a lethal weapon.

He dumped the ring into his palm, then tucked the empty envelope back into the pocket of his suitcoat.

Her eyes went wide. "Holy… How big is that rock?"

"A little over six carats." Smiling while she gaped, he glanced at the wide gold band with the emerald-cut diamond that sparkled in his palm like the tail of a comet. "Criminal Intel took it and both Rolexes off a career jewel thief. They haven't yet found the lawful owners. Meanwhile, the watches and ring are on loan to us from the property room's safe."

She held out a hand to accept the ring. "I hope you don't expect me to wear this while I'm digging in flower beds."

"No, just all other times." Instead of handing her the ring, he slid his fingers around hers…and felt her stiffen. "My touch," he reminded her, aware of how soft her flesh felt against his. "You have to get used to my touch, Morgan."

"I know." Her lashes fluttered. "I'm getting there."

"And I have to get used to yours," he added. With his hand cradling hers, he eased the ring onto her finger. He could feel her nerves shimmering against his flesh. He wasn't so sure his didn't follow their lead.

"It fits." The lightness in her voice sounded forced. "Imagine that."

He tightened his grip when she started to pull away. "I have a ring, too." He reached into his pocket. The gold band had once symbolized the vows he'd made to another woman. Now it served as a reminder of one very huge, painful mistake. "Here."

He could sense her cool caution as she plucked the band from his palm.

The instant she slid it on his finger, she stepped back. "That it? We officially the Donovans?"

He met her gaze, saw nerves and some other emotion he couldn't peg swimming in her blue eyes.

"Yes, that's it."

"Okay, I'll get my suitcase from the bedroom."

"Need some help?"

"No. I'll just be a minute."

Letting out a pent-up breath, he watched her walk away, her hips swaying beneath the black leather mini like a swing in a soft breeze. She disappeared up the staircase with one last inviting flash of leg.

When a spike of lust drove into his gut, he could all but feel the danger tripping through his blood. He didn't intend to let any woman get to him again. To dig in, then start clawing until there was nothing of him left except hollow hurt. His eyes narrowed. There was something indefinable about Morgan McCall that made him suspect she might take hold inside him, even if he didn't want her to.

Distance, he told himself, was the key to prevent that from happening.

Too bad they were about to move in together.

Shoving his hands into the pockets of his slacks, he muttered a curse. Working undercover had honed his acting skills. For him to get through this assignment, he'd damn well have to give an award-winning performance.

With the BMW's top down, the warm June air slid across Morgan's flesh as she tailed Alex's black Lincoln through the rich neighborhood of professionally tended landscapes and massive, architect-designed homes. She had grown up in a comfortable, middle-class area of Oklahoma City, had occasionally taken shortcuts through Hampton Hills on her way to somewhere else. Never in her wildest imaginings had she envisioned herself the mistress of one of these monster, million-dollar homes.

Or pictured herself married—pretend or otherwise—to a man like Alexander Blade. *Donovan,* she mentally corrected.

She nudged her designer sunglasses more firmly up the bridge of her nose as she reflected on the man driving the car in front of hers. His shaggy hair, unshaven face, rumpled shirts and worn jeans had lent him a darkly brooding mystique. Now, with his hair trimmed, his face shaved, his clothing expensive, he looked like the godfather of a Mafia empire. A cool, controlled, *dangerous* man with whom a woman could never totally feel safe.

Just thinking about spending so much time with him, parading as his sexpot wife, had her easing out a breath. On her left hand, the killer diamond sparked in the sunlight, reflecting dazzling rays in every direction. Only to herself would she admit she wasn't sure she could handle this assignment. She functioned best with rules. Solid rules. Stable guidelines. Laws and ordinances that were printed in black-and-white and could be quoted verbatim. None of those existed in the murky world of undercover work. There it was all games and illusions. Smoke and mirrors. Lies and deception. It took only one tiny, unintentional mistake to leave a hole for someone to peer through and learn the truth.

The sudden clench of nerves at the base of her neck had her palms going damp. What if she screwed up? What if Carlton Spurlock saw through her act? The man was a monster who had ordered—or carried out—the murder of at least six people, three of them cops. Her fingers tightened on the steering wheel at the thought of some mistake on her part landing herself and Alex in danger. Worse, getting one or both of them hurt…or killed.

"Stop," she ordered herself through gritted teeth. "You can pull this off. You *have* to pull this off." Spurlock was a killer. Period. It was up to Alex and her to take him down. Of lesser importance was the fact this assignment was a great career opportunity. Done right, it could help sweep her swiftly up through the department's ranks.

She was still assuring herself she could do the job with perfection four blocks later when the Lincoln's turn indicator flashed.

She had seen numerous photos of the Hampton Hills mansion in which she and Alex would set up house. No picture, however, could have prepared her for her first glimpse of the enormous sprawling structure.

"Heavens," she murmured as she swung the BMW onto the cobblestone driveway shaded with towering oaks. The Lincoln glided forward, finally stopping a few yards behind a large, white moving van. Since the bank had seized the house and all its furnishing during the bankruptcy, the cops dressed in blue overalls with a moving company logo embroidered on the back were in the process of unloading only a few pieces of furniture loaned from the Feds that had been fitted with hidden compartments. The remainder of the van had been filled with various sizes of cardboard boxes, most of them empty.

Morgan braked the BMW just before the driveway curved to nest against a columned porch wide enough to inline skate on. Planters, she decided automatically. The porch would look more inviting with stone planters holding trimmed shrubs placed on either side of the massive, double front doors.

She turned off the Beemer's purring engine. Instead of sliding out, she leaned back and studied the imposing three-story white structure with a high-peaked roof, forest-green trim, the numerous windows flanked by emerald shutters.

It hit her then—the reality of the assignment. Alex had drummed into her head how comfortable undercover cops had to become with their cover story. *Comfortable,* she thought, as panic tightened her chest. No way in hell could she ever feel at ease pretending to be the mistress of this jumbo house with its large rooms, thick walls and shiny hardwood floors.

Or the wife of the man who would inhabit those rooms with her.

"Darling." Alex's deep voice jerked her gaze from the structure. As if sensing her panic, he placed a hand over the one she still had clenched on the steering wheel. His touch was firm, steady. Warm. "Everything all right?"

She gazed up at him, his mirrored sunglasses reflecting her image back at her. It wasn't Morgan McCall she saw, but a woman with poofy blond hair and a mouth made pouty by siren-red lip gloss. Morgan Donovan, she thought, her nerves instantly calming. She now knew this woman inside and out, she reminded herself. The sexy, slinky Mrs. Alexander Donovan, with her big hair, skimpy outfits and six-carat diamond ring would feel infinitely comfortable in these expensive surroundings.

And feel totally at ease with the man who provided them.

Mentally she slid into her undercover persona role while sending Alex a slow smile. "The photos you showed me of the mansion don't do it justice. It's much more beautiful in reality."

"That it is." With his hand still on hers, he swung open the door and helped her ease out of the BMW's tooled leather comfort. When she would have automatically released his hand, he tangled his fingers with hers, edged her closer and slid his free hand against the side of her throat. When he dipped his head, her pulse stuttered, then picked up speed.

"I just used my watch to do a scan—there's no active audio surveillance at the moment," he murmured, his breath a quiet wash against her cheek. "But several cameras mounted on the brick wall behind me are aimed this way. Be careful what you say. Someone on the other side of those cameras might read lips."

Morgan didn't know if it was the feel of Alex's hands on her flesh or the knowledge they were being watched— or both—that had her stomach flipping. Trying to keep her breathing even, she adjusted her sunglasses while focusing across his shoulder. Spurlock's property was surrounded by a twelve-foot brick wall, topped with surveillance cameras, motion detectors and sensors. When she pulled into the drive, she had taken note of the ornate iron gates that blocked entry to the curvy, meandering driveway.

She gave the staring black eyes of the security cameras one last look before shifting her gaze back to Alex.

She instantly froze, aware now that if she lifted her chin, her mouth would be on his. She stood unmoving as the warm, spicy scent of his cologne slid into her lungs. Against her throat, his palm was a hard, firm presence. What would it be like, she wondered, to ease forward that one forbidden inch? To skim her lips against his wide, generous mouth? How would he feel? *Taste?* As dangerous as he looked?

The sudden burr of an engine cut through her thoughts. She took an unsteady step backward. Then another, forcing him to drop his hand from her throat.

He didn't, however, relinquish his hold on her hand.

"That's our new lawn person," he said casually as Agent Rackowitz steered a riding lawn mower into view. "Her name's Sara Jones." He shifted his gaze back to Morgan, rays of sunlight glancing off the mirrored tint of his glasses. "Sara had great references, so I hired her. She'll also clean and maintain the pool. If she can't take care of other odd jobs that need doing, she'll find us someone who can."

"Sounds like you're lucky to have found her."

"That's how I feel."

Morgan rubbed the spot on her throat where Alex's palm had lingered. Beneath her fingers, she felt her pulse race. Concentrate on the job, she told herself. The job, which she had snagged not just because of her looks, but also her knowledge of plants and flowers.

The game, she thought, had truly begun.

Squaring her shoulders, she diverted her gaze and gave

the lawn a slow, appraising sweep. "Alex, our grass is a nightmare."

He glanced at the lawn. "It is?"

"Just look at it. It's starving." Easing her hand from his, she moved to the driveway's edge and nudged the toe of one stiletto into the ground. "This type of grass should be denser and a much deeper green. Three shades deeper. It needs a regimen of nutrients. Fertilizer. Not to mention water. A lot of water."

"I'll speak to Sara. You may need to give her specific instructions on…lawn nutrition."

"Count on it." Swiveling, Morgan turned her attention to the large flower beds on either side of the wide front porch. "Does no one from the bank realize it is June and ninety degrees in the shade?"

Alex crossed his arms over his chest, his gold cuff links glittering with the gesture. "The weather never came up during my dealings with the bankruptcy department."

"I guess it would have been too much to expect a bunch of bean counters to think about turning on the sprinkler system."

Tossing her head, she strode the length of the nearest flower bed that was thick with weeds and unidentifiable brown shriveled clumps. "All the flowers in this bed have died from lack of water. At least the azaleas, hydrangeas and peonies are still alive." She reached, fingered a curled, wilted leaf. "Barely." Hands fisted on her hips, she swiveled to face him. "I'll be lucky to save them."

"If you don't, I'm sure Sara can recommend some good nurseries in the area where you can buy more flowers."

Morgan flicked a wrist in disgust. "I have to deal with the soil first. It needs an acidifier. Badly."

"You're the expert." Alex strode toward her, extending

his hand. "Why don't we discuss acidifiers later? I want to give you a tour of our new home. Like you said, pictures don't do it justice."

"Fine." Mindful of the cameras, Morgan gave a flirty dip of her head. It was a gesture she had seen Carrie use successfully around the unending stream of men who hovered around her sister. "It's not every woman whose husband gives her a mansion for a wedding gift."

"Not every woman deserves one." As he spoke, Alex's hands settled on her hips, slid up her bare midriff and paused just under her breasts. The desire zinging through her belly had her clenching her teeth.

"Alex—" Whatever it was she planned to say whooshed out when he swooped her off her feet. "I...can walk," she managed.

"Yes, and you do it quite well in those heels," he commented as he carried her across the cobblestone drive. "What kind of husband would I be if I didn't carry my new bride across the threshold?"

Only one other man had swept her off her feet, and she had vowed to never let that happen again. Balling her hand against Alex's shoulder, she resisted the urge to squirm. *His* reasons for whisking her into his arms were far different from those of the man who had sliced her heart years ago.

Alex advanced up the wide steps that led to the front porch. Several of the cops parading as movers glanced their way as they hefted the specially fitted antique writing desk across the porch. Some cops nodded; all kept their expressions bland as they continued hauling boxes out of the truck and into the house. Out on the grass, Sara Rackowitz, a baseball cap pulled low over her eyes, steered the lawnmower, her total concentration centered on her task. Everyone stayed in character. The cops assigned to this operation were professionals, doing their job.

Knowing the same was expected of her, Morgan unballed her fist and placed her palm against Alex's cheek. "You don't have to carry me. But you're sweet to have thought of this."

"I'm a real sweetheart," he murmured.

He carried her through the set of gaping double doors into a cavernous foyer where a Persian carpet pooled over cool pink marble. Although he halted at the base of the burgundy-carpeted staircase that curved up two floors, he made no move to put her down. "A lab guy who's presently hauling in boxes swept the house for bugs when they got here. It's clean. We can say whatever we need to indoors."

"Okay." She started to shift from his hold, but his grip remained firm.

"You meant all of that out there, didn't you?" The mirrored sunglasses might have hidden his eyes, but that didn't prevent her from feeling the intense scrutiny of his gaze.

She stopped squirming. "All of what?"

"The talk about the lawn. The plants, shrub and soil. You weren't faking it."

"I didn't have to. Everything's a disaster. All those shrubs on the brink of death. Just because the house and furnishing got swept up in a bankruptcy doesn't mean what's outside went into suspended animation. Somebody at the bank ought to be shot for not making arrangements to have the sprinkler system switched on."

"Shot?" His mouth twitched. "That's a little severe. But seeing as there's one or two lawyers working in the bankruptcy department, I'll see what I can arrange."

She gave him a narrow look. "My mother has spent

her life nurturing things, making them grow. If she saw the grounds here, she'd wage war.''

"I think her daughter is doing that for her.''

"You don't grow up working in a nursery and not learn to respect plants, shrubs and flowers. They do a lot for people's well-being." She angled her chin. "Haven't you ever gotten pleasure just from the scent of a rose? Or seeing a vase of gorgeous flowers all grouped together?''

"I see flowers, mostly I think of funerals.''

"What about weddings?''

"What about them?''

"They usually have as many flowers as funerals do.''

"In my mind both events have a lot in common.''

"Sounds like Mrs. Donovan had better tread lightly around her husband with an attitude like that,'' she said.

"Not necessary. At this point he's too blinded by love to have dark thoughts about the institution of marriage.''

"Lucky her.'' One of his palms gripped her bare thigh; she could feel the firm length of each of his fingers against her flesh. Too warm, she thought. Too close. *Too intimate.*

Her nerves snapping, she placed her palms against his shoulders and eased back. "We're out of camera range, which means the Donovans are offstage. You can put me down.''

"Point taken,'' he said easily. He settled her on her feet and stepped back. The gold band she'd placed on his left hand winked as he pulled off his sunglasses. "You did a good job out there, Morgan.''

She ran her palms down the leather miniskirt. "Thanks.'' She felt as if her nerves were riding on the surface of her skin.

"I'll ask one of the men to bring our luggage upstairs and stow your groceries in the kitchen. Then I'll show you around.''

She slid off her sunglasses, her gaze sweeping across the walls wrapped with pale-blue linen paper that rose from antique wood paneling. Several long-legged glossy tables nestled against the walls. Overhead, a small brass chandelier spilled light. "Judging just by the size of the foyer, that tour might take a while."

"It will. On the drive over, I got a call from Wade Crawford, the tech from the Vice detail who's assigned to get the security alarm up to snuff and install the cameras and straight-line to the safe house. He had some sort of equipment snafu to deal with, so he won't be here for at least another hour." Alex checked his watch. "That gives us plenty of time for the tour," he added, his gaze skimming back to her. "The more we're together, Morgan, the more comfortable we'll feel around each other."

"I'm sure you're right." Judging by the way her heart was hammering against her ribs, she doubted that would ever happen. But he didn't need to know that.

He dipped his head. "I'll be back in a minute."

"Fine."

Standing in the cool quiet of the spectacular entry hall, she watched him turn and stride toward the door. When he stepped out of sight, she lowered onto the staircase's bottom step.

Her mouth was dry, her knees wobbly and the ache in her belly was pure longing. Dammit, she had to get a grip. Somehow find her balance.

Hormones, she reasoned. The desire to be held and touched, *to feel,* was a human one. That heat, gathering like a fireball in her lungs whenever Alex touched her, meant she was only human. A human experiencing nothing more than an inconvenient little hormonal tug.

A tug, she resolved, she could—and would—control with a strong dose of willpower.

# Chapter 5

Dressed in a blue golf shirt and slacks, Alex walked into the kitchen late that afternoon. Centered amid cabinets topped with dark granite was an imposing cooking island with a built-in chopping block, small sink, six electric burners and a grill. A massive copper hood hung over the cooking area. A restaurant-size range sat against one wall; the motor on the nearby stainless-steel refrigerator purred like a contented cat.

Leaning against the island, Alex watched the OCPD Vice cop on the far side of the kitchen. A toolbox, its lid yawning open, sat near Sergeant Wade Crawford's booted feet. Beside the toolbox were coils of various-colored electrical wire.

The cop was in his early thirties, tall, lean and lanky. He wore his coal-black hair long enough to be considered antisocial; he'd spent enough time in the sun to turn his olive skin a shade darker. His eyes were brown and deep set, and his serious countenance was enhanced by heavy brows. Those eyes were presently focused on the wires spilling out of the small hole Crawford had cut in the wall near the door that led out to the terrace.

"How's it going, Crawford?"

"It's going, Blade."

"You sure this system is airtight?"

"Is a pig's butt pork?" the electronics guru asked in a drawl that held a faint trace of his native Louisiana. Glancing up from a grouping of wires he'd twisted together, Crawford sent Alex a grin that was pure confidence. "Blade, when I'm done here, this mansion'll have a security system almost as foolproof as the one at Fort Knox."

"Almost? You want to define *almost* for me?"

"Sure." Crawford pulled a rag out of the back pocket of his blue work pants and wiped his hands. His white shirt displayed the logo of a security company over one pocket. The logo matched the one on the van he'd parked in the mansion's driveway. "I said 'almost' because when I talk about alarm systems, I add a disclaimer." He jammed the rag back into his pocket and shifted his attention to the system's digital display while he punched numbers into the keypad. "After all, there are people on this planet capable of fooling most any security system."

"You being one of them."

"I do have the touch," Crawford agreed. "Hell, Blade, there's nothing complicated about most intrusion alarms." He punched in another set of numbers, gave a satisfied nod, then pulled a battery-operated screwdriver out of the black tool belt hitched low on his hips. "They're just metal, wires and integrated circuitry. A couple of microchips tossed in."

The screwdriver whirled noiselessly while Crawford installed a faceplate over the keypad. After dealing with the last screw, he gave the panel a pat. "This baby's solid. I've programmed in a fifteen-digit base numbering system and a forty-five-second delay."

"Meaning?"

"When the system is activated and someone opens an entry/exit door, that person has three-quarters of a minute to punch in the correct code. If they don't, the siren goes off. And I've reprogrammed it to shriek like a French Quarter hooker who's been offered a five-thousand-dollar trick."

Alex fought a smile. "I expect that's something."

"Pierce-your-eardrums loud. There's not much chance of someone who doesn't have the right access code turning off this system in time. Even if someone got through the door, unscrewed the face plate and hooked up an electronic counter to the keypad's wiring, they'd be out of luck."

"Are you talking about the same kind of counter the bad guys use to bust ATMs?"

"Exactly the same."

"From what I hear, they're pretty successful."

"You heard right." Crawford crouched and began stowing coils of wire in his toolbox. "A counter rams massive numbers of combinations into a recognition bank. It works on an ATM because a money machine is connected to the bank's megafast computer. A security alarm can't deal with info at anywhere near that speed. Plus, an alarm's got a ticking clock."

"In our case, the forty-five-second delay."

"Right. That isn't near long enough for an electronic counter to crunch the possible amount of number combos."

"That covers the doors. What about the windows?"

Crawford closed the toolbox and rose. "They're wired,

too. So is the attic's trapdoor into the garage and the walk-through door that opens between the attic and the storage room where the moving guys stacked the empty boxes they carried in. There's also a battery backup. If someone shuts off the main circuit breaker, this monster of a house stays secure.''

Alex glanced at the collection of household items Crawford had placed on the cooking island when he first arrived. The coffeemaker, desk lamp, VCR, mahogany mantel clock and pair of leather-bound books were equipped with microchip surveillance cameras. ''Give me a rundown on how the video system works.''

The Vice cop moved to the island. ''Motion activates all cameras. Someone walks by, that person's image is trapped on tape in living color. View the tape later, you'll see a date and time stamp of when the activity occurred.''

''What about lighting?'' Alex had been on enough undercover ops to know that low light conditions posed a problem for surveillance, especially when using color video cameras.

''Lighting isn't a problem ever since the department replaced all microcameras with the newest 'smart' ones. Every camera we're using has sensors that automatically switch their settings from color to black-and-white when the light level gets too low.''

''Good.''

''Got something else for you,'' Crawford said as he plucked a smoke detector off the island.

''You stick a camera in there, too?''

''Nope. A radio frequency detector. Someone drops by and happens to leave an audio bug behind, the red LED light on the detector starts flashing. It'll keep the light show up for hours.''

Alex nodded. ''You need my help in the video room?''

A small room accessible through a hidden panel had been created on the first floor beneath the staircase. Inside, Crawford had installed the video recorders programmed to tape everything the covert cameras picked up. The recorders and other equipment had been packed in boxes the movers carried in that morning.

"Yeah, I can use a hand." Crawford nodded at the items on the island. "I need you to place these in different rooms around the mansion. While you're doing that, I'll be in the video room, watching the monitors. I can tell you where in each room to place the camera, then at the angle that gives maximum view."

"How do we communicate while we're doing that?"

Crawford snagged a duffel bag, pulled two small radios from inside. "With these," he said, handing Alex a radio.

"Ready to get to work?" Alex asked, clipping the radio onto his belt. When Crawford didn't answer, Alex glanced up. The cop's eyes had widened and locked on the doorway. Alex turned his head in time to see Morgan step fully into view.

She had changed into a red halter top and a pair of cutoffs skimpy enough to showcase her long, tanned legs. Her red canvas tennis shoes matched the halter. She'd piled her blond hair on top of her head, with tendrils escaping here and there. One earpiece of her sunglasses was hooked in the halter's deep vee. Her mouth was full and wet and darkly red. If sex came packaged, this was it.

The kick of lust in Alex's gut had him scowling. As did the realization he had to remind himself to breathe. If his system survived this assignment, he could live through anything.

Gripping a legal pad and measuring tape in one hand, Morgan moved to the island, sliding a look from him, to Crawford, then back to Alex. "I've started a list of supplies we need for the flower beds and lawn. I'm going out to get Sara's input before she leaves for the day."

"Good idea." Taking a controlled breath, Alex nodded toward the window over the sink. "I spotted her going into the storage building a few minutes ago."

"While I'm outside, I'll measure and sketch all the flower beds. I can enter the dimensions into the software on my laptop and plan the exact amount of flowers and shrubs to buy."

"Fine." Alex was fully aware he wasn't the only male reacting to her presence. He could almost hear Crawford's testosterone level rocket into the red zone while the Vice cop gave Morgan a slow once-over.

"We haven't met." Hand extended, Crawford stepped around the island to where Morgan stood. "Sergeant Wade Crawford, Vice detail."

"Morgan McCall." She looked at Alex. "Also known as Donovan."

"I heard there was another McCall sister in the academy." Grinning, Crawford leaned in. "You, Carrie and Grace ought to thank your mama and daddy every night for making you so pretty."

Morgan laughed, a rippling, smoky sound that flowed across Alex's skin. His mouth went dry. His gut clenched. He realized he had never before heard her laugh…and, dammit, he liked the sound of it.

"I'll pass your compliment on to all involved, Sergeant Crawford," she said.

"Wade."

"Wade."

Alex noted that Crawford now had his hand wrapped around Morgan's. Where women were concerned, the Vice cop had a reputation for having perfected the art of smooth. Seeing him in action, Alex had to agree with that assessment.

While Crawford showed Morgan the items implanted with microcameras spread across the island, Alex studied her, his brows drawn together, the annoyance he felt self-directed.

When he'd carried her into the mansion, she had fit perfectly into his arms. She had felt right. Felt as if she belonged there.

And when he'd gotten her inside, he had held on because it had been a long time since he'd had a woman in his arms. Longer still since he'd held one he hadn't wanted to let go.

Hell.

The image of him sliding his arms around her again came through entirely too clear and too appealing. They were on the job, dammit. She was his *partner*. He had no business thinking about her in any other terms. No business wondering how her red-glossed mouth would taste. Or her flesh.

He forced himself to focus on the legal pad she held in the crook of one arm. She'd made another list. He just bet the measurements she took of each flower bed would be exact to a millionth of an inch. And he knew once she entered those dimensions into her laptop, she would come up with a mountain of lists, color charts and graphs to mull over and analyze. The woman was a superachiever. He still carried the scars that proved an ambitious woman didn't stay satisfied long with a man who had no aspirations to add more stripes to his uniform sleeves.

Still, that knowledge didn't dull the ache of need Morgan's presence had lodged inside his gut.

Standing there, Alex could almost feel himself sinking into an oozing black pit without anything to grab hold of.

"...unless you need me in here?"

He realized Morgan had spoken to him, but he couldn't pull his mind back fast enough. "Sorry, I was thinking about something else."

The diamond ring he'd placed on her finger that morning glinted as she swept her hand toward the cooking island. "I said I'll put off going outside to huddle with Sara if you need my help placing these cameras."

"I'd rather have you in view of Spurlock's cameras." Alex glanced again toward the window. From the angle he stood, he could see a sliver of the flagstone terrace and a corner of the swimming pool, its water shimmering a dozen shades of blue beneath the June sun. Far beyond was the brick wall that hid any glimpse of Spurlock's estate. "Be sure to engage the sensor in your watch to check for audio surveillance. And let me know if you see any sign of the neighbor on the other side of that wall."

Lifting a brow, Morgan moved to the glass-fronted cooler angled in one corner. "I think I've got that part of my job figured out," she said before snagging one of the plastic water bottles she'd placed there when she unloaded her grocery bags.

Pausing at the back door, she slid on her sunglasses, then sent Crawford a smile. "Nice to meet you, Wade."

"My pleasure." He gave her a long, intense look. "Morgan McCall, I *will* see you again."

Crawford tracked her until she was out the door, then turned toward Alex, appreciation glinting in his dark eyes. "Nothing like a gorgeous blonde with legs up to her ears to get a man's system running on high voltage. I could go into a serious case of the want-tos over that woman."

"Put a lid on it, Crawford."

The Vice cop slanted Alex a quick, searching glance. "You got designs on her, Blade?"

"Hell, no," Alex snapped, irritated with himself because designs were apparently what he did have. "We have a job to do and I want it done right. Morgan's fresh out of the academy, she has enough to deal with right now without you sniffing around. Bottom line, this is my operation and I don't want her distracted."

"I've got no problem with that," Crawford said, then looked back at the door. "I'll just wait to distract her until after you finish this job." Turning toward the island, he picked up the coffeemaker, held it eye level to check the lens on the camera installed inside. "Want to start with this?"

"Yeah. Fine."

With the water bottle and legal pad tucked beneath one arm, Morgan traversed the flagstone terrace, infusing a sway into her hips for the sake of any surveillance cameras aimed her way. She skirted the swimming pool, its dark-blue-tiled sides and bottom making it look endlessly deep. Beyond the pool, she took the path that led to the brick storage building, its double doors standing open.

She stepped inside just as Sara Rackowitz stowed a plastic container of swimming pool chemicals on a built-in shelf. To the right of the shelf sat a riding lawn mower, edger and leaf blower. Even with both doors standing wide open, the building's interior was dim, the hot air thick with humidity. Although she'd been outside only a few minutes, Morgan could feel a trickle of sweat between her breasts.

"How's it going, Sara?"

The federal agent turned. After hours working in the sun, her tan shorts and black T-shirt were rumpled, dirt streaked and damp with perspiration. Her dark hair was shoved up under a baseball cap; her nose and cheeks held the flush of a sunburn. "Afternoon, Mrs. Donovan."

"I thought something cold might taste good about now," Morgan said, offering the bottle.

"Yes, ma'am. Thanks."

While Sara took long, slow swallows, Morgan clicked the stem of her watch. A small green light glowed, then flashed off. The light confirmed there were no active surreptitious audio surveillance devices in the vicinity. If one came on, the watch would begin to vibrate discreetly.

"It's okay to talk."

"I haven't seen any activity next door yet," Sara said, screwing the lid on the bottle. She angled her head toward the open door. "How's it going inside the big house?"

"So far Alex and I have stashed our clothes and toiletries in a closet and bathroom big enough to rent out. I've unpacked my groceries in a kitchen I would kill to have in my own house. To top things off, I just received a massive dose of charm from Sergeant Wade Crawford."

"I just bet you did," Sara said, giving Morgan's red halter and cutoffs an appraising look. "Crawford sure knows how to say things that stir up a woman. If I wasn't married, I'd let him stir me up."

"He's got a silver tongue, all right."

Sara grinned. "You interested in letting that sweet-talking Louisiana man have his way with you?"

"No." Her insides were already revving, and it wasn't due to Wade Crawford's charm.

Morgan's mind conjured Alex's image as he'd stood in the kitchen, listening to the Vice cop give her a rundown of the items in which he'd implanted cameras. At one point she'd slid a look at Alex from beneath her lashes and discovered his gaze locked on her. His dark eyes had been unreadable, his mouth clamped in a grim line. He had looked more than dangerous at that moment. He had looked fatal. Tempting.

Then as now, the tug of desire curling in her belly made her feel as tense as an unshot arrow. She knew all too well that getting churned up over a man could lead to trouble. The jerky kick her heart gave whenever she got close to Alex warned her she might already be headed that way. That was a side trip she had no intention of taking.

"Last thing I want right now is to get involved in a relationship," she said, as much for her own benefit as Sara's. "I do better concentrating on one thing at a time. For now, that's the job."

To prove her point, Morgan angled the pad into the crook of one arm and got down to business. "I started a list of things I want to buy to get the flower beds, lawn and soil back into shape." She pulled a pencil from the back pocket of her cutoffs while adding, "I'll include whatever pool supplies you decide we need."

Sara blotted the back of her hand against her forehead. "How about I make a list first thing in the morning?"

"That's fine. Do you have time before you leave to help measure the flower beds?"

"I'm the hired help, Mrs. Donovan. I work for you. My time is yours."

"Right." Morgan shoved an errant tendril off her cheek. "I wonder if I'll ever get a handle on this type of assignment."

"It takes time. Experience." Sara drained the remaining water from her bottle, then tossed it toward a nearby trash can. The bottle landed inside with a dull *thunk*. "It's your good fortune you're dealing with Alex Blade. He's the best at undercover work I've ever seen. Watch him,

Morgan. Learn from him. Doing that, I guarantee you'll get the hang of things.''

"Sooner than later, I hope," Morgan said, then stepped out the doorway into the glaring late-afternoon sun. While Sara closed and locked the doors, Morgan slipped on her sunglasses, then glanced at the cameras mounted on top of the brick wall. Her skin prickled as though a hundred eyes watched her. Were Carlton Spurlock's among them?

An hour later she and Sara had finished measuring all flower beds in the backyard and on both sides of the mansion, and had moved into the front yard. Standing with her back to the street, Morgan jotted the dimensions of the flower bed that ran parallel between the driveway and Spurlock's high brick wall.

As she began sketching the flower bed, a sudden chill ran up the nape of Morgan's neck. The pencil stilled in her hand while instinct told her something was off. She just wasn't sure what.

Behind the dark lenses of her glasses, her gaze swept up toward Spurlock's security cameras just as Sara stepped closer.

"Don't turn around," the FBI agent murmured. Using an index finger, she pretended interest in a set of measurements on the pad.

Morgan angled her chin away from the cameras so her lips couldn't be read. "What's going on?"

"A black stretch limo rolled out of Spurlock's driveway a few seconds ago," Sara explained. "Right now the limo is stopped in the street behind you. It's just sitting there, idling."

Concentrating, Morgan caught the sound of an engine's soft hum. She continued sketching. "Can you see who's inside?"

"Not through the tinted windows. But I'd bet my next

paycheck our target is sitting in the back seat, getting his fill of Mrs. Donovan.''

A sense of unease crawled along Morgan's spine. Sara was right—it was almost a given that Carlton Spurlock, a man behind the killings of at least six people, sat in that limo yards away, his gaze crawling over her.

Not *her*, she reminded herself. Morgan Donovan. That's who she was now. Needed to be. It was Mrs. Donovan's job to get the man's attention.

As Alex had taught her, Morgan closed her eyes, pictured what the former Las Vegas cocktail waitress who wore tight, curve-hugging clothes and poofed her hair would do to accomplish that goal. It took only a split second for the image to gel in her mind.

Mouth curving, Morgan handed Sara the pad, pencil and measuring tape. ''It's show time.''

Giving no indication she was aware of the limo's presence, Morgan sauntered to the nearest flower bed, infusing a look-at-me-boys swing in her walk. With a cock of one hip, she leaned to examine an ailing azalea and felt her cutoffs ride up her thighs. *Get an eyeful, Spurlock. The sooner you get friendly with your new neighbors, the sooner we get inside your place and find the evidence to take you down.*

A moment later the soft idle of the limo's engine transformed into a purr as the driver changed gears. While pinching off dead azalea leaves, Morgan shifted her stance and watched the limo out of the corner of her eye. Shining like a black pearl beneath the sun, the big car glided down the street, then disappeared around the corner.

''All clear,'' Sara said, keeping her back toward the ever-present cameras.

Straightening, Morgan turned from the azalea. Her gaze

swept the now empty street while she swallowed around the knot of nerves that had settled in her throat.

"You sure gave whoever was in that limo something to look at," Sara commented. "Nice work."

"Thanks." Morgan ran her damp palms down the front of her cutoffs and glanced toward the mansion. "I need to tell Alex about the limo."

"Yeah." Sara returned the pad, pencil and measuring tape, then tapped a finger against the brim of her baseball cap. "See you tomorrow, Mrs. Donovan."

## Chapter 6

Pictures did not do the woman justice, Carlton Spurlock concluded.

His tall, elegant frame clad in a raven-black tuxedo, he sat in a wing chair covered with needlepoint roses, a snifter of brandy cradled in one palm. The silver wings flowing back from his temples into thick black hair enhanced his air of distinction. Across the spacious bedroom sat an enormous television, its screen displaying the silent images his security cameras had recorded that day.

With his attention focused on the television, Spurlock barely acknowledged the soft strains of his favorite Mozart opera drifting through the vast room.

On tape, the sloe-eyed blonde looked interesting. She was beautifully built—tall, busty, yet slim as a dancer. From the way she moved, it appeared she was very, very agile.

Physically she was the type of woman who appealed to

him. One who would catch his eye simply by walking into a room.

No, this one didn't *walk,* he mused. His mouth curved as he rolled a slim cigar between long, manicured fingers. His new neighbor sashayed, like a streetwalker advertising her wares.

That confident prance was another thing holding immense appeal for him.

Setting his snifter on the antique table beside the chair, he retrieved the remote, hit the rewind button. While smoke from his cigar curled toward the ceiling, he again watched her move across the cobblestone driveway, the blond hair piled on her head glinting like gold beneath the sun, hips churning under the tight cutoffs, breasts straining against the red halter.

The press of another button froze her image midstep. Yes, on tape the woman looked interesting.

In the flesh she delivered a sharp, swift, hotly erotic punch to a man's system. He knew, because he had felt that lascivious blow only hours ago.

Gray eyes as hard as icy chips narrowed on her image, just as they had while he studied her from the back seat of his limousine. Everything about her brought sex instantly to mind. Wild, uninhibited, casually available sex.

Which was the kind that suited him. The only kind.

Too bad Krystelle Vander had chosen to ignore that fact.

Even now the thought of the bitch's treachery flamed his fury to white-hot intensity. He had lavished money, gifts and time on her. Had denied her nothing, save his name. Her resentment over that one denial had transformed the woman into a revenge-seeking shrew. Her threat to go to the police, to tell all she had learned while living with him sealed her fate. As well as that of the retired cop to whom she ran for protection.

Betrayal, Spurlock believed, deserved quick punishment.

He retrieved his brandy, drained the snifter. Drawing on the slim cigar, he studied through a haze of smoke what had been his beloved grandmother's bedroom. His gaze slid over the English walnut-and-leather campaign bed clad in luxurious linens. His grandmother's jewel-colored bottles and boxes still lined the bureau. The gold silk robe she had favored lay across the crimson velvet settee.

Setting the cuffs on his formal white studded shirt, he shifted his gaze to the Waterford vase on the nightstand. A sense of satisfaction welled up inside him at the sight of the golden buds just beginning to part their tender petals. He had bred the *Rosea Midas Touch* in honor of his grandmother. In full bloom, the blossoms would be exquisite.

Every other day, fresh roses replaced the ones in the crystal vase. Beside it sat the telephone and answering machine, and his grandmother's leather-bound appointment book. Other than the roses, everything in the room was just as it had been on the day she died.

Turning back toward the table, Spurlock stubbed out his cigar in a crystal ashtray. He retrieved the remote, hit the play button. His new neighbor sauntered across the television screen, the diamond on her left hand flashing in the sun.

Intrigued, he angled his chin. The ring had surprised him when he first noticed it. She didn't look like a wife. More to the point, she looked like an expensive whore. Yet she didn't have the rapacious, calculating look of a whore. Nor did any woman he knew who routinely used her body as a commodity spend hours in the intense heat measuring and sketching flower beds, as she had done this afternoon.

A tap on the door drew his attention from the television screen. He turned his head. "What is it?"

"Sorry to bother you, boss," Peter Colaneri said after swinging open the door. "Just got a call from the gatehouse. The first guests have arrived. You said to let you know."

"Yes. Thank you, Peter."

The man who acted as both chauffeur and bodyguard remained in the doorway, his wiry, muscular build looking unobtrusive in a discreet black suit. The scars around his eyebrows, and the nose that didn't quite line up with the center of his mouth, bespoke a violent past.

Spurlock glanced at the gold watch he'd accepted from a vascular surgeon as down payment on a gambling debt. He felt a tug of regret at having to abandon the surveillance tapes, but he had no choice. Tonight, as chairman of a charity that funded heart disease research, he was hosting a dinner for twenty couples. Later, they would move en masse to the cabana he had remodeled as a casino. There they would enjoy after-dinner aperitifs, cigars, cigarettes and gambling.

Tonight, all activity in the cabana would fall well within legal guidelines.

Guests would make a donation in order to receive tokens to play blackjack, roulette or craps. By evening's end, the heart charity's treasurer would have a tidy check tucked into his pocket that included all of the guests' winnings.

"Who are the first to arrive?" Spurlock asked.

"Judge Philben and his wife," Colaneri advised.

"Lovely couple." Several years ago, bad investments

left the judge unable to pay for his daughter's schooling. Simultaneously, Spurlock Land Development was the defendant in a multimillion-dollar lawsuit over which the judge presided. At his employer's direction, Colaneri had approached Philben with an offer. The judge accepted money and granted the defense a verdict in its favor. Spurlock found it convenient to have as many judges as possible in his pocket.

He gestured toward the television. "Come in a moment, Peter. I have a job for you."

Colaneri crossed the ocean of dove-gray carpet. The instant he glimpsed the screen, his mouth formed an arrogant curve. "The new neighbor. Great legs, awesome ass."

Spurlock let the crude remark pass. He expected nothing less from a man who paid prostitutes to engage in sadistic sex, and had committed his first murder when he was barely fifteen. He kept Colaneri on his payroll precisely because he was a conscienceless, experienced killer who enjoyed inflicting pain.

Leaning in, Colaneri leered at the screen. "Broad's hotter than that stiff you had me torch."

"I didn't ask you in here to discuss Mr. Tool's predicament," Spurlock said at the reference to his former accountant. He hit the remote's off button. Although at this point his interest lay only in the woman the cameras had captured on film, experience had taught him to investigate anyone who got close. Or tried to. Since next-door neighbors fell into that category, he would have her husband checked out, too.

"Peter, I'm interested in my new neighbors. I want you to make the standard inquiries first thing in the morning."

"Will do, boss. That it for now?"

Looking back at the TV, Spurlock fought an unsettling

urge to view the tape for an uncountable time. His mouth thinned. The need to watch the woman made him feel like a common voyeur.

"Make a copy of the tape. Take the copy to our contact and have him make prints of each frame the woman is in."

"Just the woman? Not the man?"

"Correct."

"You want me to do that in the morning, too?"

Spurlock slicked Colaneri a razor-sharp look. "Tonight, Peter. I want that done tonight. Make sure the prints are on the desk in my bedroom before my last guest leaves."

"Anything you say, boss."

"Damn," Morgan muttered, slashing a knife at a handful of unsuspecting shallots spread across the cooking island's built-in cutting board. "Damn. *Damn!*"

Although several hours had passed since the limo had sat idling in the street, her skin still crawled from the sensation of being watched. Spurlock's surveillance cameras had gotten to her, too, she realized. Just knowing they'd been aimed at her had filled her with a sense of paranoia. Of *violation.*

Great, she thought. It was her job to get the guy on the other side of the high wall to leer at her. And when he did, she felt as if she should check to make sure she'd put on her clothes before stepping outdoors. What little clothes she wore, that is.

Giving her head a disgusted shake, she laid the knife aside, grabbed a hot pad and lifted the lid off a large pot. Rich, aromatic steam billowed out, confirmation her homemade chicken stock was on steady simmer.

Retrieving the knife, she went back to taking her frustration out on the shallots. With every chop, the feeling that she was being watched intensified.

She *had* to find her balance. She was used to being in control. Alex had briefed her fully about what the job entailed, and here she was, feeling creeped out over something she had *known* would happen.

Being the object of Spurlock's focus wasn't the only reason she was feeling skittish, she admitted. She thought of the huge closet off the master bedroom where her undercover wardrobe now shared space with Alex's. Of the bathroom where their toiletries lined the shelves with an intimate closeness.

It was all for show—Alex would sleep in one of the guestrooms. Still, they had to maintain appearances. Just as she and Alex planned to search Spurlock's gold bedroom for the evidence Krystelle Vander had hid there, something similar could happen here. What if they invited Spurlock over, and he—or his date or a bodyguard—slipped upstairs on the pretense of using the restroom? That person might just poke around to make sure the Donovans lived as the hot-for-each-other husband and wife they appeared to be in public.

Morgan knew she could probably heap most of the blame for her unsteadiness on the fact that she couldn't get near Alex Blade without her pulse pounding and her knees turning weak. *That* reaction was supposed to be an act, a piece of role-playing for their neighbor's benefit. Problem was, her response to Blade was as real and sharp as the knife in her hand.

"Damn," she muttered as another wave of frustration rolled over her. She had to get control of her emotions. Throttle them back before whatever was beginning to grow blossomed—

"What did those onions do to deserve death by hacking?"

She jolted at the sound of Alex's voice coming from so close behind her. When she looked across her shoulder they were suddenly face-to-face and eye to eye. Mouth to mouth. Her throat went dry. "What...what did you say?"

Moving in, he leaned against the island, examining the remains on the cutting board. He was still dressed in the blue shirt and slacks he'd worn earlier. This late in the day, dark stubble shadowed his jaw, giving his face a rawboned look.

"I asked what the onions did to deserve death by hacking?"

"They're shallots."

"Okay, shallots."

"Nothing. I was just working out a problem. I talk to myself sometimes when I do that."

"Apparently." He picked up her diamond ring from beside the small sink where she'd laid it when she washed her hands. She hadn't realized until that moment she'd forgotten to put it back on.

"Need help with your problem?" he asked easily.

"No, thanks." *You* are it. She glanced at the ingredients and utensils spread across the island. "I can move my stuff out of your way if you need the cooktop or grill. Or I can move completely and use the range." She swept her gaze around what in her mind was a storybook kitchen. "This place has enough appliances, utensils and work space for six chefs."

"Don't bother moving. Or moving anything, for that matter." He rolled the gold band between two fingers, watching the enormous diamond glint beneath the kitchen's bright lights. "The extent of my cooking ability is limited to the microwave."

"That simplifies the question, 'What's for dinner?'"

He bounced the ring in his palm. "There's a lot to be said for keeping things simple."

"I agree." Using the knife's edge, she scooped up diced shallots, dumped them into a saucepan in which she had oil heating. "I don't use the microwave often, so we won't get in each other's way."

"Wouldn't want that." Reaching, he caught her left hand in his. "You should be wearing this," he said, sliding the band onto her finger. Instead of letting go, he shifted his hold, wrapped his fingers around hers.

"I..." She looked down at their joined hands, saw he still wore the plain gold band she'd slid onto his finger that morning. "I took my ring off to wash my hands." Her voice carried a barely perceptible quake.

"And forgot about it."

She had no intention of admitting that. "I planned to put it back on after I cleaned up my dishes."

His thumb commenced a slow slide across her knuckles while his dark eyes moved over her face in sharp assessment. "Morgan, the more you wear your ring, the more it becomes habit." He released her hand. "It needs to become habit."

"It will." Diverting her gaze, she tossed more shallots into the saucepan. She could still feel the faint slide of his thumb against her knuckles. "I've only had the ring since this morning."

"Morgan Donovan wouldn't leave a six-carat diamond lying beside the sink. To a woman like her, wearing that ring would become habit very quickly."

Her lips thinned. He was right. *Her* choice in jewelry—when she bothered to wear it—ran to practical and discreet. Where this operation was concerned, her preferences didn't apply. Here, in this vast, elegant mansion, Morgan McCall didn't exist. Sultry, sexy Mrs. Alexander

Donovan, with her clothes scooped low at her breasts and cut high on her thighs ruled the roost. And that woman flaunted every bauble, trinket and diamond her loving husband showered on her.

Alex glanced at his watch. ''Guess it's my dinnertime, too,'' he commented, then strode across the kitchen. He reached the stainless-steel refrigerator, swung open the freezer's door. Morgan furrowed her brow when he grabbed a box without glancing at it.

''While you're there,'' she began, ''would you bring me the plastic bowl with the blue lid out of the refrigerator?''

''Sure.''

''Thanks,'' she said when he moved back to the island and handed her the bowl.

''What's in it?''

''Arugula puree. I brought it from home.'' At his blank look she added, ''It's like pesto. It's an ingredient in the arugula risotto I'm making.''

He sniffed the air. ''Smells good.''

''Thanks.'' She paused, wondering how long it had been since he'd had a home-cooked meal. ''Do you know what's in the box you pulled out of the freezer?''

He looked down. ''Pepperoni pizza. Thin crust. Why?''

''You didn't even look at the box until just now.''

''Your point?''

''My point is, I'm standing here with my hair poofed to the ceiling.'' She paused to give the shallots a quick stir. ''I'm wearing a hot-pink tube top, tight capri pants and ankle-wrecking heels. I have to stay in floozy mode the entire time we're here just in case someone from Spurlock's side of the fence pays us an unexpected visit.''

Alex set the box aside as his gaze swept over her. ''Mr. Donovan noticed his wife's wardrobe the instant he walked into the kitchen. Mr. Donovan approves. Morgan, your point about the pizza?''

"I'm thinking about what you taught me about working undercover. You said it's all image. That it's imperative we stay in character all the time.''

"Right.''

"What will a visitor conclude if he knocks on our door at dinnertime and we're eating different kinds of food?''

Alex angled his chin. "I've already worked that out. For example, if someone shows up tonight, I'll say I'm allergic to arugula.'' His mouth curved. "Whatever the hell it is.''

"It's a salad green. I grow it in my garden.'' She turned the heat down under the broth, then met his gaze. "We could maybe get away with that once. The reality is, married couples dine together while eating the same food. We want to keep this illusion going, so we should do that, too.''

"If you're suggesting we take turns cooking, I'm all for it. For more reasons than it would eliminate our having to come up with explanations for why we don't do something according to the norm. The only downside in the deal falls your way. That's why I didn't suggest our sharing cooking duties in the first place.''

She dumped the rice she'd premeasured into the pan with the shallots. "You thought of this already?''

"It's my job to try to anticipate everything. I knew if we stayed in on my nights to cook you'd have to settle for takeout or something from the freezer. It's not exactly fair to force fast and frozen foods on a gourmet cook.''

"I'm not a gourmet cook.'' She tapped a pink fingernail on the recipe card lying to one side of the cooktop. "I own a few fancy cooking utensils and know how to follow directions, that's all.''

"From where I'm standing, that's gourmet. What do you suggest we do about our cooking arrangement?"

"Simplify things so we don't have to come up with a lie."

"If you want to share kitchen duty, we can go out to eat on my nights to cook."

"Either that, or I can cook for both of us whenever we eat in."

"Won't that get old?"

"Not if you always set the table, then clean up everything afterward. Deal?"

"If you think I'm going to turn down that offer, you're wrong." Snagging the pizza, he strode to the freezer, tossed the box back inside. He turned to face her, his mouth curving. "Not only do I get home-cooked meals, doing this helps cement our cover. It's a good call on your part, Morgan."

"Thanks."

She stirred the rice, then retrieved a bottle of wine from the glass-fronted cooler, pouring some into the rice mixture. Alex pulled plates from a cabinet and carried them to the antique French oak table snugged into an alcove formed by a tall sweep of triple windows.

Since they had agreed to share kitchen duty and meals, she decided it would be best not to do it in silence. "Mind if I ask you a question?"

He slid her a look as he gathered up silverware. "Depends on the question."

"Why didn't you ever learn to cook? Did you maybe grow up fabulously wealthy with people waiting on you hand and foot?"

He let a minute of silence pass before saying, "I was a delinquent. I was too busy stealing and scamming people to learn my way around a kitchen."

She blinked. "Are you serious?"

He moved to the table, placed silverware beside the plates. "Growing up, my only real goal was to get kicked out of every foster home the system stuck me in."

"Not exactly the greatest goal for a kid."

"No, but at the time I thought it was." He moved back to the island, pausing on the side opposite from her.

"Not many people go from delinquent to cop," she commented while ladling chicken stock into the rice.

He raised a shoulder. "I got lucky."

"Because of George Jackson?" The instant she said the name, a look crossed Alex's face, a quick shadow. "You told me the other day he's the reason you're a cop," she said quietly.

"He is."

"If it's too painful to talk about him, don't. I was just curious."

Turning, Alex stared out the long window over the sink, his gaze riveted on the impenetrable brick wall with its surveillance cameras. Studying his hard, unyielding profile, Morgan again pictured the crime-scene photos, the glint of matted blood against George Jackson's silver hair. She wondered if Alex was seeing that image, too. Wondered if he was thinking about the man who lived on the other side of the high wall. Carlton Spurlock, who had either killed George Jackson or ordered his murder.

She busied herself with the risotto while Alex stood in silence, seemingly lost in thought. When he finally turned, his mouth was set. Something cold and menacing had settled at the back of his eyes. He had turned dangerous right before her.

Though she knew who he was, *what* he was, Morgan felt a bony finger of fear skitter down her spine.

"I never learned to cook because my mother was too

busy selling herself to score drugs and booze," he began, his voice as smooth as a polished dagger. "On my seventh birthday, she walked out of the flophouse room we stayed in and never came back."

Morgan went still. If things had been different between them, she would have reached for him. "What about your father?"

"My mother had no idea who planted the seed, so she couldn't introduce us. I figure he was a carbon copy of the losers she brought home every night. Most of them were drunks. Some got off on slapping her around. One got his kicks by beating me until I passed out."

"Alex…" What he was saying was horrible enough, but hearing it recited in a flat, empty voice froze her blood.

"By the time I was eleven, the experts labeled me 'incorrigible.' They were right. I had a smart mouth, a bad attitude and I never backed down from a fight. I was damn proud of that. Every foster home the state put me in tossed me out within days. The counselors couldn't keep me in school and juvie hall couldn't keep me locked in for long."

"Where did you live? *How* did you live?"

"By my wits. I staked a claim on a spot in a dilapidated building downtown where homeless drunks stayed. By then I had become a decent pickpocket and an even better scam artist. Most of my money came from running a sidewalk shell game. Turns out, one of the sidewalks I did business on was part of George Jackson's beat."

"He nabbed you?"

"Snatched me up by the scruff of my neck." Again, Alex focused his gaze out the window. "George was six foot four and two hundred plus pounds. He looked like a mountain and acted mean as hell. He even scared me, and after living on the street I was pretty immune. I figured the big, tough cop would give me a few knocks to make sure I stayed out of his territory, toss me back into the system and walk away. Instead he clamped on to me like a damn steel-jawed trap and wouldn't let go. He cut through red tape and got me into a youth center where I could get three squares and a bed as long as I went to nightly counseling sessions. George showed up at the sessions, even on his days off, to make sure I didn't duck out. He talked me into going back to school, got me interested in joining the wrestling squad instead of fighting with my fists.'' Alex looked over at her again. The darkness that had settled in his eyes battered Morgan's heart. ''To this day I don't know why he hung around to see the results. And I sure as hell can't ask him now.''

She bit her lip. ''He obviously saw the potential in you.''

Alex shrugged away the comment, but the gesture was jerky. ''Maybe.'' His forehead furrowed. ''Damn.''

''What?''

''I don't know what George thought. Any more than I know why I just told you all that. I've never told—'' He held up a hand. ''You asked why I don't know how to cook. Instead you got a play-by-play on how I grew up.''

''Which clearly explains why you never learned to cook,'' she commented. ''Like you said, we need to do whatever we can to feel comfortable around each other. Maybe telling me about your past is your way of doing that?''

''Maybe,'' he said, watching her closely.

She turned back to the cooktop, began putting the final touches on the risotto, while trying to conceal the unsteadiness in her hands. She had thought her reaction to him was all physical, brought on by her hormones responding to a too-long period of abstinence. By telling her about his past, Alex had opened a door into himself, given her a look inside the man with whom she would share almost every waking moment during the foreseeable future.

Now it wasn't just a chemical response that drew her to him but an emotional one. He'd been a child, battered not only by fists but by life itself, yet he'd pulled himself up, made something of himself. That he grieved for the murdered cop who had believed in him enough to give him a chance made her heart ache.

Alex Blade wasn't just a man who could distract her with a look and stir her blood by walking into a room. He was also her partner, worthy of admiration and respect.

She clenched her unsteady fingers on a dish towel, unclenched them. She had offered her heart before to a man who pulled at her senses. He'd handed it back to her, broken and scarred.

That in itself was a very practical, very logical, very sane reason for her to keep her guard up around Alex. Add to that the nature of their work, which made any sort of involvement between them beyond a professional one potentially lethal.

So she wouldn't risk her life, her job or her heart. She would do what was smart, which was concentrate on her career. She and Alex would complete this assignment, then go their separate ways. And that would be that.

Would have to be that.

## Chapter 7

His brain still muddled from sleep, Alex walked into the kitchen the following morning where the air simmered with warm, fragrant spices. Sitting on the counter beside the range was a pan of cinnamon rolls, each the size of his palm. He touched a fingertip to the side of the pan; the rolls were still warm from the oven.

Rubbing a hand over his face, he felt the crackle of stubble against his palm. He had no doubt the rolls were made from scratch. And that they would taste like paradise, just as the risotto had last night. After years of eating mostly takeout fare and food zapped in a microwave, he could get used to home-cooked meals.

And fresh-ground coffee, he added, moving across the kitchen toward the heady scent emanating from the coffeemaker. Yesterday he and Wade Crawford had agreed the prime spot for the appliance was on the counter beside the refrigerator so the lens of the camera imbedded inside would pick up all movement in the kitchen. As he filled a mug with coffee, Alex was aware his image was being transmitted to one of the VCRs in the video room concealed beneath the first floor staircase.

Carrying his steaming coffee, he moved to the French doors that led to the flagstone terrace, then pulled them open. It was nearly eight, already the sun shone down with blazing intensity. He tugged his sunglasses from the pocket of his shirt, slid them on and took his first sip of coffee.

The rich, hot taste had him stifling a groan. Hell, yes, he could settle comfortably into a life that included gourmet home-cooked meals and coffee that slid a silky whisper of caffeine into the system.

But never, he knew, into a relationship with the woman who made them.

His brow furrowed as he leaned a shoulder against the doorjamb. He had lain awake half the night wondering what had possessed him to tell Morgan about his miserable childhood. That part of his life was the thing of nightmares, and he loathed talking about it. Made it a habit not to. When he'd asked his now ex-wife to marry him, he'd told her only enough details of how he grew up to explain why he wouldn't be taking her home to meet the folks. Yet he had given Morgan all the grim facts.

That he had—and didn't know why—put a knot of unease in his chest. As did the knowledge that her almost constant presence over the past days had seemingly jumpstarted his libido.

Sipping his coffee, he pictured her as she'd looked last night, whipping up dinner while dressed in her curve-baring, sexy clothes. Standing beside her in the kitchen, he had fought the urge to drag her to the floor, peel off those maddening clothes and spend eternity with her naked beneath him, shuddering and helpless.

Biting back a curse, he raked a hand through his un-combed hair. He had no business imagining Morgan na-ked. No business fantasizing about her in any way what-soever. That he had never before felt this much pure physical hunger for a woman didn't matter. What mat-tered was that they were on the job. Partners. He had no intention of involving himself with a fellow officer during an assignment when their lives depended on staying ob-jective and keeping a cool head. He was just going to have to tether the lust crawling inside his gut. Which shouldn't be hard to do, since working undercover was all about disconnecting emotions. And camouflaging the ones he couldn't seem to get a handle on.

Truth, he reminded himself, wasn't the important thing here. What was *perceived* as truth was. He would damn well make sure no one other than himself knew his partner had his system revved like a gambler's who'd hit a hot streak.

He would have an easier time keeping his mind on business by remembering Miss Superachiever was not his type. He knew that for sure. Just as he knew a man with a drive to succeed equaling hers would present a powerful lure for Morgan McCall. When she chose a lover, he thought, she would seek out a man every bit as proficient in the business world as in the bedroom.

*He* sure as hell wasn't that man.

When this assignment was over, she would do her time on the streets, then probably shoot through the ranks to the department's top echelon. He would stay where he was, working assignments that suited him. Odds were, he and Morgan would never again work together. Hardly ever even get a glimpse of each other.

Which, considering his huge mistake in marrying a

woman who drove herself to excel, was best for both of them.

The sound of water slapping against tile drew him out onto the flagstone terrace. The deep end of the swimming pool came into his range of sight just as Morgan did a neat flip turn and used her feet to push off the wall. She glided beneath the water's surface, then propelled herself toward the pool's far end with the powerful, efficient strokes of an athlete. An Olympic athlete.

*How else?* Alex thought, sliding one hand into the pocket of his stone-gray linen shorts. Swimming, he saw, was just another thing she did to perfection.

When she again reached the tiled pool wall closest to him, he caught a shimmer of blond hair and a flash of her red suit. She whipped around with a supple twist of her body and shot back in the opposite direction. Her tanned, leanly muscled arms sliced through the water, her long legs scissored.

Beyond all sober good sense, he wanted those arms wrapped around him, wanted those long, luscious legs tangled with his.

As he watched her, his cop's sixth sense stirred, sounding a warning in his brain. He turned and moved with unhurried ease across the terrace toward the black wrought-iron table with a center canvas umbrella that blocked the sun. There, he sat his coffee aside and clicked the stem on his watch. He felt no vibration against his wrist, which meant no audio bugs were active in the area. A shift of his gaze verified several cameras on Spurlock's brick wall were now aimed at the swimming pool.

*Watching her, you bastard?* Alex asked as his jaw set. Knowing part of Morgan's assignment was to flaunt her physical attributes to lure Spurlock didn't ease the pressure in Alex's gut. Not when he knew it was almost guaranteed that Spurlock—or some goon on his payroll—was watching her tanned, shapely form glide through the water.

And probably enjoying the hell out of the show.

Irrational as he knew it was, Alex felt protective, possessive and wildly territorial when it came to the woman under observation. For an instant he entertained the notion of retrieving his Glock from the hidden compartment in the desk and taking aim at those damn, one-eyed voyeurs.

That the idiotic idea had even crossed his mind was another thing to add to the list of items he planned to keep quiet about. Irritated with himself, he snagged the towel draped over a nearby wrought-iron lounge chair, moved to the pool's deep end and waited for Morgan to complete another lap.

As if sensing his presence, she slowed her strokes when she neared the pool's edge, then surfaced.

"Hi," she said, treading water to keep afloat.

"Morning. How many laps is that?"

"One hundred seven." She dipped her head back into the water to slick her blond hair away from her face. "One hundred was my goal. I wanted to see how many over that I could manage."

"Naturally you surpassed your goal. You said something last night about jogging this morning. Change your mind?"

"No. I ran before I made breakfast. Wanted to get that out of the way before it got too hot." With the sun beaming in from behind him, she lifted one hand to shade her eyes as she looked up at him. "I made cinnamon rolls. Did you see them?"

"Smelled them before I even got halfway down the stairs. They look great. How far did you run?"

"Five miles."

She'd jogged, whipped up breakfast and swum laps barely before he'd managed to get out of bed. "Remind me not to ask again about your morning activities," he said under his breath.

"What?"

"Nothing." With her long hair smoothed back and her tanned face washed clean of any cosmetics, she again had that varsity cheerleader look. Alex narrowed his eyes, noting for the first time the scar near the hairline on her right temple.

"Something wrong?" she asked.

"No." He held up the towel. "Need a break?"

Her gaze flicked toward the cameras and her mouth formed a sassy curve. "Not really, but I'll take one. Unless you'd care to join me, sweetheart?"

He raised a brow. "What did you have in mind?"

"A race." Treading water, she glided closer to the pool's edge, a challenging gleam in her blue eyes. "I'll even spot you a one-lap handicap."

"Darling, you're too good to me." The last thing he needed was to get hammered by a woman with the stamina of a pentathlon athlete. "If I didn't have to be at the track for the first race, I'd take you up on the offer."

"Tomorrow?"

"There's always that possibility." *Only if hell freezes over,* he silently added, watching her swivel toward the nearest ladder.

When she started up the ladder's rungs, his throat locked tight. The red suit he'd glimpsed beneath the water was a couple of stingy scraps of spandex that covered barely enough flesh to stave off an indecent-exposure arrest.

She walked toward him with the confidence of the fictional Morgan Donovan, her blond hair flowing long, loose and wet over her shoulders, water sliding down tanned flesh on a body built like a centerfold's. The suit left nothing—and everything—to his imagination. Alex sensed she had the same effect on whoever was on the other side of the surveillance cameras. He didn't have to act out Alex Donovan's dark reaction to some faceless man leering at his wife. He *felt* it.

"Darling," he began with a smoothness he was far from feeling. "Of all your bathing suits, that one is my favorite."

She sent him a saucy, under-the-lashes look. "That's why I'm wearing it." Pausing a few steps from him, she cocked a hip and held her hand out for the towel while a pool of water formed at her bare feet. "Give me a minute to change, then we'll have breakfast out here on the terrace."

He knew she was in character, knew the strut, the cockiness, the sex-bomb smile were all an act. That didn't change the fact that her mouth was pale and wet, her spiky-lashed eyes as blue as the sky overhead and the damp, sun-cooked smell of her flesh shot a surge of raw need into his blood.

Later, after his system cooled, he would reason that what he did next was solely for the benefit of the surveillance cameras. At this instant, though, it wasn't the cop in him controlling his actions. It was the man with her scent drifting over his mind like mist and a fierce hunger slamming into him. All he knew was that he wanted a taste of her. *Had* to have a taste.

Just one.

"Breakfast outside sounds good," he murmured. Gripping one end of the towel in each hand, he hooked it around her neck, then tugged her closer. His gaze lowered, measuring the pulse that jumped at the base of her throat.

"First, how about our saying a proper good morning to each other?"

Her eyes registered wary surprise when he dipped his head, moving his lips within an inch of hers. He might want the kiss more than he wanted to breathe, but he'd be damned if he took it by force. All she had to do was give him a peck on the cheek and no one watching would raise and eyebrow. "Your call, Morgan," he said quietly.

She remained motionless, her cautious gaze on his, the kiss hovering for the space of several heartbeats while the air heated and churned between them. He saw the change in her eyes, an almost imperceptible darkening a second before she placed a palm against his cheek, as if to keep his mouth at a safe distance. Even as he felt the trembling in her fingers, she angled her head back in a gesture that could readily be mistaken for teasing.

"I vote we save that proper good morning for later," she said, her eyes staying on his. "Cinnamon rolls always taste better when they're still warm."

Alex let out a breath. "Yeah." As sanity overtook madness, he eased his grip on the ends of the towel, then released them. "Wise call, Mrs. Donovan," he said, taking a step back. "Very wise."

Morgan sat on the terrace, the warm breeze caressing the ample amount of her flesh not covered by the skimpy khaki shorts and low-cut top she'd changed into. Her barely tasted cinnamon roll and coffee sat on the wrought-iron table in front of her. Although over a half hour had elapsed since she and Alex stood beside the pool, her pulse raced as though she'd just swum another hundred laps.

The woman in her had wanted the kiss he offered.

Wanted that tempting, dangerous mouth on hers. Oh, God, how she'd wanted.

Still wanted.

It had been the cop in her who'd held on to sanity, reminding her that the hunger in his voice had been there for show. Just like the slithering walk and the flirty looks she'd sent him. The entire impromptu sexual dance she and Alex had engaged in poolside had been for the benefit of Carlton Spurlock's surveillance cameras. Alex and Morgan Donovan were characters in an unscripted play, their goal to lure a man who had murdered six people. The make-believe world in which they performed would fade as fast as cut roses when the assignment ended. She had to remember that. *Would* remember that.

Her eyes narrowed against the sun's glare as she stared unseeingly at the water shimmering in the blue-tiled pool. She only hoped the fierce, hungry need churning inside her would fade with equal speed.

"Lose your appetite?"

She shifted her gaze across the table. Alex was a study in calm, leaning back in his padded, wrought-iron chair, his coffee mug resting on one of his bare thighs. He wore a gray golf shirt a shade darker than his linen shorts, and a pair of casual deck shoes. The sun had shifted enough so that his chair was now partially in its rays. Dark stubble covered his jaw; his midnight-black hair ruffled in the breeze. Sunlight glinted off the lenses of the mirrored sunglasses that cloaked his eyes so thoroughly.

Just the sight of him heated her blood with a wanting she had experienced only one other time in her life. She knew full well the sense of heady, thrilling surrender that went hand in hand with that kind of wanting.

Just as she knew those mind-clouding sensations were

as dangerous as a drunk behind the wheel of a car on a rain-slick road.

She curled her fingers into her palms while a ripple of panic slithered along her nerves. She couldn't risk again. Would not allow herself to succumb to desire. Wouldn't let herself gamble away everything she'd struggled, *fought,* so hard to regain.

Taking a breath, she gave a nonchalant shrug. "Seems I wasn't hungry after all," she said, picking up her coffee cup. If she took another bite of her roll, her roiling stomach would toss it back up. She dipped her head toward the basket heaped with cinnamon rolls at her elbow. "Want another one?"

"Yes, but I've had my limit. And I helped myself to seconds of the risotto last night. I keep eating like that, I'll have to jog and swim laps with you." His mouth quirked at the edges. "I'm not sure I'm up for such a grueling workout regimen."

"I wouldn't exactly describe it as grueling."

"What do you call running five miles, then swimming over one hundred laps all in the same morning?"

"Challenging." She sipped her coffee, found it tepid and set the cup aside. "If you're worried about keeping up with me, I promise to slow to your pace."

"Ouch," he said dryly. "That's my ego you hear thudding at your feet." He glanced back at the mansion. "I'll just spend a few hours each day in the gym here in order to counter the effects of your culinary skills. You're a great cook, Morgan."

"Thanks. Like I said, I have a talent for finding good recipes—"

"And following the directions," he finished.

"That's right."

He sipped his coffee, his eyes staying locked with hers.

"Gourmet cook, imposing athlete, awesome student, experienced horticulturist. Is there anything you don't do well?"

"The list is endless." She finger combed her still-damp hair away from her face, feeling as though she'd been shoved under the lens of a microscope. "I just invest my time in the things I'm good at."

"The things you do to perfection, you mean?" Without waiting for an answer, he asked, "With all your varied talents, why did you decide to be a cop?"

Her gaze instinctively slid to Spurlock's high brick wall. Alex sat with his back to the cameras; the umbrella centered in the table angled to where it blocked her face from view of the lenses. The audio sensors inside their watches confirmed they were free to talk.

"It's what I always wanted to be."

"Why?"

She forced herself to relax, muscle by muscle. It might be good for them to talk, she reasoned. Maybe after a few friendly chats she would get used to Alex being around. If seeing him, talking to him became habit, maybe her system would stop churning whenever he got close. Anything was worth a try.

"I became a cop for two reasons. First, I like rules. Laws. Structure. When people go against them, someone needs to stop them, maintain order. Control. And get justice for the victims."

"That's reason one. You said there are two."

"Wearing a badge runs in my family," she reminded him. "And since we're Scots, so does the talent for weaving a good tale. My Granddad was the first McCall to sign on with the OCPD. My Dad was the second."

"Let me guess, they wove good cop stories?"

"The best. Growing up, we used to eat lunch every

Sunday at my grandparents' house. After dessert, Carrie, Grace and I would sprawl on this big braided rug with our brothers, while Granddad and Dad regaled us with tales about their jobs.'' Picturing the scene, Morgan smiled. ''The cops were always the 'good guys' and the do-wrongs were 'crooks.' Part of the fun was getting Granddad and Dad to show us all the cool takedown moves they used on crooks. Then all us kids practiced on each other, and wound up in a tangle of arms and legs on that braided rug.''

''Sounds like fun.''

''It was. Mostly.'' She scowled. ''Once in a while things got a little intense.''

''How so?''

''Like the time I twisted Bran's arm up his back with a little too much force and broke one itty-bitty bone in his wrist. He had to wear a cast for six weeks, and I got grounded for the same length of time. You'd have thought I tried to kill him.''

''I'll be sure not to resist if you ever have occasion to take me down.'' Leaning in, Alex sat his mug on the table. ''Since all six McCall kids became cops, those stories must have been inspiring.''

''We all wanted to be good guys like Granddad and Dad.'' She hesitated, then asked, ''Did you join the force because you wanted to be like George Jackson?''

''That, and I wanted a job that came with a steady paycheck. When you grow up not knowing where your next meal will come from, that's a big lure.''

''I can imagine.'' She propped her forearms on the table. ''So, how long have you been drawing that steady paycheck?''

''Nearly fifteen years.''

''You're halfway through your career.''

''More than that if I decided to retire after twenty years.''

Her brow knit. ''You're still a sergeant.'' Her response was automatic, one she wasn't even aware she'd said out loud until Alex slid his sunglasses down on his nose and looked at her over the rim.

''That a problem for you, Officer McCall?'' he asked, his voice as cool as his eyes. ''My *still* being a sergeant?''

''No. I hope to be a sergeant someday.''

''But you don't plan to stay one for long, do you?''

''I intend to move up the ranks.'' She lifted her chin. ''Wanting to advance in one's chosen career is nothing to be ashamed of.''

''You're right, it's not. Neither is finding a place where you fit and staying there.''

''Is that what you've done?''

''Yes.''

''Have you even taken the lieutenant's exam?''

''Meaning, do I possess the ambition to rise up the ranks like you? The answer is no. Working undercover suits me. I don't want a promotion.''

''Ever?''

He took off his glasses, swinging them from finger and thumb while he studied her. Nothing in his tanned features gave away his thoughts.

''I don't plan to take the test,'' he finally said. ''*Ever.* I imagine that makes me seem lacking in the eyes of a woman like you.''

''A woman like me,'' she repeated, lacing her fingers together. ''Exactly what kind would that be?''

''Focused. Ultracompetitive. A woman who drives herself to succeed at everything she does. If she cooks, it's gourmet. If she swims, it's in Olympic form. If she goes to the police academy, she comes out top in every subject.

And if she hits a glass ceiling at the PD, she'll make sure she shatters it on her way to the chief's office.''

"So, you think I'll be the top cop one day?"

"Sweetheart, I'd make book on it."

She furrowed her brow. "You make it sound like that's a bad thing. That I'm hungry for power."

"There's nothing wrong with your goal, Morgan. Any more than it's wrong for someone who doesn't share your aspirations to stay in a job where they feel they do their best. Get the most satisfaction. It's a matter of choice."

"I agree."

He gave her a sardonic smile. "You might honestly believe you do. You'll feel far different if you try to share your life with a man whose ambition doesn't equal yours. The relationship will be doomed from the start."

"Doomed." Light gusts of wind picked up strands of her hair, batted them against her cheek. "Is that the voice of experience I hear?"

"It is."

She thought about the comparison he'd made the previous day between funerals and weddings. "Sounds like you hooked up with a woman who had her eye on making it to the top of her career field. And the fact you didn't share her ambition in your own job caused problems."

"It caused a divorce." His eyes narrowed on her face. "And it appears, with you, I'm repeating history."

"Hardly. We're pretending to be married. It's business, not personal." She had no idea why she felt it important to point that out. "With us, feelings and emotions don't figure into the equation. Can't figure in."

"Like everything else, you've tied all aspects of our assignment into a tidy package." He checked his watch, then rose. "The happily married husband and wife who now live in this mansion are suited for each other in all ways, so let's keep our minds focused on them. So, Mrs. Donovan, what will you do today while your adoring husband makes himself known at the racetrack?''

Morgan eased out a breath. Alex was right—things would go much smoother between them if they kept their minds on the job. Which is where she now directed her thoughts.

Last night she and Alex had settled in the mansion's huge, oak-beamed study and reviewed the operation plan they'd drawn up for their assignment. They had agreed Alex would spend his days at the track, the reasons being threefold. First, his presence would solidify his cover as a professional gambler, new to the area and looking for action. Second, placing substantial, attention-getting bets would put him in position to connect with local gamblers who ran in Carlton Spurlock's inner circle. Third, a few discreet visits to the stables to interact with jockeys might unearth new information about Frankie Isom, the jockey whom Krystelle Vander claimed Spurlock murdered.

''I've got a good idea what needs to be added to the soil here to get it healthy,'' Morgan said, glancing across the terrace toward the pitiful flower beds. ''I want to make sure, though. I'll take soil samples from several spots this morning and have Sara take them to the county extension center for analysis.''

Alex walked around the table, stopping beside her chair. ''And after you're through digging in the dirt?''

''I'll finish inputting the measurements for the flower beds into my laptop. From that, I'll set up a spreadsheet to help plan what shrubs, perennials and annuals to plant in each bed, and how many. Then I'll do a chart to co-ordinate the colors that will look best in each bed.''

''Spreadsheets and charts,'' Alex said. He reached down, cupped her chin in his hand and nudged it upward.

His fingers were warm, tensed and started her stomach quivering all over again.

He studied her face for a long moment, his dark eyes unreadable. "I wonder, do you ever stop to smell them?"

"Spreadsheets and charts?" she managed to ask while her pulse throbbed hard and thick.

"Flowers. The ones you list on your spreadsheets and charts. Do you ever take time to smell the real flowers? Enjoy them?"

She ordered herself to settle. His hand was on her chin because of the surveillance cameras aimed their way. Solely because of the cameras. "Of course I smell the flowers."

He skimmed his thumb over her jawline. "I'm glad to hear it."

Just then, Morgan caught movement out of the corner of her eye as Sara Rackowitz appeared around the corner of the mansion.

"Sara's here." Morgan pulled back fractionally, forcing him to drop his hand.

Alex followed her gaze. "Right on time," he said.

Dressed in cutoffs, tennis shoes and a sleeveless top, the FBI agent strode across the terrace. She wore her dark hair drawn back in a ponytail anchored through the back of a red Oklahoma Sooners baseball cap.

That Morgan could still feel the light skim of Alex's thumb across her jaw—and the fact Sara had witnessed that moment of intimacy—sent a ripple of unease creeping up Morgan's spine. Unease that intensified when the agent's assessing gaze flicked from Alex to her, then back to Alex.

"Good morning, Sara," he said.

"Morning, Mr. Donovan. Mrs. Donovan."

"Sara." Morgan nudged the basket of cinnamon rolls

across the table. "How about a roll and some coffee before we start work?"

"I'll pass on the coffee, but not on these," Sara said, snagging a roll from the basket. "I smelled them the instant I stepped onto the terrace." She took one bite, then rolled her eyes. "These fell from heaven, right?"

"I have a similar reaction to anything Morgan cooks," Alex commented. He shifted his stance to put his back toward Spurlock's security cameras. "Sara, it's safe to talk."

"Good." She took another bite. "Before we get down to real business, I just want to say that I'm sunburned and sore as hell from all the slave labor I did around this joint yesterday. Would you guys please tell the Donovans their Girl Friday deserves a raise?"

Alex chuckled. "I'll tell the Bureau to put something extra in your paycheck."

"Yeah, that'll happen in this lifetime." Sara pulled a folded piece of paper from the back pocket of her cutoffs and handed it to Morgan. "Here's the list of swimming pool supplies you asked for."

"Thanks," Morgan said.

"The piece of paper under the list shows a description of each car that entered Spurlock's property last night for the charity do he hosted," Sara explained. "We ran the tags off the photos taken by our pole-cam to find out each vehicle's registered owner." Morgan knew Sara was referring to the camera the Feds had installed inside a nondescript-looking cylinder and mounted on a utility pole across from the massive gate that blocked Spurlock's driveway.

Standing behind Morgan's chair, Alex settled a casual hand on her shoulder as he leaned in and studied the list. "Judges, mayors of surrounding municipalities, CEOs," he read. "A lot of upstanding citizens, at least on the surface."

"Right." Sara continued to nibble on her roll. "Wonder what those citizens would say if we told them their host last night was responsible for the murder of at least six people, three of them cops?"

"They wouldn't believe it," Alex answered. "Won't believe it without our having evidence to back up our claim."

"Six people," Morgan said, her gaze drifting to the high brick wall. "Here we are, hoping we can find whatever evidence Krystelle Vander supposedly hid in Spurlock's gold bedroom that proves he killed the jockey. Even if we do, we might not ever be able to prove Spurlock killed the other five victims."

Alex's fingers tightened on her shoulder for a brief instant. "Taking him down for one murder is preferable to no conviction at all."

"True," Morgan agreed.

His hand drifted from her shoulder. "I have to get ready to go to the race track." He bent, dropped a kiss onto the top of her head. "See you tonight, darling."

"See you." With the breath backed up in her lungs, she watched his slow, confident gait take him across the terrace, then through the French doors. She'd been wrong, she realized. No amount of friendly conversation would ever get her used to being around Alex Blade. Her system would never grow complacent. Her pulse would never even out. Her desire for him would never wane.

For the second time in her life, Morgan found that her feelings for a man had her teetering on the edge of a cliff. Closing her eyes, she fought against the fluttering panic in her stomach. She couldn't let herself tumble off that cliff this time, she told herself. Wouldn't let herself fall.

"How's life with Blade?"

Morgan opened her eyes, noted she was the subject of the FBI agent's sharp, intense scrutiny. "Peachy. He's agreed to set the table and wash the dishes whenever I cook."

"How'd you manage that?"

"He likes to eat food that has never been frozen or seen the inside of a box."

"Same thing goes for my husband, but he still won't get near a sink full of dirty dishes." Sara popped another bite of cinnamon roll into her mouth. "You going to give me the recipe for these?"

"Sure."

"To tell you the truth, I'm a real slouch in the kitchen," Sara confessed. "My kids have no idea what 'made from scratch' means. How about when this operation is over, you come to my house and give me a couple of cooking lessons? I'll buy a bottle of wine to make sure the process is painless."

Morgan laughed, and found she genuinely liked Special Agent Sara Rackowitz. "Just name the date and time."

"I will." Sara tucked a hand into the back pocket of her cutoffs and looked out at the lawn. "So, Mrs. Donovan, what kind of work do you have planned for us today?"

"We're going to dig in the dirt."

"Somehow I knew you were going to say that," Sara commented, rubbing a hand across her lower back. "I definitely deserve a raise."

# Chapter 8

Two weeks later, a vicious case of frustration had Alex steering his black Lincoln into the drive behind the department's two-story brick safe house. When he pushed open the car door and climbed out, the late-afternoon heat stole the oxygen from his lungs.

"Hell," he muttered, shoving the keys into his pants pocket.

Leaving his suit coat behind on the Lincoln's front seat, he jerked the knot of his slate-blue silk tie loose then flicked open the top button of his white tailored shirt. He unhooked his cuff links and rolled up the starched sleeves while advancing up the narrow, creaking wood steps to the house's back porch.

It wasn't the searing heat or humidity thick enough to swim in that had his mood as dark as a storm about to strike. It was the job. The job he loved, that defined who he was. The job that now seemed to be driving him slowly mad.

He set his jaw. Having worked undercover for years, he knew to expect setbacks. Knew it sometimes took months to build a case. For Alex, being patient had never before posed a problem. He'd learned the higher the stakes, the more the waiting paid off.

His knowing all that, and applying it to *this* undercover operation were miles apart.

He knocked twice on the door, paused, then rapped four times in quick succession, sending Sara Rackowitz the "all is well" code.

Seconds later the trim, attractive FBI agent swung open the door. Her damp hair and crisp top and shorts told him she wasn't too long out of the shower.

"On the phone you sounded surly," she commented, flicking her gaze over his loose tie and rolled-up sleeves. "You look that way, too. Bad day at the racetrack, Blade?"

"Actually, Alex Donovan won. Huge."

"Third day running. You're on a roll, big spender."

"Donovan is, anyway."

Alex stepped into the cool, small kitchen, his gaze sliding over the faded wallpaper, chipped counters and yellowed linoleum. "Got a beer, Rackowitz?"

He wasn't surprised when her dark brows arched. He'd made it a staunch rule to shun alcohol while working undercover. That he was making an exception to that rule—and didn't much care at the moment—added to his overall sense of irritation.

"Sure, I've got a beer. And since I worked my butt off today cleaning that monster pool you and Morgan get to float around in, I'll join you." Rackowitz walked to the refrigerator, snagged two cans, handed him one, then trailed him into the small living room where a window air conditioner ground away in a monotonous tone.

"Speaking of Morgan," Rackowitz continued, "why isn't Mr. Donovan on his way to the mansion to celebrate his good luck at the track with his gorgeous wife?"

"I'll be there soon enough."

Truth was, Alex thought as he settled onto the sagging sofa, returning to the mansion every evening had begun to feel too much like coming home. He knew it was ridiculous to feel that way just by walking into the massive house that wasn't his, and becoming instantly aware of the scent of the woman who didn't belong to him.

He didn't give a flip about the mansion. But he damn sure wanted the woman. A woman who was all wrong for him. One he knew could never belong to him, not for long, anyway.

That, he thought, was the reason the frustration gripping him by the throat had brought him to the safe house. He wanted the operation over. Finished. Wrapped up in a package so incredibly tidy that even Morgan McCall would approve.

"This op is going nowhere." He popped the top on the can, took a long, slow pull of ice-cold beer. "That's going to change."

"It will." Rackowitz dropped onto the stuffed chair that looked as decrepit as the couch. "Don't forget, Blade, you've been at this for barely two weeks. And you *have* made progress. We know for sure you snagged someone's attention, because that Las Vegas cop suspected of having ties to a gambling consortium ran a check on Alex Donovan."

"Problem is, we don't know if the cop ran the background check at Spurlock's request. Could have been for one of the high rollers I met at the racetrack who's thinking of investing in the real estate deals I've been talking up."

"The cop ran an inquiry on Morgan Donovan when he did the one on you. Instinct tells me the background check run on her has Spurlock's prints all over it."

"Still, we can't be sure, since Morgan spent a couple of days at the track with me. You can bet she got a lot of attention."

"I'll bet."

Taking another swig of beer, Alex made a useless attempt to erase the memory of how it felt to have Morgan's arm linked with his as they moved among the wealthy clientele who leased penthouse suites at the track. Of how she smelled like hot, smoldering sin. Of how that scent filled his lungs, his head, making him crazy to have her.

His desire for her seemed to intensify daily. Dammit, he had to get away from her before he did something stupid.

"I want this operation over." His inability to keep the sharp edge out of his voice had his temper bristling.

Watching him with interest, Rackowitz sat her beer can on the coffee table with water marks ringing its surface. "You want to tell your control officer what's going on here, Blade?"

"What's going on is nothing. Spurlock has yet to outwardly acknowledge our presence. It's our job to get him to do that. I'm damn well going to see that happens."

"How?"

"Plan B. Call and get the ball rolling. For tonight."

"Tonight?"

"We know Spurlock is having another charity event this evening. When his guests start leaving, I'll put on a show Spurlock can't ignore. He won't like that sort of attention drawn to his neighborhood."

Rackowitz checked her watch. "You're not giving our guys a lot of notice."

"For what's left to do, it's plenty. They built the device before Morgan and I moved into the mansion. It just needs to get hooked up to the piece-of-junk seizure car, which is here, parked in the garage."

"You're sure about this?"

"I'm sure." Alex shoved a hand through his hair. "Look, Rackowitz, it's time. Morgan's got every flower bed replanted with flowers, shrubs and who knows what else. The grass is starting to look greener than emeralds. If a bunch of pretty blooms and a manicured lawn were going to appeal to Spurlock's love of horticulture enough to draw him to our side of that brick wall, they'd have done it by now."

"Probably." Rackowitz frowned. "I thought Morgan's looks would be what got him to drop by and welcome you to the neighborhood. Can't believe I was so off-track. Why do you think he's holding back?"

Alex raised a shoulder. "Maybe because of his recent problems with Krystelle Vander and Emmett Tool. One was his lover, one his accountant. Both were insiders he trusted and they turned on him. We put plan B into effect, we show Spurlock that Alex Donovan also has reasons to be concerned about his own safety. Hopefully, what happens tonight will be the shove Spurlock needs to make him realize he and I are kindred spirits."

"When you explain it like that, plan B sounds like the way to go," Rackowitz said, then reached for the phone. Five minutes later, the ball was indeed rolling.

Reclaiming her beer, Rackowitz leaned back in the chair. "Blade, when I asked you earlier what was going on, I didn't mean only with the operation."

He slid her a look. "What else is there?"

"What's going on with Morgan?"

"Officer McCall is inexperienced but capable. She's holding her own. End of story."

"I've been around her enough to have figured all that out for myself," Rackowitz countered, then eased forward, her dark hair brushing across her cheeks. "You and I have worked together on some pretty intense operations. I've never seen you wound this tight, so I doubt your comment about Morgan is the 'end of story.' Tell me what's going on between you two. Off the record."

"Nothing's going on, Rackowitz." When she continued to stare, he added, "I'm being straight with you."

"Okay, I'll buy that because you've never lied to me." She angled her chin. "Is *that* why you're wound tighter than a watch spring? Because there's nothing going on between you and Morgan and you want there to be?"

Frustration pushed him to his feet, had him pacing the small living room with a restless, prowling stride. "No that's the last thing I want, Rackowitz."

She conveyed her doubt in his statement with a penetrating look. "Is that so?"

"That's so," he responded. "Suffice it to say that Morgan might as well have been cloned from my ex-wife."

Rackowitz crossed her arms over her chest. "The only comment you've ever made to me about the ex-Mrs. Blade is that marrying her was one big screwup."

"My opinion hasn't changed." He rubbed his fingers dead center of his forehead where a headache had begun to brew. "So, how about you and I go over the details for plan B? If it works, we'll be able to pack up and go home soon."

"Sounds good to me."

In the dark master bedroom, the clock beside the bed glowed an eerie red 1:00 a.m. With the mansion gripped in the heavy hush of night, Morgan eased back a panel of the velvet drapes and peered out a window.

On the cobblestone driveway below, the black Lincoln sat in the spot where Alex had habitually parked it since the day they moved in. Several small spotlights installed in strategic locations around the mansion's front yard spread dramatic fans of light across the Lincoln's shiny black exterior.

She looked back across her shoulder. With the only light coming from a small lamp out in the hallway, she could make out Alex's silhouette, but not his expression as he stood at the foot of her unmade bed. "Are you sure that's a different car than the one you've driven since this op began?"

"Positive. Alex Donovan's primo Lincoln is locked in the garage at the safe house," he said, inclining his head toward the window. "The one you're looking at now is a seizure car the department acquired last month in a drug raid. It shifts like a garbage truck and has a skip in the engine stroke."

Letting the drape swing closed, she turned from the window to face him. "Whatever that is, it sounds bad."

"In this case, terminal," he said, stepping forward into a weak spear of light. "The Lincoln parked outside is slated for the junkyard." As he spoke, he weighed a small, black flashlight in his palm. He had explained earlier that an OCPD bomb tech had converted the flashlight into a triggering device. All Alex had to do was slide down the little silver lever on the side, and a mechanism hooked to the Lincoln's ignition would send a spark to the modest amount of explosives the tech had planted beneath the almost empty fuel tank.

"Tonight, you and I will simply speed the Lincoln's destined arrival at the junkyard," Alex added.

"You and I," Morgan repeated, resolutely telling herself to ignore the fact he wore only a pair of gray cotton drawstring pajama bottoms. The light sweeping in from the hallway might be weak, but she could see enough to know that his chest, darkened by a scattering of sleek black hair, was much too broad and too tempting for her to let her gaze settle anywhere but on the shadowed planes of his narrow, rawboned face.

Which was a huge temptation in itself.

Feeling that temptation clear to the bone, she put a hand to the lapels of her long robe of ivory silk. "Since I didn't know about plan B until a few hours ago, you should get all the credit. I'm just glad you told me what was going to happen tonight before you put things into motion."

He slid the triggering device into his pocket. "If I hadn't briefed you, how do you think you would have reacted when an explosion rocked you out of a sound sleep around one in the morning?"

Her gaze ranged across the bedroom to the antique writing desk with its hidden compartment. "Maybe grabbed my gun and badge, thinking we were under attack." She shoved a hand through her hair that she'd artfully tousled to make it look like she'd been jolted from sleep. "I don't know for sure what I would have done."

"Neither do I, which is not good when working assignments like this. Undercover partners have to keep the lines of communication open, have to tell each other exactly what they intend to do. Forgetting that can blow your cover and get one or both hurt."

"Not to mention killed."

"That, too."

She turned again to the window and eased back the drapes. The night was inky black; she could barely make out the dark shapes of trees swaying in the wind. Beyond the yard, the street dotted with wrought-iron lampposts was devoid of traffic.

When Alex moved in behind her, a faint whiff of his now familiar, musky aftershave slid into her lungs, tightening her insides. She closed her eyes against need that rose in her like a warm wave. After two weeks of living under the same roof with him, she ached to feel his hands against her flesh, to know, to finally *know* how that hard mouth would taste, how it would feel against hers.

*Don't go there,* she cautioned, struggling to force back the cloudy haze of desire. Getting involved twice in one lifetime with a man who could rob her of her faculties to think would be emotional suicide. She was back in control of her life now, her fate. She had no intention of allowing history to repeat itself with the man standing only inches behind her.

"Morgan, open your robe."

Her eyes flew open the same instant Alex's hands cupped her shoulders.

When he turned her to face him, her hands went up instinctively, settling on his bare arms that looked hard as marble and felt just as solid. The feel of flesh against flesh heated the need already flowing in her blood. Need that mixed with razor-sharp panic when she gazed up into his face and felt her resistance toward him peel away.

That quickly. That terrifyingly.

Raising her chin in defense, she tossed her hair back. "Look, you're about to blow a car to smithereens. This isn't the time—"

"Relax," he said quietly. "If I had seduction in mind, I would choose a different time and place." He flicked a look at the immense bed with its pooling, rumpled sheets. "A different time, anyway," he amended.

"Fine," she managed. "Why do you want me to open my robe?"

"An explosion jerks someone out of a sound sleep. Before they dash out of the house to see if the end of the world has arrived they *maybe* have the presence of mind to grab a robe."

"Okay. So?"

His right hand moved from her shoulder, settling at her waist. "So, they don't take time to cinch the robe's belt into a nice, neat bow," he said, tugging the belt loose.

She felt the robe's silk lapels slither apart to expose her matching ivory gown. In the weak light from the hallway, she saw Alex's gaze drop to the lace that snugged across her breasts, saw his dark eyes flicker, then sharpen.

"That's...logical." She let her hands fall from his arms and took a step back. "I guess with the belt tied, I look too together. Tidy."

His gaze rose to meet hers. "Too damn tidy for your own good." Turning abruptly, he sliced back one side of the drapes with his hand and stared out the window.

Her pulse thudding hard and thick, Morgan studied him in the silent dark. Her gaze traced his broad shoulders, moved across his muscled chest, slid down to his washboard-flat stomach. If she was so in control of her fate, her life, why did she want this man, who could stir her with one look, even more than she wanted to breathe?

And how the hell was she going to keep her hands off him when all she wanted to do was jump that gorgeous body?

Alex dipped his head toward the window. "Looks like Spurlock's party is breaking up."

Her erotic thoughts scattering, Morgan moved beside him and gazed out beyond the driveway and well-tended lawn to the street. A vehicle turned out of Spurlock's driveway, its headlights licking across the blacktop. Seconds later another vehicle followed.

Alex pulled the triggering device from the pocket of his pajama bottoms, his index finger hovering over the silver lever. He met her gaze. "Ready to see if we can get our neighbor's attention, Mrs. Donovan?"

"More than ready."

Although she was expecting the explosion, the thundering blast jolted her heart into her throat. She watched out the window as the black Lincoln jumped a foot into the air, landed hard, then burst into flames. From one story above, looking down across the driveway into the windshield was a glimpse into hell. Flames danced across the seats, the dash, bursting in blue and red-orange spikes. The lights fanning across the front of the mansion illuminated the white smoke billowing from beneath the Lincoln's hood.

Alex placed the device in the drawer on the nightstand, snagged the phone and dialed 911. With adrenaline surging like a torrent through her veins, Morgan marveled at the control in his voice as he reported the blast to the dispatcher, then answered questions.

He hung up, turned, then held out a rock-steady hand. "We'd better get out there."

By the time they rushed down the staircase and onto the front porch, the distant, urgent whip of a siren filled the smoke-laden air. Morgan spotted several luxury cars stopped in the glow of the streetlights, their faceless occupants no doubt watching the inferno. Mindful of the surveillance cameras eternally pointed their way, she put a hand to her mouth, then staggered back a few steps.

"Steady, darling," Alex said, wrapping an arm around her waist.

A siren wailed to a crescendo when a fire truck throbbing with emergency lights swung into the driveway, followed seconds later by a black and white patrol car. All sirens ceased abruptly as several firefighters in full turnout gear spilled from the truck.

Within an efficient thirty minutes, the fire was doused, equipment stowed, the fire truck and its occupants gone. In anxious, worried-wife mode, Morgan paced the mansion's wide front porch with the restless, prowling stride of a caged cat while Alex stood in the driveway conversing with a uniformed cop with a flat, masked expression. The cop nodded, handed Alex a copy of his report, then slid into the black-and-white and drove away.

Continuing to pace, Morgan glanced toward the street. Now that the excitement was over, the curious onlookers had driven off in their big, expensive cars. And Carlton Spurlock had yet to surface.

Squashing the hard jolt of disappointment, she moved down the porch steps, her open robe billowing in the night breeze. Crossing the driveway, she felt the coolness of the cobblestones beneath her bare feet. She paused when she reached Alex's side and gazed at the Lincoln's charred skeleton.

"How long do we mill around, hoping Spurlock shows?" she asked quietly.

Alex glanced down at her. "Give it time. Our quarry has an aversion to the police. No way would he come calling while they were still here."

"True."

Alex dipped his head toward the Lincoln's burned remains. "I'll have to be sure to congratulate the bomb tech on a job well done."

Morgan nodded just as the purr of an engine drifted on the breeze. Turning in unison, she and Alex tracked the sleek, black limousine gliding up the driveway.

Feeling as if a stone had lodged in her chest, Morgan watched the limo brake to a stop a few feet from where they stood.

Sliding an arm around her waist, Alex dipped his head. "Plan B worked," he murmured. "Darling, get ready to meet our neighbor," he added, then pressed a steadying kiss against her temple.

## Chapter 9

When Carlton Spurlock emerged from the long, sleek limo's rear door, Alex got his first in-the-flesh look at the man. The overall impression was one of vitality and health and well-channeled power. The imposing carriage lamps mounted on each side of the mansion's front door illuminated Spurlock's tall, powerful build in a mix of silver light and shadow. That distinctive build looked doubly impressive cloaked in a dark tailored suit with the pant cuffs breaking on a pair of expensive Italian loafers.

The knowledge that the man had murdered six people—including George Jackson and two Feds—snapped at Alex like fangs. The resolve to take him down and lock him up increased a hundredfold.

As Spurlock moved away from the limo, the wiry, athletic-looking driver who'd opened the door for him fell into step at his boss's heel. Spurlock paused, spoke a few words. The underling instantly nodded, walked to the front of the limo, then propped a hip against the hood.

And focused his cold, calculating gaze on Alex as if he were a snake that might strike his employer at any instant.

Smart guy, Alex thought.

From intel compiled by the FBI and OCPD, Alex pegged the goon as Peter Colaneri, an ex-con with a phone-book-thick rap sheet reflecting a propensity for violence. That personality trait qualified Colaneri to serve as a bodyguard—and suspected henchman—for the man advancing across the driveway like a shadow, controlled and observant. Soundless.

"Mr. Donovan?"

"That's right." Tightening his arm around Morgan's waist, Alex prodded her behind him. He wanted Spurlock to know up-front that Alex Donovan was a distrustful, hard-bitten tough guy with territorial instincts toward what was his. Including his wife. "Who the hell wants to know?"

Spurlock arched a dark brow. His face had sharp features and tanned skin that glowed with health. His hair was black, well styled, silver at the temples and all there. Eyes as hard as ice chips flicked from Alex to the charred Lincoln, then back. "I'm Carlton Spurlock. Your neighbor. I had a social gathering tonight. Some of my guests were…disturbed by the explosion. So am I."

"The line forms behind me, pal. Somebody sticks a bomb on my car and blows it to hell, you think I'm not *disturbed?*"

"This is a quiet neighborhood, Mr. Donovan. I have an interest in keeping it that way."

"So, buy yourself a set of ear plugs."

"Honestly, Alex," Morgan chided. Easing from his hold, she took a sauntering step into Spurlock's full view, her ivory robe flowing open with the movement. "There's no reason to be rude to Mr.…."

Tilting her head, she sent Spurlock a slow, apologetic smile. "I'm sorry," she began in a voice as dark and sultry as the night surrounding them. "I didn't catch your name."

It was as though she had prepared for this role all her life, Alex thought. In one simmering second the tidy rookie cop had effected a silky metamorphosis into a confident, sexy former cocktail waitress who knew all the tricks about drawing a man's eye.

"Spurlock." The gray gaze flicked to her lace-covered breasts, then rose. "Carlton Spurlock."

Oh, yeah, Alex thought, reading the silent appreciation in the man's eyes. Already she had their prey's blood running a little hotter.

"I'm Morgan Donovan, Mr. Spurlock." Offering her hand, she strolled toward him with a metronome sway of hips. "Please excuse my husband's brusqueness. He's upset about what happened to his car." She sent a wary glance in the direction of the Lincoln. "A bomb," she breathed. "One of the firemen said it was a bomb. My nerves are just jumping."

"How could they not be?" Instead of shaking her hand, Spurlock lifted it to his lips, pressed his mouth to her knuckles.

"And it doesn't help to know we've upset you and your guests," she added. Skimming a fingertip down the long column of her throat, she gave Spurlock a distressed look. "I hope you'll give us a second chance to prove we can be good neighbors? *Quiet* ones."

"Of course," he said, his mouth lingering over her hand. "And I ask you to excuse my rudeness in not welcoming you to the neighborhood when you moved in. Some business endeavors have claimed my full attention lately. I hope you'll forgive the oversight, Mrs. Donovan.''

"There's nothing to forgive." Her hair was a gorgeous mess, falling like a golden waterfall over her shoulders, curling seductively over her breasts. Alex looked at her, and all he could see was Spurlock's manicured thumb brushing across her knuckles. He felt his hatred for the man gain strength until it oozed through his blood like molten lava.

"And, please, call me Morgan," she added, then tossed Alex a chastising look with laser blue eyes. "Sweetheart, you and Mr. Spurlock started off on the wrong foot, don't you think?"

"Yeah." Reining in his thoughts, Alex sent her silent kudos for how perfectly she was playing her role. Too much open hostility on his part would either block or delay their initial goal of getting invited to visit Spurlock's kingdom on the other side of that brick wall.

Alex stepped forward, offering Spurlock his hand… which forced the scum to release his grip on Morgan's. "Alex Donovan. My wife is always telling me I'm too abrupt with strangers. Guess she's right."

"No harm done, Mr. Donovan." Spurlock returned the handshake with a hard, firm grip, then turned and examined the Lincoln with interest. "It appears you have an enemy."

"I've got more than one," Alex commented.

"That's something we have in common, Mr. Donovan." Spurlock looked back at him, his gaze narrow, measuring. "Do you have an idea which of your enemies planted the bomb on your car?"

"Maybe. When I know for sure, I'll deal with that person, one-on-one."

"Yes. I get that impression."

When Spurlock reached into the inside pocket of his suit coat, Alex's spine stiffened in reflex. Although his eyes stayed mild, his thoughts flashed to the master bedroom where his loaded Glock lay with Morgan's in the desk's hidden compartment. That was the thing about working undercover—you often had to rely solely on your wits instead of your weapon.

He relaxed only slightly when Spurlock pulled out a slim cigar and solid-gold lighter from his pocket.

Spurlock dipped his head; with a flick of his thumb a flame flared, highlighting the silver at his temples. Watching the flame, Alex pictured the crime-scene photos of Emmett Tool's charred remains that required dental records to make ID. Had Spurlock used that same gold lighter to burn his traitorous accountant alive?

Expelling a stream of smoke, Spurlock turned and examined the artfully lit flower bed that snugged against the front porch. "You've planted the *Madame Pierre Oger* rose," he said after a moment.

"Why, yes." A look of total fascination glinting in her eyes, Morgan settled a hand on his sleeve. "Are you an admirer of roses, Mr. Spurlock?"

"Carlton," he said, looking back at her. "I inherited a love of the blooms from my grandmother."

"I got my green thumb from my aunt." As if warming equally to him and the subject, Morgan slid a hand into the crook of his arm. "She had a huge yard, crammed with every type of flower and shrub you can think of. Growing up, I spent summers with her and my cousins. Every day before we could go swimming, we had to help in the yard and gardens. I never really minded, though. My aunt made me realize there's something fascinating about patting seeds into soil, then watching them grow. Thrive."

"Yes, exactly." Spurlock's smile spread as he looked deeply into her eyes, holding the moment. "Your aunt sounds like my late grandmother."

"She liked to work in the garden?"

"With roses. She grew them, bred them. They were her passion. As they are mine."

Morgan gestured toward the flower bed on the opposite side of the porch. "Then you maybe recognize the *La Reine Victoria* bush I planted there? That's the rose named for *Madame Pierre Oger*'s mother. I thought it would be nice to have the bushes paired along the front walk. Sort of a tribute to mother and daughter."

"An enchanting gesture," Spurlock commented, brushing a casually intimate hand over hers.

The frank male interest in the bastard's gaze sent a spike into Alex's brain. Narrowing his eyes, he pondered if he would have enough time to bash in Spurlock's aristocratic face before Colaneri could sprint over and jump him.

Alex flicked a quick look across the driveway. Light from the carriage lamps glinted in Colaneri's eyes, giving him the feral look of a sleek, deadly jungle cat. He still stood with one hip against the limo's hood, his black suit coat unbuttoned, his arms relaxed at his sides. Alex knew the stance allowed for quick retrieval of a holstered weapon.

"I have several hundred rose bushes planted in my gardens," Spurlock commented. "They're in bloom now. Perhaps you and your husband would like to see them?"

"I'd love to. Alex?" Morgan turned, gave him a speculative look. "I know you're not much for looking at flowers, so maybe you'd rather I go alone?"

Alex knew she'd made the comment because he had cautioned her about their acting too eager to accept any invitation Spurlock might offer. Still, knowing that didn't do anything about easing the primitive instinct to keep what was his—if only on a temporary basis—at a safe distance from Spurlock's murderous grasp.

Strolling to Morgan's side, Alex slid a hand beneath the heavy fall of her hair and settled his palm against the back of her neck. When he nudged her around to face him, the movement eased her hand from Spurlock's arm.

"Darling," Alex murmured, his body brushing lightly against hers. "I can look at plants all day, as long as I'm with you."

"So smooth," she said, her low, smoldering laugh drifting on the warm night air. She settled a palm against his bare chest and gave him a saucy look from beneath her blond lashes. "I wonder if you'll say things like that after we're married a whole year?"

"I'll not only say them, I'll still mean them." Telling himself he had a duty to play the scene as convincingly as she, he dipped his head, brushed his lips over hers.

And felt his heart stumble. His mind blur.

With the air backed up in his lungs, he fought to think like a cop and not a man suddenly trapped between infatuation and something deeper. He reminded himself it was all an illusion. An act. His and Morgan's lives depended on convincing a killer they were nothing more than a happily married couple who happened to have moved into the mansion next door. Logic, however, didn't make the need stirring in Alex's blood any less real. Or any less of a danger.

Pulling back control, he turned in time to catch a glimmer of envy in the gray eyes locked on Morgan.

*She's mine,* Alex thought with an inner snarl as he slid his hand down the curve of her spine to settle at her waist. *All mine.* He sent Spurlock a slow, meaningful smile, a message passing male to male. "My wife and I will be happy to take a look at your flowers."

Spurlock expelled a stream of smoke, the white column curling upward into the dark night while he made a long, careful study of his new neighbors.

"I'll check my schedule," he said, rolling the slim cigar between his manicured fingers. "Then be in touch."

Standing beside Alex on the mansion's front porch, Morgan tried to ignore the ferocious hammering of her heart while the red glow of the limo's taillights disappeared into the night. Wordlessly she turned and walked into the pink-marbled foyer, thankful she was barefoot and not trying to force her unsteady legs to maneuver in ankle-wrecking stilettos.

As soon as she heard Alex close the front door and engage the dead bolt, she put a hand to her chest. "Dear Lord."

He turned. Alarm shot instantly into his dark eyes as he reached for her. "You're white as a sheet."

She batted his hand away. "I have…to catch my breath." She pressed a palm against her chest as if to shove air out, but there wasn't any.

He took a step toward her. "You need to lean forward."

"No…I need…to breathe."

He snagged one of her arms. "You can't do that when you've got air trapped somewhere beneath your diaphragm." Placing a palm against the back of her head, he forced her to bend at the waist.

Instantly air heaved out of her lungs, then swooshed in.

"Better?" he asked, watching her intently while she dragged in another breath.

"Yes. Thanks." She straightened. Using the back of her hand, she shoved her tousled hair off her forehead.

"How can you stand there so calm when we did what we just did?"

He raised a brow. "You're referring to our encounter with Spurlock?"

"What else?" She flipped a hand toward the front of the mansion. "I'm standing here, hyperventilating over it and you're not even breathing heavy."

"It's called experience, Morgan. And we got Spurlock's interest, is all. We won't know if he bought our act unless he gets back to us with a firm date and time for us to take a look at his flowers."

"I hate to think I'm about to have a heart attack if what we just did is for nothing."

"Time will tell. In the meantime you need to sit down." With his hand still gripping her arm, Alex steered her across the Persian carpet to the staircase, nudged her down on the bottom step. "Stay here. I'll pour you some brandy."

"Okay." Feeling a chill, she pulled the silk robe around her and watched him move off to the study, his pajama bottoms revealing a muscular body that looked fit beyond reason.

By the time Alex returned, her lungs were working like well-oiled bellows. "Thanks," she said as he handed her a snifter.

"You're welcome."

She took a long swallow, letting the warmth of the rich, smooth brandy course through her. "I had no idea about this."

His brows slid together. "The brandy?"

"The rush that hit me. The adrenaline surge."

Alex settled onto the burgundy carpeted step beside her. Beneath the brass chandelier's bright gleam, his tanned chest and arms looked as hard as marble. "I'd call it more an attack of nerves. Something akin to stage fright."

She nodded slowly. "You remember me telling you I read those articles by undercover cops?"

"I remember."

"One of the cops called a reaction like mine 'friendly fear.' Like a natural fight-or-flight response. He said in an undercover situation, friendly fear can be the early warning that gives a cop a split-second edge."

"He's right."

She shoved her hair back, lifted it off her shoulders, then took another sip of brandy. "I'm not sure I felt fear while we were with Spurlock." She narrowed her eyes, considering. "I don't really know what I felt."

"Morgan, you're talking about emotions."

"Right. I'm trying to analyze what I felt."

"You're wasting your time. Emotions aren't something you can put on a spreadsheet and logic out. It doesn't really matter what you felt out there. What matters is that you fooled the people you had to fool. Period. You did a super job."

Alex's praise joined the warmth of the brandy scooting through her. Angling her chin, she leaned in. "You really think so?"

He studied her with those unfathomable dark eyes. "I know so."

She grinned. "It's the strangest thing. When Spurlock drove up, something in my mind clicked, and all of a sudden I was a combination of Morgan Donovan and Carrie."

"Carrie, your sister?"

"Yes. According to Grace, Carrie's been leaving men puddled at her feet since she was five. Carrie makes dealing with men look so effortless. Easy."

"Tonight *you* made it look easy."

Morgan leaned an elbow against the carpeted step just above the one on which she sat. She could almost feel the brandy dissolving the tension inside her, layer by layer. "You weren't so bad yourself tonight, Blade."

"Yeah?" With his hair tousled, his eyes dark, his jaw shadowed by stubble, he looked rough and reckless, dangerously and delectably male. Then there was that bare, muscled chest.

She nodded, trying to keep her mind focused. "You came off like a really hardcase out there. Like one of those guys who's going do what he's going to do and he doesn't care much what anybody else thinks about it."

"That description also applies to Spurlock."

"I know. But when things hit a snag, he snuffs people." She gave Alex a narrow, assessing look. "Does tough, dangerous Alex Donovan snuff people, too?"

His eyes glinted. "An interesting question, Mrs. Donovan. Don't you think you should have asked it before you married me?"

"Too late now." Without realizing she'd made the gesture, Morgan glanced down, saw her hand resting on Alex's knee. When she started to pull back, he entwined his fingers with hers.

"You're right, it's too late," he said quietly. "There's also something else Spurlock and I have in common."

With her hand linked in his, a flood of sensations washed over Morgan, from excitement to anxiety to desire to fear. She set the snifter aside, struggling to think while her pulse pounded in her head, echoed in her ears. "And that would be?"

He reached out, his fingertips skimming her cheek as he nudged her hair behind her shoulder. "We both think Alexander Donovan has a gorgeous wife."

Heat surged into her face along the path his fingers had taken. She knew she should pull away, tell him good-night and go up to her room. But she didn't. Couldn't. She settled for shifting the subject back on firm ground. "So, ah…do you think Spurlock bought the story about the bomb? That some enemy of yours planted it on your car?"

"I don't imagine he thinks it was a bunch of college kids practicing what they've learned in their advanced chemistry class."

Shifting her hand in his, Alex grazed his thumb over her knuckles. "If he wasn't behind that Vegas cop running the background checks on us, Spurlock will do it now. And if he was the reason for the first check, he'll have a more intensive one done. That check will show him there's more to Alex Donovan than what's on the surface."

"The pieces of the legitimate companies Donovan owns."

"Right. Spurlock will want to find out how a convicted gambler got his hooks into those legit operations. Our neighbor will be curious as to whether Donovan uses those operations to launder illegal gambling profits. If so, Spurlock will probably want to get in on the action. He'll dig into Donovan's background, which is airtight, thanks to the Feds. If, after all that, Spurlock figures you and I are the genuine article, he'll make good on his invitation for us to drop by and smell the roses."

"He has to. An invitation is the only way we'll get inside his mansion to look for whatever evidence Krystelle Vander hid in the gold bedroom."

"Even if that happens, it's going to take a measure of luck for us to find the evidence when we don't even know what it is."

Morgan nodded. The skim of his thumb across her knuckles was slowly, compellingly tying her insides into knots. "In the meantime, we continue to do what we've done for the past two weeks. We wait on Spurlock."

"Right." Alex angled his chin. "I'm usually good at waiting. Being patient for things to happen, for a bust to go down." She heard the subtle change in his voice, a thickening, as his gaze shifted, focused on her mouth. "Right now sitting here watching you, touching you, I find there's something I'm damn tired of waiting on."

His words went straight to her head to swirl with the haze of brandy. "I…"

"You smell like hot, smoldering sin." He tightened his hold on her fingers, then cupped his other hand around the back of her neck and eased her toward him. "I want a taste of you, Morgan McCall. I want to put my hands on you and have a long, slow taste of you."

"This…isn't…smart." Her hands rose, settled against his bare chest. She didn't push away. How could she when she, too, had been desperate for a taste of him? "You know it, and I know it."

"We both know." He lowered his head, caught her bottom lip lightly between this teeth. "One taste."

"One," she whispered in hoarse agreement, her lips parting beneath his.

He took her mouth slowly, torturously. Her pulse leaped, her breath shuddered as the taste, the textures flowed around her. Into her.

With reason fading, desire spiked to the surface where she couldn't escape it. Everything inside her whirled into a mindless rush—her heart, her blood, her head—and she forgot everything but the need to be in his arms.

His mouth angled, taking hers now, hot and hard, strangling the air in her lungs, misting the last remnants of reason still clinging in her brain. He shoved the silk robe off her shoulders, down her arms, then he cupped her hips and dragged her onto his lap.

Her arms went up, twining around his neck, her fingers shoving into his hair. *Mine,* she thought while her mouth met his, greed-for-greed.

His hands moved, sliding up her sides to her breasts. His hard, seeking fingers stroked her nipples, already straining against the silk of her gown. A moan ripped up her throat. Her heart jackhammered, heat flashed in her veins so fast and hot that it incinerated everything. Including thought.

"Every rule," Alex murmured. He wrapped her hair around his hand, tugged her head back and gazed down into her face. The raw emotion that turned his voice to a rasp glinted in his dark eyes. "Dammit, Morgan, I want to break every rule when I'm around you."

*Rules.* The word drummed in her head while his mouth feasted on her throat. Not only were they breaking every rule of the job, but she had also turned her back on the ones she had carved for herself. In stone, or so she had thought. Rules meant to keep her safe, to protect her heart, her sanity.

Sitting in Alex Blade's lap while they tried to swallow each other whole was about as insane as it got.

Her survival instinct winning out over passion, she pulled back. "We…can't…do this."

"We *are* doing it." His mouth trailed down her throat while his fingers thrust down one of the nightgown's paper-thin straps. "Let me have you, Morgan. Here. Now. Let me have you."

"I… No." Panic skittered up her spine when she felt the last threads of her resistance ripping away. In one move she pushed back, slid off his lap. "We can't do this. *I* can't."

With her blood still flowing hot, she found her legs so unsteady she had to grab the banister for support. "I can't get involved with a man like you," she blurted.

"A man like me," Alex repeated. He remained on the bottom step, his dark hair rumpled where her fingers had been, his narrowed eyes watching her, measuring. "Want to explain exactly what that means?"

"It means…" She pressed a hand to her thundering heart while she swallowed hard, trying to catch her breath. Did she really want him to know that her thinking processes scrambled when he was around? That the instant he walked into the room, her blood stirred and heated? That she had learned the hard way a man who had that kind of effect on her was suicide? That she had too much at stake to jump off a cliff twice in one lifetime?

"It means we have a job to do," she finally said. That, after all, was the most important reason to keep each other at arm's length. Their safety, even their lives might depend on their maintaining an all-business relationship. "Certain rules shouldn't be broken. Lines shouldn't be crossed. You and I are here because of the job. Only the job. That's what we need to focus on. It's just basic common sense."

"I agree." As if utterly at ease, Alex leaned back against the banister. "One hundred percent." His gaze skimmed down her, then up. "It's just that I'm having trouble lately zeroing my thoughts in on work."

His intense, examining assessment had her suddenly imagining what she must look like, standing there with her hair tousled, her mouth swollen, her too-sheer gown with one of its straps slithering down her arm. With heat rushing into her cheeks, she snagged her robe off the stairs, pulled it on and cinched the satin belt tight at her waist.

"It's late. I'm going to bed." She knew she would get little sleep, if any. Not while she could still feel the haunting slide of his touch over every inch of her body.

She turned, her gaze slicking across one of the long-legged tables nestled against the foyer's blue linen-papered wall. When she saw the leather-bound book on the table, she froze.

"Something wrong?" Alex asked.

"That book on the table." She looked back across her shoulder to meet his gaze. "Is it one Wade Crawford brought the day we moved in? One with a camera in it?"

Before she even got the last syllable out, Alex was off the step. He swore viciously. Then again, quietly. "I didn't think about the camera. That there's a damn camera sitting right there—"

"Recording everything we just did."

"Yeah."

Morgan gripped the lapels of her robe in a fist while mortification warred with a vague nausea. "Tell me you know how to open the panel on the room under the staircase where the VCRs are."

"I can get in."

"And erase the tape. The tape of us…" She closed her eyes on the image of smooth-talking cop Wade Crawford watching a recording of her and Alex getting it on.

"I can erase it."

"Good. That's good."

Looking down at her, Alex expelled a slow breath. "It was stupid of me not to remember the camera. Hell, I put the damn book on the table myself." He scrubbed a hand over his face, shook his head. "You're right."

"Right?"

"Our getting involved is a bad idea, all the way around. Especially where the job's concerned. Working under-cover, you have to maintain a professional detachment with everything and everyone. I just broke that rule, big-time."

"*We* broke that rule."

"I run this operation, McCall," he snapped, his voice going cop cold. "That makes whatever happens my re-sponsibility. I let you get into my head, get to me, and it made me careless." He looked away, his jaw muscles flexing.

The self-derision in his voice equaled what swirled in-side her. What the hell had she been thinking? She didn't want to get involved with Blade. Didn't want to be any-where near another man who could make her lose control so quickly. Effortlessly. Whatever Alex stirred in her would have to be stopped, she resolved. Or, if not stopped, at least suppressed.

With the taste of him still lingering on her lips, she reinforced that conviction by taking a step away from him. Then another.

His gaze pinned hers. "Don't worry," he said as if he'd read her thoughts. "What just went on between us won't happen again. You have my word. From now on, if I put my hands on you, it'll be all business."

"That's best." Keeping her eyes locked with his, she tried to ignore a flare of disappointment. She drew in a long breath. "It wasn't one-sided, Alex. I was a willing participant. You know that. So, I give you my word, too. I'll keep my hands off you. Whatever happens between us from now on will be in the line of duty. It has to be."

She saw emotion flicker over his face before he turned his head away.

"Agreed," he said.

# Chapter 10

Muscles bunching and straining, his body slick with sweat, Alex sat on a workout bench, counting reps. His arms ached, his biceps burned as he completed a fifth set of curls with free weights. Around him sat a dozen pieces of Nautilus equipment. Two additional weight benches and free weights at various poundage lined a rack positioned in front of a mirrored wall. Behind him were separate doors that led to the Whirlpool and sauna. The top-of-the-line setup evidenced that the mansion's previous, now bankrupt, owner had been seriously into body image.

Lately, Alex was more concerned with relieving frustration than anything else.

In the three days—and nights—that had passed since he and Morgan kissed each other senseless, he had tried to put himself into the same mind-set he used when he went deep undercover. For him, doing so had always felt like a kind of separation. Becoming someone else landed him in a different dimension, transformed him into a person devoid of feelings and emotions. Now he was close to admitting he had given his best shot at trying to get to that place but had failed. It wasn't so easy to distance himself from his feelings anymore.

His feelings for Morgan. Feelings he didn't welcome, nor have any desire to analyze.

It didn't help that whenever they were indoors, he and Morgan had begun keeping the same distance from each other as they would with an Ebola patient. For him, distance didn't much help, not when the need tethered tight inside him strained hard just at the scent of her. Then there were the dinners they had no choice but to share, since Spurlock might knock on the door or send one of his minions over any minute. So, he and Morgan dined together each evening, consuming one of her four-star meals while they discussed the specifics of their undercover operation, police work in general and current events at length. What they didn't get close to talking about was what had happened between them three nights ago.

Fine with him.

His breath hissing out through gritted teeth, he began another set of curls while sweat ran down his bare chest and back, dampening the waistband of his cutoff sweatpants. Since his divorce, the few relationships he'd involved himself in had been with women who wanted the same thing as he: insignificant forays with no emotional strings attached and zero discussions about feelings. Those comfortable encounters involved a few laughs, some quick sex, a couple of days or maybe weeks of companionship. Then both parties moved amicably on.

Why the hell couldn't he move on from those crazed minutes he and Morgan had spent on the staircase?

It worried him that she had captured his mind so totally he'd forgotten the camera recording every touch, every kiss, every damn move they made. Ate at him that, three days later, he still wanted her with a fervor that was like a sickness. He knew full well an undercover cop who couldn't control his emotions—better yet, *avoid* them— represented a danger to himself and everyone around him.

He also acknowledged he should never have gone down that particular road with Morgan. Not only because she was his partner, but he was years older—not just chronologically, but in experience. Both on the job and off, he felt sure. He had taken advantage of her, and he'd had no right to do that. Period. He fully intended to stop thinking with his glands and keep his hands away from her. Which would be a lot easier for him to pull off if he could distance himself from her. Problem was, he had no chance of doing that while this operation was active.

So, he lay in his bed each night, wondering if she was fast asleep in that big bedroom not so far down the hallway from his. Or was she lying awake like him, reliving what had happened between them? Imagining what it would have been like if they'd taken things further?

"Alex, we're in."

He nearly winced at the sound of Morgan's voice coming from behind him. Since the muscles in his arms were on fire, he dropped the weights on the padded mat beneath the bench. He turned while using his forearm to wipe at the sweat dripping into his eyes.

She stood in the doorway, dressed in black shorts that showed a great deal of leg, and a stretchy black jog top that snugged just beneath her breasts and exposed her flat, tanned midriff. Her blond hair was anchored into a ponytail. The perspiration gleaming on her face and arms and the hard pumping of her lungs told him she'd just finished her morning run.

Frustration stirred inside him, shot to the surface as every cell in his body instantly burned for her.

He grabbed a hand towel off the end of the bench and swiped at the sweat on his face and chest. Christ, all he had wanted was one taste of her. Instead, he'd acted like a man feeding after a lifelong fast, and been buried by an avalanche of need and desire he had no idea how to handle. Need and desire that this instant had him fighting the urge to drag her to the floor, bury himself in her and forget the consequences.

He fisted his hands on the towel. So much for subjecting his body to punishing workouts meant to purge his system of her. She had gotten inside him. Somehow. Someway.

"We're in where?" he asked.

"Spurlock's." She gave her moist forehead a quick wipe with the back of her hand, then took a long pull from the water bottle she carried with her. "I was jogging past his place when that huge gate blocking the driveway swung open and a man stepped into my path."

"One of the two black-suited guys who are always at the gatehouse?"

"No. This was the tall, wiry man who drove Spurlock's limo the other night—"

"Colaneri."

"Right, Colaneri. He stepped into the street right in front of me. I had to skid to a stop, nearly lost my balance. It was like he'd been waiting for me to jog by at my usual time." She raised a shoulder. "Which I did." Moving into the room, she grabbed a hand towel off a small table and blotted her face. She paused, frowning.

"Something wrong?"

"There's a malicious edge in his eyes. Even when he's being polite like he was this morning, it's there."

Alex nodded. He had felt Colaneri's hostile stare from across the driveway the other night. He damn well didn't like knowing the vicious bastard had approached Morgan in the street.

"You read the intel we have on Colaneri," Alex said. "He has a fondness for committing assault and battery, and likes to engage in kinky sex with prostitutes. Some women he's been seen with have gotten cut up. A few have wound up dead, sliced to pieces. There's never been proof he's the one who did the dicing, but I'm sure those talents are one reason he's on Spurlock's payroll."

Morgan scrubbed the towel down her neck. "Reading intel on people like that is one thing. It's a whole different world when you come face-to-face with someone that bad."

"Welcome to police work," Alex said, giving her a thin smile. "Which person are you referring to? Colaneri or Spurlock?"

"Both." She took another drink from the bottle. "I'm not sure which one of them creeps me out more."

"Remember Spurlock calls the shots. These days, Colaneri doesn't do anything without instructions from his boss. We've got three cops and three civilians dead because Spurlock either did the killings or ordered them." Alex wadded his towel, tossed it into a galvanized hamper. "What did Colaneri say?"

"That his boss, Mr. Spurlock, would like us to come for drinks and dinner tonight."

"What time?"

"Six o'clock." She arched a brow. "We're supposed to drive over instead of walk. That's because Spurlock's Dobermans get nervous when they smell strangers."

"I have that same reaction to Dobermans." Alex felt

the familiar rush, the lift that came when an investigation picked up speed. ''Sounds like we made the first cut.''

''Sounds like.'' Morgan strolled to the StairMaster angled near the mirrored wall and gazed idly at its control console. After a moment she rolled her shoulders as if to ease tension that had settled there. Not tension, Alex amended. Apprehension.

He expelled a slow breath. It was the man in him who needed to distance himself from her. It was the cop who was responsible for preparing his partner for what faced them tonight.

''I won't go to the racetrack today.'' He rose, hefted the weights off the mat and replaced them on the rack. ''I'll take a quick shower, then meet you in the study. We'll go over every step of the operation again.''

She turned, a smile shadowing her mouth as she handed him the water bottle. ''Thanks.''

''Morgan, some amount of apprehension is good. It keeps you on your toes. Just remember you've proved you can handle yourself around Spurlock. Tonight you'll just be handling yourself around him in a different location.''

''On his turf.'' She pulled her bottom lip between her teeth. ''I keep thinking about everything that can go wrong while I'm looking for the gold bedroom. Then snooping around in it for the evidence Krystelle Vander hid there. Whatever the heck it is.''

''Snooping?'' Alex angled his chin. ''I think of it more along the lines of your performing a sensitive investigative technique.''

She let out a little laugh. ''Thanks, Blade, I needed that.''

''Anytime, McCall.'' He took a step toward her. ''Remember, in this business, there's no way you can anticipate what might happen. The key is to be flexible enough so you can modify the flow of your character as needed to meet changing situations.''

''Flexible. Right.'' She tugged off the band tying back her hair so it cascaded over her shoulders like golden sunlight. ''I need to hit the shower, too. I'll see you in the study.''

''Yeah.''

He watched her reflection in the mirrored wall as she moved toward the door, her black shorts snug on her slender hips and trim bottom. What *he* needed was to touch her.

Closing his eyes, he took a deep, greedy gulp from the water bottle…and tasted her all over again. He barely prevented himself from heaving the bottle against the wall.

Hours later Morgan gave her appearance a final check in the mirror at the top of the staircase. With her blond hair teased into a dense, wild mane and a red cat suit clinging like skin to her body and dipping low over her breasts, she definitely took on the essence of her undercover persona.

She pressed a hand to her jittery stomach. She might look like the self-assured, sexy woman who had once waited tables in a Vegas cocktail lounge, but right this minute she lacked Morgan Donovan's cocky confidence. On the inside she was all Morgan McCall, and her nerves were scrambling. She didn't want to think about the upcoming venture on the other side of Spurlock's high brick wall. Didn't want to consider the possibility she might take an unintended misstep, but it was there, like the ticking of a detonator, pounding ceaselessly in her brain.

Her almost nonexistent sense of calm wasn't helped by the fact her nerves had grown raw over the past three days. She and Alex had walked on eggshells around each other since their hot-blooded encounter on the staircase. As if by some unspoken agreement, they had kept their conversations after that cordial, centered mostly on their assignment with a few detours into local and world events.

Through it all Alex had treated her with straightforward indifference.

No, she amended instantly, frowning at her mirrored image. Not indifference. She knew he was aware of her, that was the problem. He *exuded* awareness beneath his cool, incisive exterior.

And she was aware of him.

Good Lord, she was aware.

Before she could switch off her mind, she pictured him as he looked in the gym this morning, leaning on that padded bench, wearing only ragged gym shorts, his muscles bulging while sweat rolled down his tanned flesh. It had taken all of her self-control not to jump his bones, peel off those shorts and have her way with him.

Closing her eyes against the thought, she admitted to herself it wasn't just what lay ahead of her tonight that had tension snapping inside her. It was her partner, a man she had grown to respect and admire. A man who she knew without a doubt would be totally bad for her on a personal level. A man she'd promised to keep her hands off. A man with whom she wanted to have crazed, mindless sex.

God, she was in deep trouble. Damn Alex Blade. Damn him for stirring up all this need that she'd managed to control for years.

"You look…"

Jolting, she pivoted at the sound of Alex's voice. She hadn't heard him coming down the carpeted hallway, and now he stood, leaning against the banister, studying her. In his tailored camel slacks and white silk shirt he presented the perfect image of a well-to-do man who owned a mansion, expensive cars and had a young trophy wife hanging on his arm.

She forced a nonchalant smile. "I look what? Okay? Sort of okay?"

His eyes slid from her face, down the traffic-stopping red cat suit to her sling-back red stilettos that brought her eye to eye with him. "You look dangerous," he said, shifting his gaze back to her face. "Lethal."

"Is that a compliment?"

"Yes."

She raised a hand, her manicured fingers playing with the thin gold chain of her tiny leather evening bag. "Well then, since we're going into hazardous territory, I should fit right in."

"More than." He pulled a black, sleek lipstick tube from his pocket. "I gave the camera a last check." Pushing away from the banister, he moved toward her, handing her the tube.

"Thanks." She tried to ignore the skip in her pulse brought on by the scent of his musky aftershave. Instead she forced her thoughts to how he had patiently walked her through the paces with the camera during their time in the study. Because of that, she felt confident using it.

She gave him a smile. "I guess I owe Sergeant Wade Crawford a big kiss for figuring out how to fit a microchip camera into this tube and still leave most of the lipstick intact."

Alex studied her, his brown eyes looking a shade darker against his tanned face. "A handshake will suffice." He dipped his head. "You ready to pay a visit next door, partner?"

Easing out a breath, Morgan slid the lipstick into her purse. "Ready as I'll ever be."

* * *

Spurlock's mansion looked quietly elegant, built in the style of an English manor house complete with ivy creeping up the brick walls. The English motif extended indoors in the form of antique woods and classic fabrics, ultraconservative furnishings done in warm colors. Breathtakingly expensive original oil paintings decorated the walls; needlepoint rugs blooming with flowers in muted colors pooled across the polished wood floors.

When their host escorted Morgan and Alex onto the mansion's expansive back terrace, the seemingly unending gardens of lush, velvety roses completed the image that they had been transported to England.

After an hour's tour of the gardens and greenhouse, they returned to the terrace. The nearby arbors and trellises crawling with blooming rose vines, and ornate urns overflowing with a variety of flowering plants made Morgan think of a secret garden. "Carlton, your home, your gardens are beautiful," she said, meaning it. "Magnificent."

"Thank you." Dressed in tailored black slacks and a gray linen shirt, Spurlock poured champagne into crystal flutes. The sun had disappeared in a burst of color, illuminating the terrace in pale-pink evening light. The soft, indirect lighting tucked beneath the house's eaves highlighted the silver at Spurlock's temples.

Morgan smiled. "Your gardens remind me of my aunt's. On a larger scale, of course."

"I'm honored," he said. "Considering the amazing improvements you've made already to your yard and flower beds, I consider you an expert." He handed her a flute. "I believe you mentioned your aunt grew all types of flowers and shrubs."

"That's right."

"Perhaps you can help me with a problem."

"Surely not with roses." Morgan flicked a look at Alex, standing a few feet away. She knew he also had to wonder if she was about to be tested.

"Not roses," Spurlock confirmed. "See the grouping of oak trees beyond the swimming pool cabana? Their leaves form such a thick canopy that grass won't grow beneath them. I carpeted the area in moss."

"Makes sense," Morgan commented.

"Yes, but there are bare spots where I can't get the moss to fill in. I'm wondering if you know of a solution?"

Morgan looked past the swimming pool, noting the dark cabana. "Buttermilk," she said, looking back to meet his gaze.

"Buttermilk," Spurlock repeated.

"Mix a pint of buttermilk with a gallon of water and paint the mixture on the bare spots. The moss should settle in."

His gaze slicked down her red cat suit. "You're not only an expert on plants, you're a gorgeous one."

"Thank you."

A short, thin Oriental man in a white coat appeared, carrying a silver tray with the unopened bottle of water Alex had requested. Spurlock slipped the bottle from the tray, waved away the servant and shifted his gaze to Alex. "Mr. Donovan, are you sure I can't interest you in something other than bottled water?"

"No, thanks, and call me Alex," he said amicably as he accepted the plastic bottle and twisted off the cap. "I like to keep a clear head when I'm talking business." Giving Morgan a smooth smile, he slid an arm around her waist. "And I agree with you, *Carlton*. My wife is gorgeous."

"Extremely." Spurlock sipped from his flute, then inclined his head. "I wasn't aware you and I had business to discuss."

"I'm looking for advice on an investment," Alex explained. "I've got the chance to buy a small vacant shopping center on the city's northwest side." He took a drink of water. "Someone at the track mentioned you own a land development company."

"Among other things."

At that, anxiety built in Morgan's belly. According to her and Alex's plan, his mention of business was the catalyst that would give her time inside the mansion to search for the gold bedroom where Krystelle Vander hid the evidence that would prove Spurlock ordered the hit on the jockey.

"So," Alex continued, "I thought you could give me the pros and cons of opening certain types of businesses in that area."

"Perhaps." Spurlock eyed him. "What type of businesses?"

"I plan to convert most of the space into a movie theater."

Spurlock arched a brow. "A movie theater?"

"To show low-budget, independent films for select clientele. I'd put a bookstore in next door to the theater. There'd probably be room for a novelty shop, too."

Easing out a bored sigh, Morgan glanced at Spurlock before shifting her attention to a nearby trellis, thick with thousands of white clematis blooms. She could almost see the man's mind working behind those steel-gray eyes. Alex had clearly gotten the message across that the theater would show porn films, with an adult bookstore and a shop for sleazy sexual paraphernalia nearby. Businesses like those had customers who paid in cash. Capacity and sales numbers, especially for the movie theater, could be easily manipulated on the account books to show a lot more profit than what actually came in. That made the operations excellent devices for laundering large numbers of small bills.

A man who operated a gambling casino—and other criminal endeavors—was perpetually looking for ways to wash illegal money.

"Yes, Alex, I believe I can give you some advice." Spurlock glanced at his solid-gold designer watch, then swept a hand toward a round, glass-topped table. "My cook will have dinner ready in about twenty minutes. We can discuss the potential of your investment now if you'd like."

"I'd like." Alex tucked Morgan's hand into the crook of his arm as they strolled toward the table. "Darling, I know business discussions bore you."

She gave her hair a petulant pat. "Can't you put this off?"

"I would, but I have a meeting with the property owner tomorrow morning," Alex explained. "So I need to talk to Carlton now."

She gave a sulky shrug when they reached the table. "You did just spend an hour looking at roses without complaining."

"True." He turned toward the table, pulled out one of the padded chairs for her. "This won't take long." She knew the comment was Alex's reminder they had agreed she would spend no more than five minutes on her first search for the gold bedroom.

"Actually, I think I'll go powder my nose while you talk business." She set her flute on the table near a crystal vase from which magnolia boughs spilled. Fingering the gold chain on her evening bag, she met Spurlock's gaze. "You'll excuse me?"

"Of course."

"Didn't I see a powder room when we came in through the hallway?"

"Yes. I'll be happy to summon Chan and have him show you the way."

"Don't bother," she said, even as she moved off with a confident swing of hips toward a set of French doors. "I remember where it is."

Morgan stepped inside the doors, checked her watch. When they first arrived, she had casually ascertained from Spurlock that his massive home had four bedrooms downstairs, eight upstairs.

There was no time to get upstairs tonight. If luck was with her, she'd find the gold bedroom on this level.

She moved hurriedly through an expansive living room past a grouping of leather sofas and chairs, polished tables and bookcases filled with leather-bound first editions. The air was ripe with good, rich scents coming from the far-off kitchen.

She turned into a softly lit hallway wainscoted in silky mahogany. The pounding of her heart matched the staccato click of her heels against the wooden floor. As she moved, she turned the clasp on her leather bag. If any kind of surveillance camera was recording her movements, a small tone would sound. She heard nothing.

The first door she came to was the small powder room she'd passed earlier. She cast a look up and down the hallway, then reached into the room, flicked on the light, then pulled the door to the powder room closed.

Retrieving the lipstick tube/camera from her purse, she continued along the hallway, turned down another, wishing she had some idea of how many servants were in the mansion. She had to assume a couple, all of whom might appear and confront her.

She edged open the first door she came to and flipped on the light. She found a huge bedroom, done in crimsons and gray blues, and felt an instant flare of disappointment at not finding the gold bedroom on her first try. Aiming the small tube, she snapped two pictures, turned off the light, shut the door.

Shoulders tight, spine stiff, she hurried down the hallway, telling herself she would maybe relax again in about ten years. Right now, her body felt razor-sharp and all edges.

She continued her search, repeating the picture-taking process in a bedroom with a hunter-green motif, and another decorated in soft, oyster-white hues. All the bedrooms she had seen so far looked obsessively neat and had an unlived-in feel.

She checked her watch. Over two minutes had passed. *Hurry.*

Even the silence around her seemed laced with tension as she stepped to the door at the end of the hallway. Easing it open, she caught a whiff of lavender as she flicked on the light, illuminating a large bedroom done in French blue and pale coral. The bed was massive, covered in a luxurious velvet spread. A vase of yellow roses sat on the nightstand, giving the room a lived-in feel. Morgan was about to snap a photo when she heard the distant scrape of footsteps advancing along the hallway's wooden floor.

Heart in her throat, she rushed across the expanse of dove-gray carpet into the small adjoining bathroom. She locked the door behind her then leaned against it, dragging in air as her body trembled. She strained to make out any noise coming from the other side of the door, but couldn't hear past the pounding of her heart.

Instinct told her someone had come looking for her and she would find them waiting for her when she opened the door. Was it Spurlock? His servant Chan? The cook or a housekeeper? Maybe even the hired bodyguard, Colaneri, who had stopped her in the street this morning, and had yet to make an appearance tonight?

She knew how to play this. She and Alex had prepared for something like this happening, had worked out a scenario for what she should do if someone confronted her. All she had to do was keep her cool. Maintain cover. Get through it.

After waiting an appropriate length of time, she flushed the toilet then moved to the long marble counter, turned on the solid-gold tap and stuck her hands under the cold water. Taking a series of deep breaths, she checked her reflection in the mirror ringed in lights. Despite a tan and the blush she had applied earlier, her skin was pale as a sheet.

She dried her hands on one of the thick towels hanging nearby, then pinched her cheeks to put color back into them. Sliding an unsteady palm down one red spandex-covered hip, she drew in a last deep breath, forced a nonchalant look on her face, then pulled open the door.

She shrieked when Colaneri shoved her back, her icepick heels nearly skidding out from under her on the ceramic-tiled floor. Like a charging bull, he rushed into the bathroom, slammed the door, then took a step toward her.

Fear shot up her spine in a single, icy arrow as she grabbed the counter to keep her balance. "What the hell do you think you're doing?" she demanded.

His mouth curved while a hovering cruelty glinted in his dark eyes. "What've you got under that cat suit, blondie?"

# *Chapter 11*

When Colaneri reached for her, Morgan skittered two steps back. "Keep your hands off me."

On the edge of her vision, she checked the doorknob. He had set the lock when he shoved her back into the bathroom and shut himself inside with her.

"You wearing a wire under that cat suit, blondie?"

She kept her face blank. The situation would only get worse if he caught a whiff of the fear slithering along her nerves.

"An *underwire* bra?" she asked, purposely misunderstanding.

"Cute." His mouth curled on one side. He wore black trousers and a white silk shirt open at the throat to expose several gold chains around a neck in which the tendons looked as taut as guy wires. He wasn't overly muscular, but he was taller than her and wiry, which gave him the advantage of height and strength. He had scars around his eyebrows and mouth, and his nose looked as if it had been hit once or twice too often. All were physical signs of someone whose rap sheet listed numerous assault arrests.

"Hey!" she protested when he grabbed her evening bag and jerked the chain off her arm.

"Shut up."

Stay calm, she told herself. If she acted like a victim, she would wind up one. And if he found the camera hidden in her lipstick tube, she definitely had the potential for coming out on the bad end of this encounter.

"What the hell do you think you're doing?" she demanded.

"What the hell do you think you're doing snooping around?" he asked, mimicking her words.

He pulled out the lipstick tube, yanked off the top and twisted the end. Glancing down, he checked the slim column of red lipstick that swiveled up.

Morgan swallowed hard when he jammed the cap back on the tube, then dropped it into her purse.

"Snooping?" she asked. "Who's snooping? I had to use the bathroom." Deliberately careless, she swept her arm to one side. "This is a bathroom, isn't it?"

"You bypassed four others on your way to this one," he pointed out in a low, bloodless voice. He examined her compact, then her small atomizer of perfume. Finally he tossed the purse onto the counter.

When his gaze settled on her breasts, cold fear prickled on the back of Morgan's neck.

"You wearing a wire, blondie? Maybe got a bug hidden in your bra, thinking you'd plant it around here some place?"

"Why would I do that?" she demanded with a lot more bravado than she felt.

He smirked. "To spy on my boss. There's lots of people who'd like to know all about his business dealings."

"Well, I'm not one of them." She tossed her hair back even as her legs trembled. "For your information, I don't care what Mr. Spurlock does."

"I do. And I get real suspicious when someone starts snooping around, sticking her nose where it doesn't belong."

*"I had to go to the bathroom!"*

He took a step toward her. "Here's the deal, blondie. I'm going to pat you down to see if you've got more than just the usual goodies under all that red spandex. You don't, I'll apologize. You do, you and I will have something new to talk about."

Her pulse beat at a furious pace as her mind echoed the intel information she'd read on Colaneri. The image of the crime-scene photos of Krystelle Vander's cut throat and bloody, knife-shredded flesh loomed in Morgan's vision. If she gave in to Colaneri's request, she had no guarantee he would stop at a pat down. He could have her stripped—maybe raped, maybe dead—in minutes.

That wasn't going to happen. She was a cop. Just because her partner was dealing with another bad guy and not around to back her up didn't mean she couldn't get herself out of hot water. She had, after all, come out top in the academy's self-defense training.

She just had to defend herself like a woman, not a cop.

Silently cursing her ice-pick heels, she spread her feet for better balance. "You want to *pat me down*," she repeated coolly, then leaned in, narrowing her eyes in disdain. "Isn't that a police term? Are you some kind of undercover policeman who gets his kicks fondling defenseless women?"

"Do I look like a damn cop?" Colaneri's voice sounded like chipped glass, and she could see in his eyes the brutality was only a whisper away.

Her throat was raw and hot, and she felt a trickle of sweat between her breasts. She had to get out of there fast.

"Do I look like a woman who's going to just stand still and let some pervert feel her up?"

"You asked for it, blondie," he said, then reached for her.

Quick as a snake, her hand lashed out, grabbed his thumb, and forced it back into his wrist. At the same instant she stomped a stiletto heel into the top of his foot. Roaring in pain, he dropped to one knee, his free hand flailing for the marble counter.

"Don't ever touch me again," she hissed. She grabbed her purse; in seconds she had the door unlocked, opened and was racing down the hallway, air heaving in and out of her lungs.

She knew the performance she was about to put on for Spurlock would determine whether she and Alex got out of there alive.

Shoving through the French doors, she rushed onto the terrace. The sky was now black as pitch. Lamps illuminated the round table where Alex and Spurlock sat, their intent expressions confirming they were still talking business.

She marched toward them on unsteady legs; with Spurlock's back to her, she met Alex's gaze, sending him a look of urgent warning. She saw the skin beneath his eyes tighten, then relax. He leaned forward, watching her face intently when she slapped her palms on the table top and gave Spurlock a fiery look.

"What kind of sick place are you running here?"

Alex lunged to his feet, gripped her arm. "What happened?"

He couldn't have known—had no way of knowing—how just his touch had the power to reassure.

"Yes," Spurlock said, rising from his chair, his gray eyes cool as they took her in. "I'm curious to know why you believe I'm running a *sick place*."

"Your goon tried to feel me up, that's what happened." She gave Spurlock a look as hot as his was cool. "He takes orders from you, doesn't he? Did you know he was going to do that?"

Alex wheeled on Spurlock, his hands fisted. "What the hell is this?"

Spurlock dipped his head. "I assure you both, I don't know what this is about. If you'll excuse me, I'll find out."

He turned just as Colaneri burst out of the French doors. He limped halfway across the terrace before Spurlock held up a hand. Like a trained dog, Colaneri stopped in his tracks. The look of red-hot hatred in his eyes chilled Morgan's blood.

"Him!" She stabbed an indignant finger into the air. "That ape said if I didn't *let* him feel me up he was going to do it anyway."

"Bastard," Alex spat with snarling fury. When he took a menacing step forward, Morgan grabbed his arm.

"No. Alex, he didn't lay a hand on me, I made sure of it. Just take me home. Now."

Spurlock turned back to face them. "Mrs. Donovan, *Morgan*, I would prefer you not leave, at least until you tell me what happened." He sliced a look at Colaneri, then remet her gaze. "If one of my employees has treated a guest badly, I need to know so I can deal with the situation."

"Well…" Putting a hand to her throat, she glanced toward the mansion. She had made progress tonight. She had determined the gold bedroom was not on the mansion's first floor. That meant it was one of the eight bedrooms on the second level. It was a sure thing neither she nor Alex would be taking another tour of the mansion tonight, which meant they had to play this so their host would invite them back.

She met Spurlock's waiting gaze. "I went in to use the powder room in the hallway, just like I said I was going to do," she began, relating the story she and Alex had devised earlier. "But the door was shut and I could see the light on underneath it, so I figured someone was in it." She flicked her wrist. "This being a mansion, I assumed you had more than one powder room on the first level, so I just went on down the hall. I opened doors, and all I found were bedrooms. It seemed a little personal for me to tromp through someone's bedroom to get to the adjoining bath, so I kept going, thinking the next door I opened would be one to a separate powder room. When I got to the end of the hallway, I opened the last door and saw it was another bedroom. I…" She swept her lashes down demurely.

"You what?" Spurlock prodded quietly.

"Well, by then I had to really *go* so I went on through the bedroom into the powder room and took care of business." Lifting her chin, she sent Colaneri a blazing glare. "When I opened the door to leave, that *animal* shoved me back inside. He searched my purse while accusing me of wearing a wire and planting a bug. Then he told me he was going to pat me down."

Alex gripped both her arms. "Did he?"

"No—"

His hands tightened and he almost pulled her off her toes.

"Dammit, Morgan, I want the truth," he demanded,

his voice tight with barely controlled fury. *"Did the bas-*
*tard touch you?"*

"No." She patted his chest, and felt his heart racing.
"Baby, I swear he didn't get the chance." She sent Spurlock a self-satisfied look. "A girl doesn't serve drinks in
Vegas for long without learning how to stop lechers from
copping a feel."

Spurlock's gray eyes narrowed as he measured her and
Alex with a long, assessing scrutiny. "Please give me a
moment to speak privately with my employee," he said,
his voice holding the same politeness it had as when he'd
escorted them on a tour of his rose gardens. "I'm sure
this is a misunderstanding that can be resolved if we all
keep cool heads."

"Don't count on it," Alex grated, the muscles in his
face looking hard and tense.

"Alex, I'm okay," she soothed. "I really am. We want
to get along with our neighbors, so let's give Mr. Spurlock
a few minutes."

Alex kept his murderous gaze locked on Colaneri. "If
that's what you want, darling."

"It is."

Spurlock dipped his head. "I'll have Chan refresh your
drinks while you're waiting." He moved with fluid grace
toward the mansion, snapping his fingers when he reached
Colaneri. Like a trained dog, the thug turned and limped
after his master.

Morgan waited until the men disappeared through the
French doors, then sagged against Alex. "Heaven help
me, I need to sit down."

He prodded her into a chair, then settled on the one
beside hers. He glanced at the door, then leaned in, his
eyes glinting with fury. "You okay?"

"Barely. I didn't—"

''Darling.'' He snagged her hand, placed it over his watch. She felt the fluttering vibration against her palm. Spurlock had activated a listening device the instant he and Colaneri stepped indoors.

She kept her gaze locked with Alex's. ''I didn't know what to do,'' she extemporized. ''That gorilla had me shaking like a leaf. Thank goodness Bruno taught all of the girls who worked in his club self-defense.''

''Yes,'' Alex agreed, and placed a hand against her cheek. ''Thank goodness for Bruno.''

Hours later Alex sat on the couch in the Donovans' darkened living room, reviewing the events of the night and wondering if Spurlock had truly bought Morgan's story.

When their host returned to the terrace after having a supposed talk with Colaneri, Spurlock had acted totally gracious. Apologetic. Effusive in his request that both Donovans forgive the rude behavior of his employee, who Spurlock assured would be disciplined.

Yeah, right, Alex thought.

Colaneri hadn't shown his face during dinner, or when Spurlock escorted his guests to their car.

To Alex it appeared Spurlock had bought the story he and Morgan had devised. If not, most likely Colaneri would have been on the evening's dinner guests like hot sweat.

Alex hoped to hell he was right, and that his and Morgan's cover was still intact. In this line of work, he could never be one hundred percent sure.

Dressed only in pajama bottoms, Alex leaned back on the couch and stared unseeingly across the room at the black-and-white war movie flickering on the big-screen TV. Working undercover was the equivalent of living in a world infected with murderers, thieves, drug pushers, addicts, pimps and whores. Some of who thought no more of killing someone than they would have of squashing a bug. The very nature of the work was loaded with danger. Over the years Alex had experienced numerous close calls, both for himself and his various partners.

Like tonight.

Closing his eyes, he raked a hand through his hair. He had known all along Morgan could take care of herself physically. That was one reason he had spent hours sitting in the gym at the academy, observing her during self-defense training. He knew she was every bit as capable of protecting herself as he was.

Tonight that knowledge hadn't seemed to matter. Not when he had wanted to rip out Colaneri's heart for what the scum had done to her. The bastard hadn't even touched her, and Alex wanted to kill him.

Even now, hours later, the urge was so strong it shocked him.

He could maybe get by with telling himself his reaction was normal. Write it off as a partner's instinct to protect. But he knew it was more, much more. This time, against all reason, against his considerable will, he found himself half-obsessed with a woman who happened to be his partner.

And that made him nearly as dangerous as the scum they were after.

He could continue to remind himself Morgan McCall was not his type, but that didn't stop him from wanting her. He could keep shoving thoughts of her into the back of his mind, but even then she continued to pull at him. She was a beautiful, talented, intelligent woman who had earned his respect, and he'd already had a taste of her. Even if he fooled himself into believing there was a place for her in his life, and he in hers, he knew she would not stay with him long.

And that was the problem.

Where all he had wanted since his divorce were brief sexual flings, he knew that wouldn't be enough for him this time. Not near enough, not with Morgan.

He lifted his gaze to the ceiling. She was upstairs in her bedroom. The instant they returned home, they had settled in the study—with the desk separating them—and she'd debriefed him on what had transpired between her and Colaneri. She had been totally calm, her voice level, her expression businesslike. Later she excused herself to go write her report on the incident. Alex figured by now the report was written, signed and efficiently filed with the other paperwork in the writing desk's hidden compartment.

If Morgan had been anyone else, he would go upstairs, knock on her bedroom door and assure her again she had handled the encounter with the goon just right. Then he would ask if she needed to talk things out again over a cup of coffee. Do whatever it took to make sure she was handling the aftereffects of the event okay.

But Morgan wasn't just anyone. Dealing with her involved a lot more complications than those that came with the job. So he would do them both a favor and stay on the couch, staring at the TV screen where tanks rolled across a snow-covered hill. While he was there, he would continue to remind himself that a cop seasoned in undercover work was damn well capable of suppressing his emotions and controlling his feelings.

Even if that knowledge did nothing to ease the tightness in his lower body.

When Alex opened his eyes the following morning, he was still sacked out on the couch, and the living room was bathed in sunlight.

He sat up stiffly and winced when pain shot up his neck and his head began aching like a fresh wound.

Narrowing his eyes against the glare coming through the floor-to-ceiling windows, he noted that a TV talk show with a bubbly redheaded hostess had replaced the black-and-white war flick. Snagging the remote off the coffee table, he aimed it at the TV and silenced Miss Perky.

He scrubbed a hand over his stubbled jaw and winced when pain razored across his forehead. The last time he'd had a headache that was almost off the scale, it had been part of a well-deserved hangover.

All he'd had to drink last night was water.

"Damn," he muttered when he rose and got hit by a wave of light-headedness. Rubbing his temples, he headed for the kitchen, figuring a hit of Morgan's strong, fresh-ground coffee was what he needed to clear the thick, sticky cobwebs that had spun in his brain during the night.

He halted in front of the coffeepot and scowled. For the first time since they'd moved in, Morgan hadn't made coffee. Because he hadn't bothered learning how to operate the bean grinder, he was out of luck.

Still scowling, he turned and swept his gaze across the cooking island. He'd hoped to find a plate of fresh muffins, a basket of rolls, maybe a platter of just-baked bread. Nothing. Nor did the air hold the warm, spicy scent of cooking that had greeted him every morning.

He was aware now of the silence around him, broken only by the distant, low hum of the central air-conditioning system.

He'd left his watch on the coffee table in the living room, so he checked the clock over the range. It was after ten. Late even for him to sleep.

Morgan would have been up for hours. *Should* have been up.

His cop's sixth sense tightened his gut as he walked across the kitchen. He had activated the security system last night; now, the red light on the alarm's control panel glowed back at him. Morgan always turned off the system each morning before going out for her run. If she'd acted according to habit this morning, the green light would be glowing, not the red.

Thinking she might have reset the alarm when she left to jog, Alex stabbed in the code to disarm the system, pulled open the French doors and walked out on the flagstone terrace. It was the first day of July; the air was still as death, already thick and hot. The water in the swimming pool sparkled like diamonds beneath the blazing morning sun.

He knew Morgan usually left a towel draped over one of the chairs so she could swim after finishing her run. Today there was no towel.

No Morgan.

A cold fist of apprehension tightened his chest. Something was wrong. Everything around him *felt* wrong.

Whipping around, he strode back into the kitchen while fresh pain knifed through his temples.

"Dammit," he hissed. He hadn't had any alcohol, so his problem wasn't a hangover. His stomach wasn't roiling, so he hadn't picked up a bug.

He paused just inside the kitchen, scrubbed a hand across his stubbled jaw and forced his aching brain to work. Could this heavy, lethargic feeling be the aftereffect of a drug? *Had* he been drugged? If so, when? Not at Spurlock's, he was almost sure. He'd been careful to drink only water from a bottle he'd opened himself. Morgan had sipped champagne poured from the same bottle from which Spurlock had served himself. The food had been served buffet-style and tasted fine. Neither he nor Morgan had experienced any aftereffects during the hours after they'd eaten.

All the logic in the world didn't hold back the familiar stab of awareness in Alex's gut that always warned him of danger. Had Spurlock not bought Morgan's story and somehow broken their cover? Had one of his thugs somehow bypassed the alarm system during the night, drugged *him* and gotten to Morgan?

Hurt her. *Killed* her.

Alex's jaw clamped tight against the possibility. He had to focus, he told himself, shoving back cold panic. He wouldn't—couldn't—let his mind start imagining the worst. Not until he knew for sure.

He closed the French doors and set the lock. Now the silence in the house seemed ominous. Overwhelming. He pulled open a drawer, withdrew a knife. He nestled the long blade against the inside of his right wrist to keep it out of sight, then moved silently out of the kitchen and down the hallway.

He passed through the living room where he'd spent the night, walked down another hallway past the study. Nothing looked out of place, he could see no surface signs that a search had been conducted. He stepped into the foyer, the marble floor cold against his bare feet.

He glanced at the hidden panel beneath the staircase that guarded the small room in which Wade Crawford had installed numerous monitors and VCRs. Alex would know for sure if someone other than Morgan and he had been inside the mansion by watching the tapes recorded from the cameras placed in various rooms. First, though, he had to find Morgan.

The sense of urgency, the brutal need to hurry intensified as he moved to the staircase. There, he glanced up, then froze. The red LED light in the smoke alarm Crawford had outfitted with a radio frequency detector strobed in two-second intervals. The flashing light signaled that at least one audio bug had been planted in the mansion.

Alex had checked the unit after he and Morgan returned from Spurlock's, and the light hadn't been flashing. Confirmation that someone had breeched the mansion's security system during the night brought Alex a rush of useless emotions—anger, outrage, a hated sense of vulnerability.

Had Colaneri been the person who'd been inside? The bastard was violent, vicious and had a grudge against Morgan.

Fighting for calm and logic, Alex told himself the bug had been planted so conversations between him and Morgan could be overheard. He sent up a prayer that she was *alive* to have those conversations.

He kept repeating the prayer, a tape-loop of reassurance against the dread curling in his gut.

Although he wanted to rush to find her, years of training forced him to pause at the top of the staircase. Holding his breath, he listened for movement, strained to hear any sound past the pounding ache in his head. He checked the long, carpeted hallway in both directions. All the doors stood open, except the one to the master bedroom—Morgan's room. Alex knew he needed to search the entire mansion to make sure whoever had gotten in was gone. He would do that, as soon as he found Morgan.

His lungs working overtime, he tightened his grip on the knife and edged along the hall, keeping his back to one wall. He paused at the door to the master bedroom, took a controlled breath to counteract the twisting in his stomach, then turned the knob.

His heart simply stopped when he saw Morgan sprawled facedown on the bed, a pool of crimson surrounding her.

# Chapter 12

With his stomach encased in ice and his heart paralyzed, it took an instant for Alex to realize the crimson pooling over the bed wasn't blood. It was Morgan's robe.

That knowledge didn't stop the fear he felt for her from spiking inside him.

He did a quick crouch to make sure no one was hiding under the bed, then he rushed across the room, his gaze flicking toward the walk-in closet then to the adjoining bathroom. Although he didn't *sense* another presence, he knew whoever had broken in could be hiding in either location, waiting to ambush him.

Getting to Morgan first was a chance he had to take.

The minute he touched her, felt the heat in her skin, relief poured through him.

*She was alive.*

"Morgan?" He laid the knife on the nightstand, gripped her shoulder and rolled her onto her back. "Morgan."

When she didn't respond, he placed his fingertips against the pulse point of her throat and realized his hand was trembling.

Her pulse beat steadily, but when he brushed her long hair away from her cheeks her face looked too still, too white.

His breath came fast and harsh as he gripped her shoulders, pulled her up and gave her a gentle shake. "Morgan!"

Her eyes fluttered open, shut.

"Babe, wake up." Seeing the glazed look in her eyes confirmed his suspicions they'd both been drugged. But he had no idea how, or with what. If they both received the same dosage, her smaller build probably meant the drug had a deeper effect on her.

He had one moment of dread when he thought about the possibility she'd been raped by whoever planted the audio bugs. But her crimson robe was belted tight and her nightgown flowed to her ankles, both signs she hadn't been physically assaulted.

She groaned when he dragged her up against the pillows and tapped a hand against her cheek. "Morgan, open your eyes. Look at me."

Her hand flailed, knocking his away. "Leave...me alone." Her voice sounded weak and thready.

He grabbed the knife, again nestling the blade against the inside of his right wrist. He did a quick inspection of the bathroom and walk-in closet. They were clear.

He shut the bedroom door, locked it and moved back to the bed, sparing a look at the desk which, thankfully, appeared untouched. He considered retrieving their weapons from its hidden compartment, but decided against it. If audio bugs had been planted throughout the mansion, that left open the possibility a few wireless surveillance cameras had also been left behind. A camera could be filming them right now. The last thing he and Morgan needed was someone on the outside watching them conduct a police-type search of the place with their service weapons drawn.

Since they were both still alive, Alex figured their cover remained intact. He wasn't going to blow things now.

"Darling, wake up," he prodded, keeping his voice light for the benefit of anyone listening. When she tried to roll away, he slid an arm under her shoulders, his other under her knees and lifted her. "We both overslept," he added as he headed toward the bathroom.

He had to get her out of microphone range—he knew she would be disoriented when she came to, and might blurt something about being a cop. He also needed to tell her what happened so they could plan what to do next.

"A cold shower should help get our blood going, don't you think?" he asked. With her head pillowed against his shoulder, he moved into the bathroom, shoved the door closed with one foot, then set the lock.

Somewhere in the hazy recesses of her mind, Morgan felt herself being carried as she drifted up toward consciousness and a painful pounding in her head. "No..."

"Darling, trust me, a cold shower is the way to go. For both of us."

Alex's voice sounded a great distance away, but how could that be when he was carrying her? *Carrying her.*

She forced her eyes open, tried to focus, but his face was wavy, like images in a mirage. She felt groggy, and searing pain was shooting up from the base of her skull. Even her tongue felt thick. "What...happened?"

Alex shifted her weight. "We overslept," he murmured against her ear as he used his free hand to pull open the door of the shower constructed of wavy glass blocks. He twisted knobs; water sprayed, echoing against the glass enclosure. "We've been drugged. At least I think we have."

His words sparked an instinctive sense of urgency at the edges of her awareness, but her entire body felt like a lead weight, and she didn't seem able to move. Couldn't think past the pain that now pulsed behind her eyes. She grimaced. "My head…"

"It'll clear," he said. "This ought to help us both," he added, then stepped under a spray of water that was as cold as winter.

Morgan yelped, her eyes popping open.

"My exact sentiments," Alex grated through clenched teeth, before sticking his own head under the spray.

"Christ," he muttered, giving his head a shake. He adjusted the knobs; seconds later the blasting spray heated.

"Someone broke in last night," he whispered over the hiss of the water and clouds of steam that began curling around them.

While water streamed over their bodies, Morgan forced herself to concentrate on Alex's voice, the meaning behind his grim words. Someone had somehow managed to drug them. He, she or they had gotten past the security system, planted audio bugs, maybe cameras inside the mansion.

Fear welled inside her as she used an unsteady hand to drag her wet hair away from her face. "He…they could…have killed us."

"Yeah." Alex kept his gaze locked on hers. "Whoever it was could have done a lot of things." His eyes were no longer cop's eyes, flat and cool. They were full of swirling storms and emotion.

As her sluggish thought processes caught up, she felt

the blood drain from her cheeks and freeze around her heart. She tried to read any signals her body was sending her, but the drug still hung too heavy in her system. "Was I...raped?"

"I don't think anyone touched you," Alex answered, his voice even and steady. "When I got to you, your robe was still belted and your gown pulled down. The bed linens aren't overly rumpled."

Despite the logic of Alex's words she felt vulnerable, exposed, confused. Even her sense of time felt distorted. "Put me down. Alex, please." She desperately needed to regain the control stolen from her while she lay unconscious.

"Morgan—"

"I'm okay. I'm okay." When her body gave an involuntary shudder she felt his arms tighten around her. "Just put me down."

"All right." He settled her on her feet, keeping one supportive hand gripped on her arm. "You'll probably feel light-headed. I did."

"Yeah." She leaned back against the glass wall and waited for the world to stop tilting. Her head pounded and her legs felt as wobbly as if she'd jogged ten miles. She just needed to get warm again, she told herself, even as steam swirled and the hot spray pounded her flesh. She glanced down, aware for the first time that the sheeting water had transformed her crimson robe and nightgown into a cloying second skin.

"I want you to stay in the bedroom while I search this place," Alex said.

Her gaze jerked up to meet his. "You think whoever broke in is still inside?"

"It doesn't *feel* that way, but I could be wrong. Someone—I'll call them *he*—somehow got in without deactivating the alarm or setting it off. It's a good bet he left the same way and is long gone. I just need to make sure.''

''I can help you search.''

''Not a good idea. He planted at least one audio bug inside, maybe a camera or two. If someone is watching, we don't want them to see us conduct a search. I'll just start looking around, casually ask if you know where the movers left a certain box of records I need. Something like that.''

''Okay.'' Morgan put a hand to her aching temple. ''What do you want me to do?''

Alex remained silent, the muscles in his jaw tightening. She could almost see his mind working in the dark depths of his brown eyes.

''Get dressed,'' he said after a minute. ''If whatever you put on has a pocket, check to make sure there's not a transmitter in it. If everything's okay after I do the search, I'll give you a signal. You go down to the kitchen, look in a cabinet, then say we're out of the flavored coffee beans I like. Grab your purse and keys and drive to the nearest grocery store that has an indoor pay phone.''

''Has to be a grocery store?''

''Has to be. There might be a transmitter planted on the Beemer. If someone hears you say you're going to the store to buy coffee beans, that better damn well be where you go and what you do. Use the store's pay phone to call Rackowitz's pager.'' Alex narrowed his eyes. ''When I went outside this morning I didn't see her car. Where is she?''

Morgan slicked back her wet hair and forced herself to think. ''The pool supply company delivered the wrong chemicals. Sara said she'd go by there this morning and make the exchange. She mentioned something about running a couple of other errands while she was at it.''

"Okay. Let Rackowitz know what we're dealing with. Tell her I want Wade Crawford here on the double to check his not-so-state-of-the-art security system so we'll know how it got breeched. Have her remind Crawford we've got audio bugs so when he gets here he needs to talk like he showed up to do routine maintenance on the alarm system. Also tell Rackowitz to have one of the department's chemists put on a disguise and get over here to take a sample of our blood. I want to know what drug knocked us out."

"All right." Morgan paused. "Spurlock sent whoever it was who got in, didn't he?"

"Spurlock is the logical suspect."

"Because I defended myself against Colaneri. I wasn't wearing a wire or carrying a bug, so I should have just let him pat me down like he wanted." She closed her eyes against the imagined feel of the thug's hands groping her flesh. "If I had let him search me, this wouldn't have happened."

"You don't know that." Alex's expression remained cool, but the anger was there, darkening his eyes and his voice. He stepped closer, the spray hitting him in the chest, plastering his dark hair against his flesh. "What we both do know is what Colaneri is capable of. There's no telling what that bastard would have done if you had let him put his hands on you."

"That's what I told myself while I was locked in that bathroom with him," she said. Her throat was raw and hot, and her heart was beating in hard, jerky pulses. "Now, I'm not so sure what I did was the right thing."

"Don't waste time second-guessing yourself, Morgan."

She saw the hesitation in his eyes before Alex settled his hands on her shoulders. She knew he'd given quick thought to the promise they'd made not to touch each other unless duty called. His hands were warm, steady and reassuring, and she was glad, very glad, he'd ignored his promise.

The steam rose, clouding the room, blocking out everything around them. The sole person in her world at this moment was Alex Blade.

"Spurlock showed a lot of interest in the business proposition I discussed with him last night," Alex said. "He's too careful, though, to jump into something. He's wary and distrustful and he'll keep checking everything about us until he's satisfied we're not cops. What happened here last night could have everything to do with that, and not your encounter with Colaneri."

"So you think Spurlock sent someone over to see if we're who we claim to be?"

"Yeah. You can bet whoever came in checked to make sure my clothes were hanging in the same closet as yours and our toilet articles shared space in this bathroom."

"Thankfully, they do." She frowned. "He could have seen those things if he'd broken in while we were both gone."

"True, but that wouldn't have clued him in to our sleeping arrangement," Alex pointed out. "Cops working undercover don't sleep together as part of their assignment." He shoved a hand through his wet hair. "We're damn lucky I fell asleep on the couch in front of the TV. If I'd been sacked out in the bedroom down the hall, we'd be in bad shape."

Morgan closed her eyes, opened them. "Dead maybe."

"Maybe. I intend to make sure Crawford turns this place into a fortress so what happened last night doesn't get repeated. Just in case though, I'll sleep on the couch from now on."

A small panic budded in Morgan's chest. "I don't want

to think about this happening a second time. About someone drugging us again, breaking in, doing God knows what to us when we can't defend ourselves.''

''It won't happen again.'' Alex's fingers tightened on her shoulders. ''After we figure out how they drugged us and bypassed the security system, we'll know how to prevent a recurrence.''

''Can't we get an idea of that by watching the tapes from our own surveillance cameras?''

''Probably. But we can't chance opening the panel on the hidden video room until we know for sure our uninvited visitor didn't leave his own cameras sitting around.''

''Right. I should have thought of that.'' Morgan rubbed at the throb in her forehead. ''My brain is operating at half speed.''

''It'll take time for the drug to wear off.'' Alex glanced down at the cotton pajama bottoms plastered to his legs. ''Just in case there's a camera planted in the bedroom, I've got to peel these off before I walk out of here.'' He arched a dark brow. ''Thought I'd better warn you.''

She forced a weak smile. ''All this fog, I won't see a thing,'' she said, then pulled in a breath that was as shaky as she felt on the inside.

As if reading her thoughts, he took her face in his hands, running his thumbs gently over her cheeks. ''We had a close call, Morgan,'' he said quietly. ''We'll probably both feel a sharp twist in the stomach whenever we think about what could have happened to us.'' The shrug he gave was in direct contrast to the look of intense concern in his eyes. ''We got lucky and survived. In undercover work, survival is what counts. You going to be okay, partner?''

She stared up at him, absorbing the comfort of his touch. She'd learned enough to know that luck was a small, very small, part of the picture. Cops who survived undercover work did so because they kept a cool head, thought fast on their feet and had good instincts. This man who had taken care of her when she couldn't care for herself possessed all those qualities.

Between one heartbeat and the next, she knew. She'd gone and done it after all. Let him sneak into her, right through the walls she'd erected. She was on the verge of falling in love.

Oh God, no, that was wrong, she countered while desperately trying to reinforce the walls she felt crumbling around her. What she felt right now was physically weak and very out of herself. And, despite the fact she was a cop, the woman in her was experiencing an attack of sheer feminine distress. She was human, after all, susceptible to certain basic fears. Knowing what could have happened to her while she lay unconscious had nausea roiling in her stomach. So, it wasn't surprising she felt vulnerable and very grateful to the man who in a sense had rescued her. The man who currently stood between herself and danger.

When her system rid itself of the drug and her queasy stomach settled, her sense of control would return, she reasoned. Her emotional state would calm and her thinking processes level out. At least, she hoped all those things happened.

"Morgan?"

"I'm okay, partner." Which was a lie. She was immensely not okay. On several levels.

Alex nodded. "Let's give the audience our best performance."

He turned off the water and stepped out of the shower. "Darling, that was great," he said, sliding into his Alexander Donovan persona. "Your skills in the shower never cease to amaze me."

"Alex," she said quietly. When he turned and looked at her through the steamy air, she mouthed the words *Be careful.*

His expression went solemn. "Count on it, Mrs. Donovan."

Late that afternoon, Alex stood in the small room secreted beneath the mansion's staircase. He stared at the wall of video monitors, his gaze tracking the intruder's shadowy figure as he stepped out of the master bedroom, a flashlight's pencil-thin beam leading his way. The man wore a black T-shirt and jeans, black gloves and a black gas mask. There was no way to ID him.

Movement in the doorway caught Alex's attention. "I figured out how he got in and out without setting off the alarm," Wade Crawford said as he stepped inside.

When the Vice cop arrived at the mansion, he had used a "sweeper" to determine last night's visitor had planted five audio bugs. Instead of destroying them, Crawford scrambled their codes so each transmitted static, leaving anyone listening on the other end to wonder if their equipment had been discovered or was simply malfunctioning. Crawford then began running a systems check on the alarm to determine how the intruder bypassed it.

"How?" Alex asked.

"He got on the roof and went through a wall into the attic."

"A wall?"

"A hole in the wall," Crawford amended. As on the day he'd installed the alarm, the Vice cop wore blue work pants and a white shirt that displayed the logo of a security company over one pocket. A leather thong tied back his shaggy, dark hair from his unshaven face.

"There are several peaks in the roof covered by

grates,'' Crawford explained. ''They match the exterior so you don't really notice them. Take off a grate and a man can sometimes fit through the hole.''

Alex looked back at the monitors, watching the intruder's image as he used the penlight to navigate across the kitchen, followed the beam down a hallway, through the study, then back up the staircase.

''The guy's wiry,'' Crawford said, watching the monitors. ''Probably wasn't a tight fit for him to slip through the hole after he unscrewed the grate.''

Alex gave Crawford a level look. ''You told me you armed the attic's trapdoor into the garage, and the walk-through door that opens between the attic and the storage room. If the wires to either of those doors had been cut, the alarm should have sounded.''

''It would have, if the wires had been cut. They weren't.'' Crawford dipped a hand into the tool belt slung on his hips and pulled out a magnifying glass. ''It took this and a couple of hours of my time to spot how he did it.''

''Did what?''

''Used a length of jump wire with an alligator clamp on each end,'' Crawford explained. ''Standing in the attic, the intruder attached one clamp to the alarm wire on one side of the door, and the second clamp to the alarm wire on the opposite side of the door. Doing that allowed electricity to flow through the wire connected to the clamps. He then picked the lock on the door and walked in.''

''And since there was no interruption in the electrical current, the alarm didn't know it had been breeched.''

''You got it. And if the alligator clamps hadn't left marks in the alarm wiring, I still wouldn't know how he got in.''

''Hell.'' Alex shoved a hand through his hair. ''So we

know how he got in and out. From the tapes we've got, we know he took his time looking around while planting five audio bugs.''

''One location being the master bedroom. Good thing you maintained cover when you found your partner drugged on the bed.''

The mention of Morgan had Alex setting his jaw. The memory of her lying drugged and helpless on that bed plagued him. Knowing the man who'd broken in could have done anything he damn well pleased to her, *anything,* tightened the knots already in his gut.

Alex clenched his fists as emotions swirled and tightened and threatened to strangle him. His reaction was more, much more than a cop wanting to protect his partner. He was a man, craving a woman who had unearthed feelings in him he had never before felt. A man who knew full well how huge a mistake it would be to involve himself with this one woman.

A man who was beyond caring about consequences.

''Blade?''

Alex turned to find Crawford examining him with curiosity.

''Where'd you go, man?''

''Just thinking.'' Alex looked back at the monitors. ''He's wearing a gas mask, so it's obvious they used some sort of gas to drug us. I just wish I knew for sure how they did it.''

''Yeah,'' Crawford nodded. ''Can't help you there, pal.''

''I can.''

Alex shifted at the sound of Morgan's voice, and instantly felt the ache of need settle inside him. She stood in the doorway, dressed in cutoffs and a plunging, electric-blue halter top. Her blond hair was piled messily on her head and her mouth was glossed a rich red. She appeared for all the world like the confident, self-assured Morgan Donovan. But Alex knew her now. He looked past the veneer and saw the same wariness in her blue eyes he'd seen that morning when she stood in the shower with him, ashen-faced and trembling.

He had to forcibly stop himself from reaching out to her.

"You figured out how they drugged us?" he asked.

"Sara and I did," Morgan said. Easing into the already crowded room, she held out her palm, displaying a small length of black plastic tubing. "We spent most of the day digging around in the flower beds next to the house, looking for footprints and whatever." Morgan shifted her gaze between the two men. "You know that bed on the east side where the big hydrangea is?"

Crawford flashed a grin. "I don't know a hydrangea from a swamp lily," he said, his voice sliding into a deep Louisiana drawl. "I'd be more than willing to let you teach me."

Alex aimed a cold, level look at the Vice cop. "Officer McCall's duties don't cover botany lessons."

Anchoring his thumbs in his tool belt, Crawford arched a dark brow. "I see."

Alex met Morgan's gaze. "I know where the hydrangea is." He scowled. "Maybe."

She rolled her eyes. "I'll show you later. Anyway, Sara spotted some chips of mortar in that flower bed. We looked closer and found a hole drilled in the mortar between the bricks. I came in and checked—the hole goes all the way through the baseboard in the study." She handed Alex the piece of rubber tubing. "That was sticking out of the baseboard."

"Now we know how they drugged us," he said. "They

sed a length of tubing to pump in some sort of knockout as.''

"Makes sense," Crawford agreed. "It would have been irculated throughout the entire place by the central air-onditioning system. All they had to do was pump it in, ait for it to take effect, then put a ladder up to the roof."

Morgan blinked. "Ladder?"

"Crawford figured out how they bypassed the alarm," Alex said, then gave her the details.

Morgan slid Crawford a look. "What's to stop that rom happening again?"

"I wired all the grates."

"To the alarm system?" she asked.

"Yeah." He smiled. "I also connected all the grates to battery-operated device that works on the same principle s a stun gun, only with more kick. Anyone touches one f those grates, they'll find out what it feels like to get umped into a hot frying pan."

"Drilling the hole would have made a lot of noise," Alex said, rolling the piece of tubing between his thumb nd finger. "It had to have been done while Morgan and were both gone."

"Last night," she said. "Otherwise the flakes of mortar ould have soaked into the dirt after one watering from ne sprinkler system." She met Alex's gaze. "That's robably why we didn't see Colaneri again after he and purlock went inside to confer. Spurlock sent him here to rill while we ate dinner."

"Sounds like you two have it figured out." Crawford ulled a plastic evidence bag out of his tool belt and held out so Alex could drop the tubing inside. "I'll take this ) the lab to see if they can peg what kind of gas went rough it."

Crawford slid the bag into the pocket of his shirt, then

looked back at the monitors where the man's shadowy form prowled past the hidden cameras. "Since you guys are still among the living, I'd say your cover held up."

"I think this confirms that," Morgan said, then tugged an envelope out of the pocket of her cutoffs and handed it to Alex.

"What is it?" Crawford asked.

"An invitation," Morgan explained. "One of Spurlock's gatekeepers trotted it over just as Sara was driving off."

Alex slid an engraved card from the envelope. "Spurlock's throwing a Fourth of July party."

"He got confirmation last night that we live like the married couple we claim to be," Morgan said. "That combined with our conversation picked up by his bug this morning must have convinced him we're on the level." Her glossed mouth curved. "His party is my chance to search upstairs for the gold bedroom."

Alex kept his gaze locked with hers, and felt a punch low in his gut. He realized he could no longer look at her and see only a cop. She was the woman he loved.

*Christ, he loved her.* He had broken all his own rules. Broken them for a woman who he knew could never be content to stay with him. Not forever.

Yet he couldn't stop himself from wanting her. Couldn't hold back the churning need he felt.

That need had him fisting his hands against his thighs. He and Morgan could have been killed last night. Neither of them could afford to be distracted for a single second.

And here he was, stupidly, irresponsibly in love with her.

Nothing could be more impossible or more dangerous.

# Chapter 13

By late that night Morgan had put into perspective the fact that the nameless male intruder had, for a time, possessed total control over her. She was a cop, after all. Had grown up around cops. Her brother-in-law had died in the line of duty; she knew full well the danger that came with the job. She'd had her eyes wide-open when she signed on with the department.

Going undercover was dangerous. So was working traffic detail when every time you pulled over a car, you had to wonder if the driver had a gun. Responding to domestic violence calls was worse—people drinking, doing drugs, sometimes would just as soon waste a cop as one another. When you carried a badge, any assignment spelled risk.

So Morgan acknowledged last night's possible brush with death, accepted it and sent up silent thanks that all was well.

She also took comfort knowing that anyone who attempted a similar break-in would receive a brain-

scrambling electrical shock, compliments of the inventi
Sergeant Wade Crawford.

The dangers that were an inherent part of police wor
however, weren't the only ones facing her. She had ru
head-on into another kind of danger just as great, just
real, coming from her own heart.

Which was why she presently stood in the mansion
kitchen at nearly one o'clock in the morning, whippi
up a batch of cookie dough loaded with white chocola
chips, macadamia nuts and pecans. All because of the m
bedded down on the couch in the living room.

Blowing out a breath, she tightened her hold on t
mixing bowl propped in the crook of one arm and used
wooden spoon to give the dough a final jerky stir. Sh
had known, *just known,* the roller-coaster thoughts that l
her while she and Alex stood in the shower's steam
intimate confines had been nothing more than emotio
gone haywire. Yet, try as she might over the hours th
had followed, she'd been unable to write off those em
tions as a result of a sudden attack of vulnerability. Sh
*had* let Alex Blade sneak through the walls she'd erecte
She wasn't on the verge of falling in love with him, sh
*had* fallen. Smack on her face.

She was sure of that. And it scared her to death.

The last time—only time—she'd given her heart to
man, she had lost her direction, her sense of self-wort
her college scholarship and wound up in an accident th
put her in a coma. Her party-hearty boyfriend couldr
even be bothered to wait until she regained consciousne
before moving on.

She'd woken up to an "it's been fun, see you aroun
babe" letter and a shattered heart.

Not her best experience. Nor one, she had promise
herself, she would repeat. She had resolved to finish co

lege, then begin her career without outside distractions. To excel as a police officer. *To stay in control.* She had succeeded by keeping a close watch on her heart and running for cover the instant she got near a man who made her pulse throb and her mind go blank.

A man like Alex Blade.

If only she weren't forced day after day to live with him, *be* with him. She felt as if she were existing in a cocoon with nothing in the world but Alex's dominant figure, the mansion, the need to find the evidence to put Spurlock away so they could call it quits and go home. Home.

The assignment had taken on such a surreal quality she was beginning to think of the mansion as home. It wasn't.

What was real, very real, were her feelings for Alex. He was there, in her heart. And she had no idea how to handle that.

Which meant she needed a sensible plan. If she had a plan, she reasoned, she would feel more in control. Since she did her best thinking on a full stomach, she intended to settle in bed with a plate of cookies and get to work formulating that plan. Figure out how to deal *calmly, logically* with the emotions that had avalanched on her.

She settled the bowl onto the cooking island and began dropping spoonfuls of dough onto a greased baking sheet. Yes, she thought, coming up with a plan was practical, rational—

"What are you making?"

Spoon in hand, she whirled.

Alex stood with a shoulder propped against the doorjamb; he wore a black T-shirt with a damp vee down the chest and gray gym shorts. His dark hair was rumpled, his jaw stubbled. A fine sheen of sweat covered his flesh.

He looked tanned and tough. Incredibly sexy.

Morgan's heart bounced high and hard. He had amazing muscles. Everywhere. "I...thought you were asleep on the couch."

He roamed into the kitchen, settled a hip against the island. "And I thought you were asleep in your bed."

His dark, seductive, overtly male scent had her throat going hot and dry. "Guess we were both wrong."

"Guess so." He glanced at the baking pan. "What kind of cookies?"

"The kind with a gazillion calories."

His mouth curved. "My favorite."

She felt pressure building in her chest, felt her flesh heating as they stood there not quite touching. Nerves jittering, she dug the spoon into the bowl, dropped another glob of dough onto the baking sheet. "Do you often exercise at one o'clock in the morning?" Her voice was as unsteady as her grip.

"When I can't sleep."

She raised a brow. "Something bothering you?"

His gaze slicked down, taking in the white crop-top tied beneath her breasts, her snug shorts. "That would be an understatement." He crossed his arms over his chest and studied her while she dropped more globs of dough onto the sheet. "Do you often cook at one in the morning?" he asked finally.

"When I can't sleep."

"Something bugging you?"

"I've got things on my mind." *You.*

The intense, measuring way he studied her brought out her need, a low and nagging ache. Her pulse hammered everywhere at once. All thought of taking her time to plan how to sensibly deal with her feelings for this man flowed out of her brain. She wanted him. Desperately.

"Things on your mind," he repeated quietly.

"Yes." She scooped up more dough, plopped it onto the pan.

"Morgan, stop what you're doing and look at me. Just look at me."

When she did, he stared into her eyes with such intensity she knew instinctively he could read every shift and flicker of emotion. Then she saw his own eyes darken with desire and felt the raw echo of that desire curl deep inside her belly.

He dipped his head. "Think it's possible the same problem is keeping us both from sleeping?"

"I...think so." She dragged in a breath. "I'm not sure how to deal with the problem."

He remained silent for the space of a dozen heartbeats, then said, "I've got an idea."

Turning, she watched him move to the counter near the huge stainless-steel refrigerator. He swiveled the coffeemaker around, opened a small slit on its back. Anticipation snaked through her when she saw him switch off the microchip surveillance camera inside.

He retraced his steps, stopping inches in front of her. Leaning back, she felt the edge of the island against the small of her back. She didn't realize she was still holding the wooden spoon until he took it from her hand. She didn't move, didn't speak, just waited.

He laid the spoon aside and used his hands to grip the counter on either side of her body. "I promised to touch you only in the line of duty. I'll keep that promise," he continued, his breath warm against her lips, "unless you tell me you don't want me to."

Heat had flooded beneath her flesh and her heart was revving like an engine. "I can't think when I'm around you. I need to think, but I can't."

"I was right, we both have the same problem."

To stop herself from reaching out to him, she fisted her hands against her thighs. "I'm not sure touching each other is a smart thing to do."

"I'm positive it's not," he agreed. "But I'm at the point where I don't give a damn about smart. I want you, Morgan. I want the hell out of you. If you don't want my hands on you, tell me now and I'll back off."

Everything that had once seemed so dream-like to her became stark reality. And the only reality that mattered at the moment was the flesh-and-blood man standing before her. Without another thought to reason or consequences, she wrapped her arms around his neck. "If you don't put your hands on me, I'll go crazy."

"Another thing we have in common," he said, bringing her against him with one hard pull. He fisted his hands in her hair, tugged her head back and crushed his mouth to hers in a kiss that tasted of dark, swirling frustration.

Her senses cartwheeling, she tunneled her fingers through his hair and kissed him back with all of the searing, pent-up hunger that had been driving her insane over the past weeks.

Groaning her name, he gripped the back of her head, holding her still while he deepened the kiss.

Morgan clung to him, feeling as if she were being swallowed alive. The edge of the counter dug into her back, but she was too aware of his hips, his chest molded against her, to notice the discomfort. His masculine scent filled her lungs, his taste swirled through her system, distancing her further from reason, muddling her thoughts, driving feelings to the surface where she couldn't escape them.

It had been so long, so very long since she'd allowed herself to tumble into searing, seductive, dangerous oblivion. All she wanted now was to feast and be filled.

His hands streaked over her, hotly possessive. His fingers slid over her breasts, covered only by the cotton crop-top. Her nipples tightened, then strained beneath his touch.

Her head fell back on a moan; his mouth moved to ravage her throat, while his thumbs tormented her nipples through the thin material. Her skin was on fire, her blood pumping like a river of lava. She gripped his shoulders for balance while sensation after sensation stormed her system. She had never wanted anything more than him. Any *man* more than him.

She felt the hard pulse of his need against her belly. His name slid across her lips with husky passion as her urgent hands shoved beneath his T-shirt, then dragged it over his head and let it fly.

Her lips conducted a slow exploration of the muscled planes of his chest while the primal male taste of him coursed through her system. Her fingers raked through the mat of crisp black hair. Her pulse pounded thick and fast, matching the rhythm of his heart.

"Morgan..." His hands slid down her back, cupped her bottom. He lifted her up against him and used his teeth on her throat.

Vaguely she felt the room shift, then realized Alex was carrying her. He stopped on the opposite side of the cooking island, slid her onto the edge. Moving in, he pressed her back until she lay flat, her legs dangling. She was aware of the coolness of the tiled surface against her back as he stood intimately between her spread legs.

Leaning over her, he manacled a hand around both of her wrists, stretched her arms over her head. She saw scalding need in his eyes an instant before he fastened his mouth on one of her breasts and suckled greedily through cotton.

Pleasure arrowed through her system. Her breath es
caped in burning gasps while her body melted like wa>
beneath a flame. His mouth shifted to feed on her othe
breast while his free hand jerked the crop-top loose. Rais
ing his head, he shoved the cotton aside to expose he
breasts. She felt his gaze on her flesh as hot and physica
as his touch.

"You're beautiful." His voice was a rough whisper o>
the still air. "Magnificent."

Her gaze slid across the muscled contours of his ches>
then dipped lower to his washboard-flat stomach, to the
waist that tapered to narrow hips and long legs. "So are
you."

"We'll get to me. Later." The dangerous edge sh>
heard in his voice glinted in his eyes as he used a fingerti>
to trace the curve of one breast, then the other. Her entir>
body quivered in response.

Slowly his hand skimmed downward across her bar>
midriff, his fingers hovering over the waistband of he
shorts. "Much later."

He tugged the shorts down over her hips, off her legs
tossed them aside. He raised a brow. "Why, Morgan,'
he murmured, "you forgot to put on underwear." He sli>
his hand between her legs, cupped her and began a slov
massage of her flesh.

Her body vibrated like a plucked string; the hard, we>
pulse between her legs hammered against his palm
"When I dressed…my mind was on…baking cookies,'
she managed.

Her vision grayed as his fingers continued movin>
against her, slowly, erotically.

"What's on your mind now?"

She could have sworn the kitchen had started to spin
"Nothing. You melted…my brain."

He gave her a slow, feral smile as he slid a hand beneath each of her thighs and lifted her hips. "Let's see what else I can melt."

Her last tenuous hold on sanity rocketed away when he lowered his head and used his mouth on her.

Staggered by a sharp lance of pleasure, words strangled in her throat, images swirled in her brain. The wanting was huge, recklessly primitive. And for now it was all that mattered.

Stars seemed to explode in front of her eyes as he brought her to mind-blinding, shattering release.

"Alex..."

"Again." His dark eyes warrior bright, he tightened his fingers on her hips, lifted her higher, spread her even more. Something close to a purr sounded in her throat as he urged her up again and sent her soaring.

When he lowered her hips she reached for him, panting his name. At the same instant he hauled her off the counter.

His face was set in almost savage lines, his eyes so intense they seemed to burn her flesh. "My turn."

"Yes." With her body still shuddering from his onslaught, she wrapped her long legs around his waist and fused her mouth with his.

She could taste herself on his lips, feel the urgent hammering of his heart against hers. Her hands gripped his shoulders. Beneath her palms his muscles felt hard as iron. "I want you," she murmured against his mouth. "Inside me. Now. *Now.*"

The next instant they were on the floor. Driven by her own need, she tugged off his shorts, desperate to feel his body against hers, *in* her.

Gripping her hips, he dragged her over him, lifting her up to straddle him. Arching back, she took him into her, all of him. Her body trembled as he opened her, filled her. She gave herself over completely, moving with him, welcoming the deep, smooth strokes of his body inside hers. She rode him, her muscles milking him.

His fingers dug into her flesh when he reached his peak. Groaning her name, he lay back, panting, his chest heaving as he gulped in air.

She slid down on top of him, her body boneless, her flesh slick with sweat. Pressing her face into his shoulder, she gasped for air like a woman drowning, then expelled it on a long, languorous sigh.

Later Alex watched Morgan as she lay beside him in exhausted sleep. She was on her side, one arm flung across his waist, one long, sleek leg intertwined with his, her hair a wild, golden tangle over the rumpled sheets. Her breathing was even, relaxed. In the soft moonlight streaming in through the bedroom windows, her skin glowed like warm honey.

The same way it tasted.

If he'd harbored any lingering doubts over his feelings for her, those doubts had been erased during their frantic mating in the kitchen, then later when they moved upstairs and taken each other slowly, tenderly.

He was totally, crazily in love with Morgan McCall.

It was, he knew, the biggest mistake he had ever made. A mistake that had several very real, very serious problems staring him in the face.

One being the fact he wasn't—couldn't be—the type of man she needed. A man whose ambition paled in the face of hers. He acknowledged she wouldn't believe the difference in their outlooks could someday matter to her, but he knew differently. He had, after all, experienced a similar nightmare with his ex.

As Morgan rose through the department's ranks—and she would—the difference in insignia on their collars would dig a chasm between them, one that couldn't help but widen over time. She would wind up getting bored with him and slowly lose interest in the relationship. Just the thought of her treating him with cool aloofness sometime down the line sliced him to pieces. He knew he needed to start trying to build some sort of defense against that, against her. He would. Still, that wasn't the biggest problem he had at the moment. Morgan's safety was.

He stroked a palm down the length of the exquisite curves and hollows that had driven him mad since the first moment he'd laid eyes on her. He could no longer think about her and not feel cold fear over what the vicious bastard Colaneri could have done while locked with her in that bathroom. Nor could Alex ignore the panic that jabbed into his gut at the thought of what might have happened to her last night while she lay drugged and at the intruder's mercy.

Alex was very aware that Spurlock had been ultimately in control of the above events. He pulled the strings. Issued orders. Decided who lived and died. And he had just sent over an embossed invitation, summoning his new neighbors back to his turf, where geography alone gave the slime the advantage.

The knowledge that his and Morgan's assignment could turn deadly intensified, crouching darkly in Alex's brain.

He shifted his gaze to the shadowy ceiling and turned his thoughts to the six people who had died because of Spurlock. The jockey, Frankie Isom. Spurlock's former lover, Krystelle Vander. When Alex ticked off George Jackson's name, his chest tightened against a shimmer of pain for the man who'd been the only father he'd ever known. Then there were the two FBI agents, poisoned while guarding Spurlock's accountant, Emmett Tool, who'd been on the verge of implicating his boss in at least three murders. And Tool himself, his body burned so badly that ID had to be made by using dental records.

Alex thought about all the hours of intensive training he'd received on how not to panic, not to lose focus during an undercover operation. Despite that, he was no longer sure he could keep a cool head or hold on to control while watching Morgan deal with Spurlock and his homicidal bodyguard.

Looking back at her, he tangled his fingers in her thick, golden hair. Her scent drifted over him like a gentle stroke of hands. He had never needed the way he needed her, not with any other woman. No other woman. He intended to protect her. Keep her safe.

He would like nothing better than to cut her out of the operation. Explain to Spurlock that Mrs. Donovan had gone to an out-of-state health spa for a couple of weeks of pampering. But Alex knew his going into Spurlock's territory without backup would make the operation too dangerous. Maybe suicidal. Since Morgan was the only person who could go in with him, he had to come up with the best way to protect her.

He had to keep her safe.

Morgan woke facedown in the massive four-poster bed, sprawled amid rumpled sheets and tangled pillows. Shoving her hair away from her face, she blinked against the sunlight spilling through the bedroom windows.

Groggy, it took her a moment to remember all that had happened between her and Alex last night. Her lips curved as she snuggled into the cozy nest of pillows. She felt alive. Replenished. Sore and swollen and wonderful.

Languid as a cat, she gave a little stretch, her smile

deepening at the minor aches that registered in her body. After a moment she slid her arm sideways, felt the coolness of the creamy white sheet on what had been Alex's side of the bed.

Vaguely she wondered how long he'd been gone…and how soon he would be back.

She burrowed into the crisp linens, inhaling deeply of his clean, masculine scent. An instant shaft of heat streaked straight up her spine. It had been so long since she'd felt anything this intensely. Since she'd *wanted* so intensely.

Feeling more than a little decadent, she summoned the energy to turn over and prop her naked body up on a bank of pillows. Her insides jolted when she looked across the bedroom and spotted Alex sitting motionless in one of the wing chairs angled in front of the green-marble fireplace. He'd been watching her sleep, she realized. Sitting there, quiet as death, watching.

He was dressed in a dark knit pullover shirt that made his eyes look almost black, khaki pants and loafers with no socks. In the bright sunlight his face looked tense, his eyes grim.

Morgan felt her chest tighten. His was hardly the expression a woman hoped to see on the face of the man she'd taken as her lover. Still, his expression might have nothing to do with her. *With them.* He might have something totally unrelated on his mind.

She smiled. "Good morning."

"Morning." He didn't answer her smile with one of his own, just nodded toward the foam cup sitting on the nightstand. "I went out and picked up coffee."

"Thanks." She checked the time as she retrieved the cup. "It's early for you to be up."

"You're right."

Her heart stirred when he stood and walked toward her. Stirred again when he cupped his palm against her cheek. She placed her hand against his, lacing her fingers through his, thinking he would rejoin her in bed. Instead he gazed down at her in silence, looking solemn with something akin to regret in his eyes.

*Regret.*

"Morgan, we need to talk." He untangled his fingers from hers, then moved to the antique writing desk with the hidden compartment that held their weapons and badges. She noticed now the papers on the desk's surface that hadn't been there the night before.

She closed her eyes. This man who had touched her so intimately throughout the night, who had touched her in ways no other man ever had, had left her bed to buy convenience store coffee and deal with paperwork. Now instead of crawling back into bed he looked at her with regret and he wanted to talk. Not good.

She sipped her coffee and tasted nothing. She conceded she hadn't known exactly what she was getting into when she'd thrown common sense out the window and stepped into Alex Blade's arms. Still, she hadn't expected him to give her the "see you around" treatment the following morning. This was why, *exactly* why she'd been so careful after her one relationship fiasco to avoid taking further risks. There were good, solid reasons for not opening oneself up to pain. She should have heeded them last night.

"I refined our operation plan," Alex said when he reached the desk.

She tightened her fingers on the cup. "Refined it?" she asked evenly.

"I had Rackowitz research the Fourth of July parties Spurlock has thrown over the past years. They're huge. Hundreds of people all over the house and grounds. That means security is even tighter than usual, inside and out. I've decided it will be better if you to stay downstairs and mingle with the other guests while I check upstairs for the gold bedroom.''

"That wasn't our plan.''

"Like I said, I refined it.''

"What about photos?''

"What about them?''

"We still need pictures of the upper floors so our guys who serve the warrant will know the mansion's layout ahead of time.''

"I'll take them.''

"With what? You can't exactly walk around upstairs using the camera in my tube of lipstick.''

"I called Wade Crawford while I was out getting coffee. He's fitting a micro camera into a pager I can hook onto my belt.''

"Having Wade go to that extra trouble when I already have a camera is a waste of time, equipment and manpower.''

Alex leaned against the desk. "You sound like a number-crunching bureaucrat, McCall. You'll fit right in when you make it to the chief's office.''

"Thank you,'' she said coolly, her eyes narrowing. "Want to tell my why you suddenly lost your common sense?''

"I haven't,'' he said mildly. "This is my operation. I call the shots. The plan's changed. Period.''

She sipped coffee, watching him over the cup's rim. Her mind was too analytical to let things go at that. Nothing had happened to require his sudden revision of their plan. The only thing that had changed since the night before was her and Alex's personal relationship.

"We already have a workable plan in place," she pointed out.

"Like I said, there's been a change."

The coolness in Alex's demeanor started a slow, molten anger burning inside her. She set the cup on the night-stand, shoved back the sheets and rose.

She had a good idea how she looked, standing naked, her hair tousled and curling around her breasts, her mouth still swollen from his kisses, her skin chafed from the stubble on his chin.

It was satisfying, very satisfying to watch his gaze heat, then drop and slide down her bare flesh. She had the sensation he was absorbing her with his eyes.

"Why, Alex?" she demanded. "Why change the plan?"

His gaze slowly lifted. There was more than heat in his eyes now. There was emotion. Something she couldn't decipher, but it was there.

"How smooth do you think things will go for you if Colaneri catches you snooping again?" he asked quietly. "What if the next time the bastard gets you alone he has a knife? A gun?"

"I'll defend myself. Again." She eased out a breath, forced herself to think. "With so many people at the party, I can just about guarantee I won't be the only one wandering around upstairs. If I am questioned, I'll claim I'm browsing, admiring the decor." She angled her chin. "Think you can slide by with an explanation like that, Blade? That you're interested in Spurlock's choice of wallpaper?"

His smile was thin and sharp as a scalpel. "Whatever happens, I'll deal with it."

"So will I. Like I did the other night with Colaneri. And Spurlock."

"That's not going to happen again."

"Aren't you the one who keeps telling me there's no way to know what might happen while working undercover?"

"You can try to anticipate certain events. And prevent them."

"Last night our plan was fine," she persisted. "This morning it isn't to your liking. What changed in the past hours?"

Leaden silence fell between them; Alex studied her, his face expressionless. "This revision to our ops plan isn't something you need to analyze to death, McCall," he said finally. "You just need to accept."

"If there was a logical reason for the change, I would."

She grabbed her ivory robe off the end of the bed and jerked it on. "I'll tell you what I think is going on. You woke up regretting what happened between us last night." She cinched the robe's sash around her waist so tight she could barely breathe. "Fine, Alex, that's your right, I'll deal with it. But I'm still your partner until this assignment's over, and you have no right to treat me like I'm suddenly incapable of doing my job."

"Dammit, Morgan!" He pushed away from the desk, his hands clenched against his thighs as he moved toward her. "That's not what I think."

"That's what it *feels* like," she tossed back, unable to keep the hurt out of her voice.

His hands shot out with such speed she had no time to react, could only utter a gasp when he jerked her against him. "I'm trying to keep you out of the line of fire. I want you safe. Is that logical enough for that computer-chip brain of yours?"

"I—"

"I care about you." His fingers dug into her arms like

shafts of steel as he leaned over her, his eyes as dark as thunderclouds. "A hell of a lot more than I should. That's the problem. Going onto Spurlock's turf is dangerous enough as it is. I need to keep a cool head. Need to maintain focus. I can't do that when I'm worried about you."

The words shocked her, hinting at a vulnerability she never would have suspected he felt. "You changed our plan because you think the way we had things worked out puts me in too much danger?"

"I don't want you hurt. It makes me crazy to think about you getting hurt."

"I don't want *you* hurt."

"I can take care of myself."

"So can I." She stared up at him as the reason for his aloofness cut through her pain. "If something happens while I'm upstairs, you'll be there to back me up. I trust you to be there."

His fingers gripped her shoulders so tight she knew she'd have bruises. "How much backup was I for you while you were locked in that bathroom with Colaneri?"

"If I had needed help, you'd have gotten to me in time."

"That happened days ago, and I still want to kill the bastard. I want to rip him apart with my bare hands just for *breathing* on you. You still trust me to keep a cool head, Morgan?"

"I trust you with my life." *Doing that is not as dangerous, unpredictable or high risk as falling in love with you.* She cupped her palm against his cheek. "And I care about you, too. A lot. Does that mean you no longer trust me to back you up?"

"You're my first choice for a backup." He slid his fingers through her hair. "Remember, I watched you take down every hulking guy in your recruit class. You can be scary, lady.'' He eased out a breath. ''You scare the hell out of me.''

''So we stick to our original plan? I do the upstairs work while you keep Spurlock occupied?''

''Dammit.'' He slid his hands in one long, possessive stroke down the sides of her body. Then back up. ''Anyone ever mention that stubborn streak of yours, McCall?''

Her mouth curved. ''I'm not stubborn, just focused. So we're staying with the original plan?''

''Yeah.'' His gaze dropped from her face, lowered. ''It'd be best if we tabled things between us for now.''

''Table them?'' she asked, feeling a hollow sinking in her stomach.

He stepped away, turned and paced back to the fireplace. After a moment he shoved a hand through his hair. ''We both need to concentrate on doing this job and walking away in one piece.''

Morgan nodded. It was ridiculous, she knew, to feel a drag of hurt over how seemingly easy it had been for Alex to switch off his emotions. To shift what had happened between them last night into the background.

A dull ache settled in her belly. Maybe Alex was right, she conceded. Maybe right now, there was too much to say. Entirely too much to feel. Too much emotion in play to try to coolly sort out where—or how far—they each wanted their relationship to go.

As if to seal his intent, he moved to the desk. ''We'll spend the time between now and the party going over the original plan. We look for holes we've left open, minute slits something could fall through. We double-check our surveillance equipment. Triple-check it. We try to anticipate everything that can go wrong. And how to deal with it if it does.''

He paused, his sober gaze locking with hers. ''Nothing

goes wrong, Morgan. No one gets hurt. Everything goes as smooth as silk. It has to.''

''Silk,'' she agreed, even as an involuntary shiver skittered down the back of her neck.

# Chapter 14

Just as intel predicted, Spurlock tightened security for his Fourth of July party. Black-suited bodyguards with masked expressions halted vehicles at the gate, checking identification against a list of authorized guests.

After he and Morgan passed inspection, Alex steered the pearl-white BMW up the long drive framed in red, white and blue lights, stopping in front of the massive curving entry. He handed the keys to the uniformed valet who scurried over. Another minion opened Morgan's door. When Alex reached her, he placed a hand at the small of her back where a slither of midnight blue sequins dipped to the waist.

"Ready?" he asked.

"Ready." The confident smile she gave him belonged to her alter ego.

He focused on the task before them, not the soft flesh against his palm, nor the profound wariness that dogged him. He had learned long ago not to ignore his instincts.

Still, this ominous feeling had hung over him since he'd admitted to himself how he felt about Morgan. He was both a cop and a man worried about the woman he loved. No big surprise his need to protect had shifted into high gear.

They advanced up the steps to the long, sweeping front porch decked out with shrubs and sweet-scented flowers. As they followed another couple inside, Alex glanced at the woodwork surrounding the double front door, knowing the ornate carvings concealed a metal detector that scanned each guest for weapons.

He would have preferred to have a gun or knife strapped to his ankle, but if that were the case, this would be as far as he got. Other than his own abilities, his sole means of defense was the solid-gold designer watch that, with three clicks of its stem, would transmit an SOS to Rackowitz's pager.

A few steps inside the marbled foyer, a waiter approached with a silver tray loaded with champagne in long-throated glasses. Alex took one of the flutes, handed it to Morgan. He waved the server away, saying he didn't want a glass for himself.

She slid a hand into the crook of his arm. "There's our host," she murmured.

Alex settled his hand over hers and surveilled Spurlock as he moved across the foyer greeting male guests with handshakes and kissing women on the cheek. Several of those females gave Spurlock a last fawning look before moving off with their escorts toward the living area that was ablaze with lights and color and packed with people standing elbow to elbow. Alex suspected Krystelle Vander had displayed the same keen interest when she'd first laid eyes on the man. Too bad that had earned her a slit throat and a bullet in the head for George Jackson.

The thought tightened Alex's chest. If everything went according to plan tonight, the good guys would be on the road to avenging not only George's death, but five others.

Spurlock moved fully into view, his tailored black suit draping elegance over his tall, honed frame. His dark hair with silver at the temples looked perfectly styled; his gray eyes held a polite, unreadable expression.

Until they focused on Morgan.

The razor-sharp appreciation that sliced into the bastard's gaze had Alex wanting to slam a fist into his face. Still, he understood Spurlock's reaction. It mirrored his own when he had caught his first glimpse of her in the short, sequined dress that was a curve-clinging statement of femininity. As an added bonus, the dress had slits up both sides that yielded a blood-pumping view of endless, long leg. Her blond hair cascaded across her shoulders in a wild tousle, the way Alex knew it did after a session of hot, steamy sex. Smoky shadow highlighted her laser-blue eyes; peach-colored gloss gave her full lips a pouty look.

Alex knew a man would have to be stone-cold dead not to appreciate the beautiful young woman on his arm. *His woman.*

Spurlock took her hand and pressed a brief kiss on her knuckles. "Morgan, you take my breath away."

"Thank you, Carlton." She tilted her head, one long, crystal earring brushing her shoulder. "We appreciate you inviting us over again so soon. Don't we, Alex?"

"It's good to get to know your neighbors."

"Yes," Spurlock agreed, slicking his thumb over Morgan's knuckles. "Both personally and professionally," he added as he offered Alex his hand. "Speaking of business, I'm anxious to hear about what progress, if any, you've made on the venture we discussed the other night."

Alex spared their host only a glance before refocusing

on Morgan. "I've made substantial progress and we'll talk about it. Tomorrow," he added before tracing a fingertip along her jawline. "Tonight I plan to pay attention to my wife." As if on cue, low, pulsing music drifted on the air. "Dance with me, darling?"

"Love to." Morgan shifted her gaze. "Carlton, I hope you'll save a dance for me later."

"Several." He looked back at Alex. "I'm the last man to fault you for wanting to spend time with such a beautiful woman," he said smoothly. "However, an associate, a financial advisor adept at certain…ventures is here tonight. He's leaving town in the morning. I would like to meet with both of you so we can finalize the arrangements you and I discussed the other night."

As if weighing the matter, Alex let a few seconds pass. He figured the advisor was some middle man Spurlock planned to put to work in the porno theater to keep an eye on his boss's money while it was being washed. The third man's presence was a bonus, Alex decided. It would extend the meeting, which meant he could keep Spurlock busy for a longer period while Morgan searched upstairs for the gold bedroom.

"All right," Alex agreed, meeting Spurlock's gaze. "Since he's leaving in the morning."

Just then, a distinguished-looking man and woman approached. Spurlock greeted them saying, "Let me introduce Alex and Morgan Donovan, my neighbors. This is Judge and Mrs. Howard Philben."

Alex smiled as he and Morgan made polite chitchat. Five years ago he had testified on a case in Philben's courtroom. Then Alex had long hair and a full beard. The judge thought he was shaking hands with a total stranger.

Spurlock explained that he and Alex had business to discuss, and asked the Philbens to keep Morgan company.

''Happy to,'' the judge said, sending Morgan an admiring look.

Alex arched a brow. Taking Mrs. Philben's scowl into account, he doubted Morgan would have a problem dumping them.

He tightened his hand on hers, knowing in only minutes she would slip up the winding staircase just a few feet away. Again his instincts sent the message that something about the assignment was off. Yet he had no idea what. And it was highly possible he was simply a man letting his emotions get in the way.

Morgan squeezed his hand. ''We'll dance when you get back.''

''Count on it, darling.''

Her fingers tense on her small evening bag, Morgan watched the two men walk away, each wearing a dark tailored suit. Tonight Spurlock looked as dashing and relaxed as usual. Alex seemed controlled and intense, yet somehow different.

She wasn't sure why. Perhaps his years of covert work made him far more expert than she at disconnecting emotion in order to do a job. Right now she wished fervently for some of his ironclad calm to quell her roiling stomach.

She accompanied the Philbens into the vast living area where a wall of French glass doors were open to the starry night. People moved around the room, out to the terrace, drifted back in, in constant motion. Morgan spied a small combo of musicians set up on the terrace and felt a tug of regret for the dance she and Alex would not share.

''Mrs. Donovan, you haven't touched your champagne,'' the amiable gray-haired judge observed. ''Can I get you something else to drink?''

Morgan smiled. Judging by his wife's glare, His Honor

was due to get an earful for not taking her drink order first.

"Thank you, no. I missed lunch, so I don't want to drink on an empty stomach," she added, setting the champagne flute aside. "If you'll excuse me, I'll go fill a plate from the buffet."

Morgan moved into the elegant dining room where an imposing mahogany table and sideboard seemed to groan beneath the weight of food-laden trays. She made a pretense of surveying the array of pâtés, meats, seafood, breads and pastries, but her interest wasn't food. It was pegging the security personnel, especially Colaneri. The last thing she wanted was another encounter with the thug.

Although she spotted several hulking bodyguard types standing apart from the guests, she saw no sign of Colaneri.

In the foyer, clusters of guests chatted while sipping drinks and nibbling from plates filled from the buffet. Getting upstairs proved no problem, as Morgan simply joined several other elegantly clad women in search of unoccupied powder rooms.

Fifteen minutes later she had used the camera hidden in her lipstick tube to snap pictures of every upstairs bedroom.

None of them were painted or papered gold.

She made her way downstairs, scouting for Alex and Spurlock, but saw neither. *What now?* she asked as she stepped out on the dimly lit terrace where the musicians had just ended a set and were beginning a break.

She snagged a champagne flute off the tray of a passing waiter, then moved away from the knots of guests to stand by herself. Lights tucked across the landscaped grounds illuminated the vast rose gardens. The delicate scent of the blooms drifted on the warm night air, filling her lungs as she reviewed the events that had set Alex and her on what seemed now a useless safari to find a *gold* bedroom.

Frankie Isom, a jockey, had been murdered. Krystelle Vander—Carlton Spurlock's lover—called retired cop George Jackson, head of the race track's security. According to the notes Jackson drafted in his computer during that call, a hysterical Vander claimed she had proof Spurlock ordered Isom's murder. Unable to safely smuggle that proof out of Spurlock's mansion, Vander hid it in the gold bedroom.

Problem was, Morgan had found no gold bedroom.

*What now?*

"The roses are beautiful."

Recognizing Judge Philben's voice, Morgan forced a smile, then turned. "Yes, they are. I envy Carlton's green thumb."

"Which he inherited from his grandmother."

"He's mentioned her several times." Morgan glanced across the man's shoulder, and saw no sign of his grim-faced wife. "I get the impression he was very fond of her."

"Very." The ice in the judge's drink rattled when he took a sip. "In fact, Carlton adored Goldie."

Morgan felt herself go still. "I thought Mrs. Spurlock's name was Emmaline." That's what the intel info said, anyway.

"Yes, that's right. She had masses of blond hair and a very pale complexion. Growing up, Carlton always called her Goldie. Her death three years ago hit him hard." The judge dropped his voice to a conspiratorial level. "I don't believe Carlton has fully recovered. He remodeled the mansion, but wouldn't let the decorator touch Goldie's bedroom. He still has the special strain of roses he bred for her placed beside the bed."

Morgan's already pounding pulse picked up speed. George Jackson had gotten the information wrong in his hurriedly typed notes. Krystelle Vander hadn't hidden the evidence in a gold bedroom, but in *Goldie's* bedroom.

Morgan's mind scrolled back to the search she'd conducted of the downstairs bedrooms. They had all struck her as obsessively neat with an unlived-in feel to them. Except the last bedroom she'd come to. The one she'd rushed through to reach its adjoining bathroom when she heard footsteps. *That* bedroom had felt occupied, lived in. She remembered the scent of lavender, a vase of yellow roses on the nightstand.

Smiling, Morgan met Philben's gaze. "Excuse me for running off again, Judge. I simply must find a powder room."

Seated in one of the blood-red leather chairs in front of Spurlock's massive desk of mahogany and inlaid teak, Alex glanced at his watch. Morgan had been out of his sight for nearly half an hour. The more time that passed, the hotter the spot in his gut burned that always sent out warning signals.

His gaze ranged across the elegant, dark-paneled study, lit by brass sconces. The one positive angle to being stuck with Spurlock in his lair was that Colaneri stood guard just inside the door. Studying the hired muscle out of the corner of his eye, Alex decided Colaneri's tall, wiry build mirrored that of the man who'd broken in two nights ago. Still, there was no way to know if the bastard had been the dark, skulking figure on the surveillance tape. Right now, with Colaneri in his sights, Alex figured the threat level to Morgan remained low.

Still, his gut burned and he wanted her where he could get to her in case of trouble.

He sent Spurlock a cool look across the desk. "I'm done waiting," he said, his tone low and controlled. "It's too damn bad your advisor got held up in traffic. You want an update on my business venture, I'll give you the abbreviated version right now. Otherwise, I'm going to go dance with my wife."

Just then the phone on Spurlock's desk rang. He answered it, then instructed, "Send him in."

"My associate has arrived," Spurlock said, replacing the receiver. "Again I apologize for the delay. He lives out of town, but his family resides here. That's why he's here—his son is in the hospital." Spurlock angled his head. "My advisor is a CPA, a very good one. That's why I want him to hear the details of our pending business arrangement."

Alex steepled his fingers and regarded Spurlock silently. So, he was about to meet Emmett Tool's replacement. He doubted the new bean counter knew Spurlock had turned his predecessor into a flaming briquette.

When a knock sounded on the door, Colaneri pulled it ajar, nodded, then swung it open.

Alex was seldom at a loss; he had been trained not to panic, to maintain focus. But when Spurlock's business associate stepped into view, he felt the impact of the man's presence as if he'd been punched in the gut. A person who burned to death—and had to be identified by dental records—was not supposed to be walking around, looking as healthy as he had on the day Alex had arrested him.

He had time only to triple-click the stem on his watch to send an SOS to Rackowitz's pager before the resurrected Emmett Tool spotted him.

The man froze in his tracks, his gaunt face paling.

Spurlock gave the accountant a quizzical look. "Something wrong, Emmett?"

"Yeah, boss. Why the hell you talking to a cop?"

Hands fisted on her hips, Morgan stood in the center of the immense bedroom that smelled faintly of lavender, assessing the status of her search. She had first checked all the drawers filled with clothing that had been Emmaline "Goldie" Spurlock's.

The drawers had not offered up whatever evidence Krystelle Vander supposedly hid in the room.

Morgan had gotten the same results in the enormous walk-in closet after sticking her hands into an uncountable number of pockets, purses and shoes. She'd also checked the obvious places—between the bed's mattress and box springs, the back and bottoms of all drawers, under the cushion of the needlepoint wing chair. She'd even used a nail file to unscrew all the outlets, since sometimes dummy outlets concealed small hiding places.

Nothing. Nada. Zilch.

She bit back frustration. Whatever she was looking for was here. She could *feel* it.

Turning slowly she slid her gaze across the crimson-velvet settee with a gold silk robe draped across it, past the enormous television, then to the nightstand where a crystal vase held fresh-cut *Rosea Midas Touch* blooms. She and Alex had discussed what Vander's evidence might be, and the potential hiding places in a typical bedroom. Morgan had even studied pictures of furniture—modern and antique—that were known to have hidden compartments. Nothing.

She started roaming. One by one she picked up the jewel-colored bottles and boxes off the bureau, held each up to the light. All contained either oil or powder. She moved to the nightstand, flipped through the leather address book lying beside the crystal vase. Nothing out of the ordinary. She lifted the receiver on the combination phone/answering machine, listened for a dial tone, then hesitated when she got silence. Had the phone line to this room been a private one which Spurlock disconnected after Goldie died? Morgan checked the phone for a number, but the plastic sleeve that held the label was blank.

She tugged on the unit's cord, found it had been unplugged from the wall. She pursed her mouth. If the line was dead, why bother unplugging the phone? If the line was still active, on the other hand, you'd unplug the phone if you didn't want calls coming in and messages left.

She flipped up the machine's cover, nudged the microcassette out of its slot, turned it over. Written on the label were the words "Spurlock—Isom." Morgan's heartbeat picked up. This, then, had to be Krystelle Vander's proof that Spurlock ordered the jockey's murder. Just before she'd been killed nearly two months ago, Vander must have hidden the cassette in the answering machine, then disconnected it so no messages could tape over the evidence.

Morgan replaced the cassette, closed the cover. The Vice guys would "find" it when they served the search warrant.

She slid on the backless heels she'd taken off to conduct her search and grabbed her beaded bag off the bed. She did a quick survey to ensure she'd left nothing amiss, then turned for the door just as it swung open.

Colaneri stepped in, his dark eyes almost frightening in their coldness. "Been looking for you, blondie. You and I need to take a nice, friendly walk to the basement."

She tossed back her hair. "I'm not going anywhere with you."

He raised a hand to show her the cell phone gripped i
this palm. "My boss is listening. You make a wrong mov
during our stroll, he'll put a bullet in your partner's brair
Got it?"

A slick, sweaty fist of fear lodged in Morgan's stomach
Colaneri had said *partner,* not *husband.* Something o
someone had blown her and Alex's cover.

And Spurlock had a gun on Alex. *Alex.*

She gave Colaneri a curt nod. "Got it."


"Stop here," Colaneri ordered a few minutes late
when Morgan reached a metal door at the end of a murk
corridor.

They had left Goldie's bedroom, walking from the sec
ond floor down the winding staircase. The numerous part
guests they'd passed hadn't given them a second look
Why should they? Colaneri hadn't brandished a gun. Fo
Morgan, the cell phone he held with Spurlock listenin
on the other end was a much more controlling weapon.

As they'd descended into the basement, the air ha
gone from cool to refrigerator cold with an edge of dank
ness. Still, she knew the surrounding temperature ha
nothing to do with the icy fear in her stomach.

Colaneri reached around her, slid a key into the lock
twisted it, let his hand drop. "Open the door," he ordered

The instant Morgan obeyed, he kicked her center back
sending her stumbling forward. Her backless heels wer
out from under her on the slick concrete floor; somethin
popped inside her left ankle as she went down crashin
onto her side.

She lay stunned, her lungs heaving from having the ai
knocked out of them. Pain ripped at her ankle in viciou
spasms.

She heard a savage curse, realized it came from Alex

Raising her head, she spotted him across the small, windowless room. He was standing, his arms stretched over his head, his wrists bound to a metal rod that hung a few feet down from the ceiling. They'd stripped him of his suit coat. She checked his white shirt for blood but saw none. His eyes were locked on her, his expression set. She'd never seen anger so cold, so controlled.

Spurlock stood a few feet from Alex in front of a waist-high workbench with tools hanging on the plaster wall above it. Spurlock held a small, nickel-plated automatic in one hand, a cell phone in the other. Morgan knew he'd controlled Alex not with the gun, but with a threat to harm her, the same way Colaneri had gained her total cooperation.

Levering herself into sitting position, she bit back a whimper when the pain in her ankle intensified. Her foot had already begun to swell. Her shoes had flown off in the fall and lay just out of reach. If she could grab one, the spiked heel could make a deadly weapon.

With Colaneri standing only inches behind her and Spurlock gripping a gun, she didn't dare make a move.

"An unfortunate injury," Spurlock murmured, pulling her gaze back to him. He slipped the cell phone into the pocket of his suit coat. "Peter, was such rough handling necessary?"

"The bitch is dangerous. Gotta show her who's in charge."

"I have every intention of showing both of these police officers who is in charge." Keeping his gaze locked with Morgan's, Spurlock pointed the automatic at Alex, his finger ready on the trigger. "If you resist in any way, I will shoot your partner. Do you understand?"

With a gun pointed at Alex's heart, she had no choice but to cooperate. She knew at the first sign of trouble he

would have used his watch to send Rackowitz an SO
Both of their watches were equipped with satellite trac
ing chips. Their best bet was to play for time and wait f
the cavalry.

"I understand," she said, keeping her voice dull, h
face slack in order to project an image of weakness. Ju
in case backup got delayed, it would be to her advantag
for Spurlock and Colaneri to think her mentally and phy
ically incapacitated.

"Good," Spurlock said. "This type of encounter a
ways goes more smoothly when my guests cooperate. P
ter, bring her to me."

"I want her," Colaneri protested. "I got a debt to sett
with her."

Spurlock arched a brow. "You may have her after I'
done. Bring her to me *now*."

Colaneri loomed into Morgan's view, the scars arou
his eyebrows and mouth making him look even more on
inous. Her heart pounded so hard she could feel her pul
throbbing under her skin.

"Hear that, blondie?" he taunted. "When the boss ge
done with you, you're mine."

Morgan wrapped her fingers around her ankle. S
could move her toes, so she didn't think she had brok
any bones. Colaneri was close enough that a well-plac
kick would crush the inside ball of his knee. Yet, if s
made a move right now, Alex would die. A tremor ra
through her as she pictured the automatic aimed at h
heart. Her best defense—only defense—right now was
act like a victim. She knew that was the reason Alex ha
voiced no further protest. He was waiting, coiled energ
held in check, ready to spring in case Spurlock lowere
his guard.

"Please don't hurt me," she whispered.

"That bitch, Krystelle, begged me, too," Colaneri said, his eyes lighting with a hovering cruelty. "Didn't do her no good. I had her, then I cut her. Same as I'm going to do you." He pulled a length of yellow plastic rope from the pocket of his suit coat. "Put your hands out."

With her wrists bound together, Morgan felt a cold twist of panic. Colaneri wrapped the excess rope around his fist, hauled her to her feet and dragged her across the room. She limped behind him, pain tearing at her ankle as the rope's stiff fibers cut into her flesh.

He tied a second length of rope to her wrists, led it over the opposite end of the rod to which Alex was already trussed. Colaneri jerked her arms above her head, then tied off the rope. She and Alex were now standing six feet apart, facing each other. His expression was set in savage lines, his eyes so bright they seemed to burn her. He knew as well as she they were positioned to watch each other die.

"Good," Spurlock said. He laid the automatic on the workbench, eased out of his suit coat, and moved toward Morgan.

"I overlooked your presence in my grandmother's bedroom the first time because your explanation for being here was plausible. My mistake." He raised a shoulder in elegant dismissal. "Did you find what you were looking for tonight?"

Morgan thought of the tape in the answering machine. Why hadn't she called Rackowitz when she found it? At least someone else would know the tape was there.

"I wasn't looking for anything. I had to go to the bathroom again—"

"Don't play me for a fool," he said softly. "Peter, did you check her purse?"

"Yeah." Colaneri patted the pocket of his suit coat

where he'd slipped the beaded bag after he'd taken it from her. "Ain't nothing unusual in it."

"Which means she didn't find anything," Alex countered. Morgan had never heard a voice so quiet. So lethal.

Spurlock turned. "You might be right, Alex—or whatever your real name is. But I'm sure you'll understand why I intend to check for sure."

He closed in on Morgan like a hunter moving through the woods. All she could do was shut her eyes and bear it while Spurlock's long, hard fingers swept over her breasts, her abdomen, then lowered, finally skimming up each of her thighs.

Finding nothing of consequence, he gripped her chin, jerked it upward. "If I had time right now, I would torture the information out of you. But I have a house filled with guests who I must get back to."

"I'll do it," Colaneri volunteered. "I'll make her talk."

Spurlock paused as if weighing the offer. "Later, Peter. Right now I want you to go upstairs."

Spurlock moved back to the workbench. He pulled a slim cigar from the pocket of his suit coat, lighting it with a sharp thumb flick against his gold lighter.

With his attention momentarily diverted, Morgan wrapped her fingers firmly around the metal rod. Testing, she put a slight amount of weight onto her injured ankle, then more. The pain was intense, but bearable. Enough so that she might be able to deliver a couple of good kicks.

She risked a look at Alex, could almost see his mind racing as he watched her, weighing danger and benefits. He dropped his gaze to her ankle then looked down at his own legs. She understood his meaning, and the unspoken question in his eyes. *Could she deliver a strong enough kick with her injured ankle?* She gave him a slight nod.

"Peter, on your way upstairs go by my office and get

Emmett. I want both of you to search the bedroom until you find what holds such interest for the police.''

Morgan's head snapped up. Was Spurlock talking about *Emmett Tool?* If so, the accountant had not been burned to death as the police believed. She saw the verification in Alex's eyes. Tool, then, must have been the financial advisor Spurlock mentioned when they'd first arrived at the party.

"Search the bedroom carefully, Peter," Spurlock instructed, turning the gold lighter over and over in his hand. "You are not to damage my grandmother's belongings. Do you understand?"

"Yeah, boss." The thug hesitated, then swept his arm Morgan's way. "What about her?"

"I'll deal with her, then rejoin my guests." Spurlock checked his watch. "After that, you may do with both of these police officers as you wish."

"I got a lot of wishes where blondie's concerned." Colaneri gave Morgan an insulting once-over, his eyes lingering on her chest. "Think about me while I'm gone," he said, then strode across the room and out the door.

The thought she might soon be at Colaneri's mercy sent a swell of nausea up Morgan's throat. She clamped her jaw tight, forced back the sick taste. The more immediate problem was the man lounging against the workbench.

Spurlock lifted his chin, expelled a stream of smoke. "I deal harshly with those who betray me," he said softly. "Both of you are about to find that out."

Alex jerked at the rope binding his wrists. "Deal with me first, you bastard."

Morgan flashed him a sharp look. She knew Alex was trying to draw Spurlock's attention away from her, *to spare her*. Alex could possibly take down Spurlock without her help, but their chances of success were far greater if she could first deliver a stunning kick to Spurlock's head.

"There are many styles of torture," Spurlock continued, ignoring Alex's challenge. "I can think of none more vicious for a man than to be forced to watch the woman he loves being abused. Then taken by another man." He examined the glowing tip of his cigar. "Don't you agree, Alex?"

"Hurt her, I'll filet you into fish bait," Alex said, his voice low and deadly.

"You love her," Spurlock said in quiet confirmation. "I watched you closely. Studied you. That's one reason you fooled me so thoroughly, Alex. No man is that good an actor."

Morgan's heart gave a powerful thud that made her feel even shakier than she already was. For an instant time stopped. She stared at Alex, wondering what was going on behind that cold, impenetrable brown gaze.

It didn't matter, she thought, her mind snapping back. For now nothing mattered but drawing Spurlock's attention. She wrapped her fingers tighter around the metal rod and gave him a pleading look. "I'll do anything you want, Carlton," she said, her voice a breathless, whisper. "Anything."

"That's right, you will." Rolling the cigar between his thumb and fingers, he moved toward her. She saw his gaze slide down from her face, watched a mix of lust and cruelty come into his eyes. "Your skin is so lovely it's a shame to burn it. A necessary shame."

The instant he extended the cigar's glowing tip, Alex exploded into motion. Cursing viciously, he jerked hard on the metal rod. When Spurlock turned, Morgan lifted her legs and slammed both feet into the side of his head.

He oofed out a grunt. The cigar flew from his fingers as he stumbled backward, arms flailing.

Gripping the rod, Alex hoisted his body. He caught Spurlock around the neck with his thighs, locked them tight. Spurlock struggled, his hands desperately trying to break the iron grip that deprived him of oxygen.

His eyes rolled back in his head just as the door to the room burst open.

# Chapter 15

Morgan whooshed out a breath when Rackowitz charged through the door, followed by a blur of plainclothes and uniformed cops. Seconds later a hulking patrol cop cut Morgan down. Rackowitz trailed along while the cop toted Morgan to a vacant corner. She quickly advised the FBI agent about Goldie's bedroom and the cassette tape she'd found in the answering machine.

Just as Rackowitz stepped away to transmit the information over her hand-held radio, a paramedic with a bushy red mustache moved in. His initial probe of Morgan's ankle sent stars exploding in front of her eyes.

"I've still…got one…good foot, pal," she gasped as knifes of pain sliced her leg. She could actually feel beads of sweat popping out on her forehead. "Touch me again, you get the same treatment as the other guy."

Mustache twitching, the paramedic glanced behind him, where a cuffed and bleeding Spurlock was being loaded onto a stretcher. "I'll be gentle as springtime," he assured her while settling an ice pack across her ankle. "All the way to the hospital."

"Can't go now. I have reports to make."

"Look, Officer, I don't think your ankle's broken. But you've probably got ligament damage. That's just a guess, though. We won't know for sure until it's X-rayed."

"Later. I'll hitch a ride—"

"Now." Alex crouched beside her, his face grim. "I'm sorry you're hurt," he said calmly. "I didn't want you hurt."

He might have his voice under control, but emotion swam in his eyes. "We're both in one piece," she reminded him, and forced a smile through the pain. "Did Rackowitz brief you on the tape I found?"

"Just now. Goldie's bedroom, not a *gold* bedroom." He shook his head. "Good work, McCall."

"You did some pretty snazzy work yourself, Blade. That was some thigh squeeze you put on Spurlock's neck."

Rackowitz hunched down beside Alex, the radio in her hand spitting static. "Our guys found the tape in the answering machine," she reported.

"What about Colaneri and Tool?" Morgan asked.

"Not yet. Alex clued us in about them being upstairs, but they weren't in Goldie's bedroom when our guys got there." Rackowitz shrugged. "They probably figured out the end was near when they heard the party guests stampede. We've got cops swarming the grounds, searching for them."

Alex's gaze sharpened. "Morgan, didn't Colaneri say he has your evening bag in his pocket?"

"That's right," she said, instantly following his thoughts. "It's bugged."

Rackowitz's face lit up. "Most do-wrongs aren't thoughtful enough to carry an evening bag with a tracking device sewn into its lining." Keying the radio's mike, she transmitted an update to the lieutenant supervising the search for the two men. After signing off, she said, "Okay, you both need to make separate statements about the overall operation. And a slew of other reports about what happened tonight. Alex, you and I can get started here. Morgan, I'll hook up with you after you're done getting checked out."

"At the hospital," Alex added.

Rackowitz's radio crackled to life. She stood, responding to the dispatcher as she moved off.

The pain biting at Morgan's ankle, combined with the steely look Alex sent her, had her backing down. "Fine. I'll go."

"Good." He took her fingers, folded them into his hand. "I'll get away from here as soon as I can." He ran his palm down her hair. "We'll talk then. You and I need to talk."

When he would have pulled away, she tightened her hold on his hand. "What Spurlock said about your feelings for me," she said quietly. "Was he right?"

Alex's mouth tightened and he looked away. When he remet her gaze, that look was back in his eyes, that grim solemn countenance that brought to mind regret.

*Regret.*

"We'll talk later, Morgan. About everything."

Alex finished briefing Rackowitz just as he received orders to report to his lieutenant's office. Biting back frustration at having to head to the opposite side of town from the hospital where Morgan was, he pulled into the lot behind the nondescript building that housed the department's covert units. Inside, he gave an overview of the operation to several members of the brass, along with OCPD's public information officer. With Spurlock having numerous pillar-of-the-community associates, the department was making sure it had all its ducks in a row.

After typing his report, Alex headed to the hospital's E.R. A nurse informed him Officer McCall had been treated, released and driven home by a second Officer McCall.

*Home.* He steered toward the house the McCall sisters shared, fully aware his own definition of home no longer computed without including Morgan in the mix. She was the one. She was his match. Tough luck for him it was a match that wouldn't last.

He could brood over that all he wanted, but there was no way to stop the inevitable. No way to change the fact he was so in love he would settle for whatever time he had with her.

He turned a corner and spotted a sporty little lipstick-red MG in the driveway of the two-story house. Carrie's car, he deduced.

Alex parked by the curb, cut across the postage stamp-size lawn and scaled the steps leading up to the small porch with its columns wrapped in ivy. When he rang the bell, he had the sense it had been years since his last visit, instead of weeks.

"Hey, Blade." Carrie answered the door while balancing a can of beer and a can of soda in one hand. She was dressed in shorts and a halter top. With her fiery auburn hair piled on the top of her head her wide-set eyes looked huge. "Sounds like you and my baby sister have had quite a Fourth of July."

"One I'll never forget." Alex stepped into the hallway and closed the door behind him. "How is she?"

Carrie slicked a look down the hallway toward the living room. "Shaky, but okay," she said, lowering her voice. "A little too pale for my liking."

Before Alex could switch off his mind, he saw it again. Colaneri smashing his foot into the center of Morgan's back, her body crashing against the cement floor. The pain in her eyes when she'd lifted her head and looked at him. His absolute helplessness at being unable to get to her. Protect her.

"I didn't want her hurt," he said. "I didn't want…"

"Of course you didn't," Carrie said, watching him closely.

"I know it's late. My lieutenant detoured me to the office for an update on what went down. I tried to catch Morgan at the E.R., but you'd already picked her up. Thought I'd drop by and take a chance she's still awake." He raised a hand, let it drop. "Dammit, I need to see to her. Tonight."

A look of awareness slid into Carrie's eyes. "You about to become a familiar sight around this place, Blade?"

"Yeah." He eased out a breath. "Maybe. If I can swing it."

Flashing a grin, Carrie shoved both cans into his hands. "Morgan's in the living room—she wanted to wait up for

Grace to get home. Baby sis is on pain meds, so she gets the soda. The beer's yours.''

''Thanks, Carrie.''

''Knock 'em dead.'' She winked and headed for the staircase.

Alex moved down the hallway, pausing at the door to the small living room, where a single lamp speared long shadows to the high ceiling. Morgan sat on the tan couch amid an assortment of rose and smoky-gray pillows. An elastic bandage swaddled her left foot and ankle, which she had propped on an oversize ottoman. Her eyes were closed, her head back against a pillow. She was so still, so quiet, he thought she had fallen asleep.

He moved silently into the room, pausing a few feet from the couch. The blue-sequined dress she'd worn earlier had been replaced with an oversize T-shirt and shorts. She'd slicked back her hair into a ponytail and wiped off the makeup. The sultry Morgan Donovan had morphed back into the wholesome cheerleader.

He had begun backing out of the room when she opened her eyes and locked her blue gaze with his.

''Hi,'' he said quietly. ''Sorry I woke you.''

''I wasn't asleep. Just resting my eyes.''

''How's the ankle?''

''Not broken.'' She wiggled her toes, then winced.

Alex felt his chest tighten when pain clouded her eyes.

''I tore some ligaments,'' she said after a moment. ''Guess I won't be jogging for a while. Or working the streets.''

''You'll get there. I thought you'd want to know the latest on the case.'' *Coward*, he told himself. That wasn't why he was there.

She eyed him for a long moment. "Sure. Have a seat."

He stepped around the crutches propped against the coffee table, eased down on the couch and popped the top on the soda can. "Compliments of Carrie," he said.

"Thanks." Morgan craned her neck toward the door. "Where'd she go?"

"Upstairs. I got the impression she had some things to do."

"Okay." Morgan took a sip, then set the can on the table beside the couch. "So, what's the status on the case?"

"Thanks to the bug in your evening bag, Colaneri and Tool got nabbed in Spurlock's cabana." Alex opened his beer, took a long swallow. "They were hiding behind the roulette table."

"Either of them talking?"

"Tool. He's hot to deal for a lighter sentence." Alex scrubbed a hand over his face. "He said Spurlock ordered the jockey killed after Isom agreed to fix a race, then got a case of conscience and didn't come through. That cost Spurlock a cool million."

"Is that what's on the tape in the answering machine? Spurlock ordering Isom's murder?"

"Yes. Tool said Spurlock somehow got wind that Krystelle planned to go to the police about him, so he had Colaneri grab Vander and George Jackson. According to Tool, Spurlock had them tied in his basement, just like us. He had a go at Vander with a lit cigar, then a knife. Colaneri finished them both off and dumped the bodies."

"You loved George," Morgan said quietly. "I hope it helps to know you took down his killers."

"*We* took them down. And, yeah, it helps."

"What about Tool? We thought he'd been burned alive. Whose body was it?"

"A homeless guy's." Alex raised a hand, dropped it. "Tool not only has a wife, he has a girlfriend no one knew about. She's a hygienist at his dentist's office. Turns out, the dentist donates time at a men's shelter. The burned body was a homeless guy the dentist treated there."

"How did they set up things?"

"After I arrested Tool, he used his one phone call to let Spurlock know he'd been busted and we were putting pressure on him to testify. Spurlock sent the lawyer who showed up to represent Tool. He worked an immunity deal, agreeing Tool would testify to Spurlock's involvement in the murders of the jockey, Jackson and Vander. As a part of the deal, Tool was moved to a hotel for questioning."

"Which was to give Spurlock easier access to him?"

"Right. We suspect Colaneri slipped the poison into the food room service delivered to the room. Tool told the two FBI agents guarding him that he was too nervous to eat." Alex raised a shoulder. "He waits for them to eat and die, then walks out. Colaneri picks him up, they find whichever homeless guy the hygienist girlfriend tells them to grab and they set him on fire. She replaces Tool's dental records with his."

"Tool disappears, only to walk into Spurlock's study tonight and ID you as the cop who arrested him."

Alex nodded. "His appearance falls under the heading of one of those unforeseen events that can occur when you work undercover." He sipped his beer. "I met with some of the brass before I came here. You'll have a commendation in your file from this case.'' His mouth curved. ''Not a bad career boost for a rookie.''

''You deserve a commendation, too.''

''One will probably show up in my file.'' He set the can on the coffee table. ''Doesn't much matter to me. I'm not looking to get promoted.''

''No, you'll just change identities and melt into the shadows of the next undercover operation. Fool someone else.''

The sudden bite in her voice had him hesitating. ''That's my job.''

''You do it well.'' She looked away. ''Just think how totally you fooled Spurlock.''

''I deceived him about a lot of things. But not about you. He was right, Morgan.''

When she remet his gaze, Alex saw the change in her expression. Shock? Astonishment? ''You going to explain what you mean by that?''

''I'm in love with you.'' Now that he'd said the words, he felt too unsettled to sit. Snatching the beer off the table, he stood and roamed across the room to the fireplace, where an enormous bouquet of garden flowers bloomed instead of flames.

''I don't know exactly when it happened, why it happened.'' He tried to read Morgan's expression, but nothing in her features gave away her thoughts. ''I only know it did happen,'' he continued. ''Up until tonight, I had everything worked out in my head how to handle things. Told myself it was all for the best.''

''*What* was for the best?''

''Our going separate ways when the assignment ended.''

Her mouth tightened. ''Why don't you explain how you came to that conclusion?''

''We're nothing alike, Morgan. We want different things, have different goals. I went down that road with my ex, and it was a disaster. Hurt like hell, and I swore I would never again hop on a ride like that. It might be great while it lasts, but that's the point—it doesn't. I knew it would be best in the long run if you and I went our separate ways.''

''Best for whom?''

''Both of us.'' He took a long swallow of beer. ''I thought that, until the minute you and I were in that basement. I saw you hurt, strung up, manhandled.'' When his fingers trembled, he clenched his hand into a fist. ''I thought I had an idea what it would feel like when you were no longer in my life, but I didn't have a clue. All I knew was if we survived, I couldn't let you go. Not now. Not for a while.''

''A while?'' Her eyes sharpened, narrowed. ''Are you saying you want us to have some sort of short-term affair?''

''I want more from you than just a body in the night, Morgan. The morning after we made love, you told me you cared about me, more than you should. I don't know how deep your feelings go, but I want everything you're willing to give. For as long as you'll stay.''

''For as long as I'll…'' She shook her head. ''You're willing to enter into a relationship with me that you have no expectation will last?''

He slid her a look. ''I'm not saying I'll like it. I'm saying I'll do it.''

''How do you *know* it won't last?''

"Like I said, I've been down that road before. You won't stay with me, Morgan. Right now you can't see that. You think we'll work. It doesn't bother you at this point I'm content to stay a sergeant, that I have no desire to move up. But once you start getting promoted, once you outrank me, it will matter. A lot."

"So, this is the reason for the regret." She pressed her fingertips to her eyes. "Since the night we made love, every time you looked at me I saw regret. Even tonight in the basement when it was all over..." She pulled her bottom lip between her teeth. "While I was sitting in the emergency room, I forced myself to accept you'd been playing a role with me, too. Your job demands that you not let anyone get close enough to touch you emotionally, so why should I be any different from anyone else? I convinced myself you didn't care."

"I love you," he said with sudden fury. "How am I supposed to look at you when I know from the start you'll someday decide I'm not good enough? That I no longer meet your expectations. Hell, yes, I regret that."

She gave a short, explicit curse, snagged her crutches and levered up.

He shoved the beer can onto the mantel. "Where are you going?"

"To get what I want," she said, crutching across the room to stand in front of him. "Now that I know what's going on in your head, it's time you know what's in mine."

Dread tightened his stomach. He had no idea how she felt. All he knew was he wasn't going to let her walk away now. He couldn't let her walk away. "I'm listening."

"My junior year of college, I went nuts over a guy who made my heart pound just by walking into the same room. His only goal in life was to have a good time. Since I was gaga over him, I jumped along with him into the party scene. My grades dropped through the floor, but I didn't care. All I cared about was *him*. One night he wrapped his car around a tree. He was okay, but I wound up in a coma. I woke up to find he'd taken a hike, and so had my full-ride scholarship. It took me three years to climb out of the hole I'd dug for myself."

"Sounds like we've both got reason to be skittish about getting involved."

"Where you're concerned, Blade, I've been skittish from the start. That's because when you showed up at the academy to check me out, my heart flipped the same way it had for party boy. That scared the hell out of me. All my life I've wanted to be a cop. No way did I intend to let another man who could make my hormones stand up and salute mess me up. The last thing I wanted was to work with you, be anywhere near you. And there I was, *living* with you." Emotion swam into her eyes. "I didn't want to, but I fell in love with you. I—"

"Hold on." He framed her face with his palms. "You love me?"

"Unfortunately," she said, jerking from his touch. "I trusted in you—in *us*—enough to stop playing it safe and work without a net. Now, here you are, telling me you'll *settle* for our having an affair, that you don't *trust* me enough to stay with you for the long run."

"Trust isn't the point. Being realistic is. I know what it's like to get tangled up with someone who wants different things out of life."

"Has it ever occurred to you that our relationship might be different from the one you had with your ex?"

"I'm talking human nature. When people no longer fit together, they move on. Period."

"Did your ex-wife ever work undercover with you?"

He frowned. "She wasn't a cop."

"Then she had no way of knowing how good you are. No real understanding that you work every day in a world where a deal gone wrong can blow your cover, and staying in one spot too long might get you killed. That someone walking into the same room with you can turn into a life-and-death situation, like it did tonight. No concept of what kind of ice-cold nerve, fast thinking, and off-the-chart courage it takes to do your job."

He shoved a hand through his hair. She was making him into something he wasn't. "I'm just a cop doing my job."

"From where I'm standing, you're a hero. It wasn't one of my charts or spreadsheets that kept us alive during our assignment. It was your skill, your knowledge, the things you taught me about working undercover." Her eyes started to soften. "I've been in the trenches with you, Alex. After this, do you truly believe I could ever look down on the work you do? That I might think some cop who sits behind a desk and shuffles paper is to be admired more than you?"

The sudden shaft of hope for a future together was almost too painful. "How can you possibly think I'm what you're looking for?"

"You weren't what I was looking for when this started," she answered. "But you're what I found." Shifting her weight onto one crutch, she placed a palm against his cheek. "I don't just love you. I admire and respect the man you are. You grew up on the streets and you kept yourself alive by your wits. You're still doing that. I don't care about your credentials. I care about you. Will care, for the rest of my life." She angled her chin. "If you don't like the sound of that, tell me now. *I'm* not willing to settle. I want all or nothing."

Her words put a pressure in his chest. She was willing to take him just as he was. Love him just as he was. All he had to do was trust. Have the same faith in her she had in him.

He spent a moment simply looking into her eyes. He could see the love there. It was real. As real as his for her.

He chose his next words carefully. "It suddenly occurs to me that, deep down where it counts, we've got a lot in common."

"So, you're saying you like the sound of our spending the rest of our lives together?"

"Yeah, that's what I'm saying."

Her expression lightened. "Now that we've got that settled, Blade, what are you going to do about it?"

He gave her a slow grin. "Something that will appeal to your baser instincts, McCall." He used a fingertip to trace the outline of her jaw. "Something—" his finger took a detour down her throat, dipped beneath the neckline of her T-shirt, "…that will get your blood churning like hot lava."

Her lips parted. "Like what?"

He lowered his head, let his mouth hover just above hers. "Develop a plan," he murmured. "Put it in spreadsheet format. Print a copy so you can analyze the hell out of it.''

She jerked back. ''A *plan?*''

He raised a brow. ''Aren't you the woman who likes to have things mapped out before she acts? A well-ordered, sensible blueprint?''

''Most of the time.'' She speared him with a look. ''However, I'm a big proponent of spontaneity when it comes to certain things.''

He wrapped his arms around her. ''Such as?''

''Such as your kissing me,'' she said. ''Right now, Blade. This minute.''

''My pleasure.'' When his mouth settled on hers and he dove in deep, every emotion he was feeling suddenly doubled.

His arms tightened around her. ''Are you willing to go for broke, Morgan?'' he murmured against her lips. ''Willing to take a life-long gamble on us?''

''There's no risk involved.'' Smiling up at Alex, she pressed her palm against his cheek. ''We're a sure bet.''

\*   \*   \*   \*   \*

*Look for the second book in Maggie Price's*
*exciting* LINE OF DUTY *miniseries,*

*HIDDEN AGENDA,*

*on sale in January 2004,*
*wherever Silhouette Books are sold!*

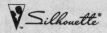

The Wolfe twins' stories—
together in one fantastic volume!

*USA TODAY* bestselling author

# JOAN HOHL
## *Double* WOLFE

The emotional story of Matilda Wolfe plus an original short
story about Matilda's twin sister, Lisa. The twins have
followed different paths...but each leads to true love!

**Look for DOUBLE WOLFE in January 2004.**

"A compelling storyteller who weaves her tales
with verve, passion and style."
—*New York Times* bestselling author Nora Roberts

*Silhouette*®
*Where love comes alive*™

**New York Times
bestselling author**

# DEBBIE MACOMBER

### A moving, emotional tale
### from her famous Navy series!

NAVY *Brat*

Erin MacNamera had one
hard and fast rule: never,
never, never fall for a navy man.
But she quickly changed her
mind when she met
Lieutenant Brandon Davis....

*Coming to stores
in January 2004.*

*Silhouette*®

*Where love comes alive*™

# INTIMATE MOMENTS™

### is thrilled to bring you the next book in popular author

# CANDACE IRVIN's

#### exciting new miniseries

*Unparalleled courage, unbreakable love...*

### In January 2004, look for:

## Irresistible Forces
### (Silhouette Intimate Moments #1270)

It's been eleven years since U.S. Air Force captain
Samantha Hall last saw the man she loved...and lost.
Now, as Major Griff Towers rescues her and her colleagues
after their plane crashes in hostile territory, how can Sam
possibly ignore the feelings she still has for the sexy soldier?

### And if you missed the first books in the series look for...

## Crossing the Line
### (Silhouette Intimate Moments #1179, October 2002)

## A Dangerous Engagement
### (Silhouette Intimate Moments #1252, October 2003)

*Available wherever Silhouette books are sold!*

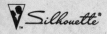

# Silhouette®

# COMING NEXT MONTH